You NEEDED Me

A Love Story

3

A NOVEL BY

SHVONNE LATRICE

CHAPTER ONE

Britain Quinton

*A*s soon as I pulled out of the parking structure of my condo, three police cars came out of nowhere. One blocked me from the front, and there were two more behind me to make sure I didn't reverse the other way I guess. Throwing my car into park, all kinds of shit ran through my mind as I wondered what the fuck all of this was for. I mean three police officers? What the hell could this possibly be about? I knew it had nothing to do with the crime family, because we had that shit completely under control. We had so many people in our pocket that it was nearly impossible for it to be about that.

One of the officers walked towards my vehicle and wound his hand to tell me to roll the window down. I did as he asked, but kept looking straight because I didn't want to acknowledge him. *Please let one of these niggas be on my father's payroll.*

"Britain Quinton?" he asked as he looked at a piece of paper.

"Is there a problem, officer?"

"Step out of the car, Mr. Quinton."

"Oh my gosh yo." I shut the engine off and got out of the car. As soon as I did, one of the other officers slammed me into my vehicle, and began patting me down. "What is this for?!" I hollered.

"Britain Quinton, you're under arrest for the murder of Tekeya Mitchell's unborn child, also known as feticide. You have the right…"

Are you fucking serious right now? Why didn't I murk that bitch?

***

At the precinct…

"Sit him down." A black man walked in wearing a gray suit.

I was still handcuffed and perplexed. I was being charged for some shit I had never even heard of and ultimately didn't do. I didn't even know killing a fetus was a crime for one, and secondly if I knew I was gonna be getting accused of doing the shit, I would have killed Tekeya's ass when I had the chance. Something told me to get rid of that hoe when she tried to drug me, but because I had love for the grimy bitch I chose to let her go. I saw why my father gave no fucks, because in this life no one gave a fuck about you. Speaking of my father, I was sure he would get in my ass once he found out about all the passes I gave Tekeya's ass.

I knew she was behind this not only because she was named as the victim, but also because I saw her bitch ass brother, Stewart, an officer, when they brought me in. That nigga had way too much fear in his eyes to be fucking with a nigga like me. If I could scare you just from making eye contact, you had no business coming for me.

"Good evening, Mr. Quinton, or night I guess." The black detective smiled and sat down. He stared at me for a bit wearing a smug expression, before scratching his too thick mustache and fixing his suit jacket. "I guess we're not gonna be polite to one another," he chuckled, referring to me declining to respond to his greeting.

"Why am I here?" I glanced towards the corner of the room to see another white detective staring me down with his hand on his gun. Really? I'm cuffed, yet he feels the need to be prepared to shoot. The fuck was I gonna do while cuffed?

"Well, first of all, I'm Detective Michael Jackson," he cheesed as if I was supposed to laugh. "And um, this is Detective Zack Campbell." He pointed over his shoulder with his thumb. "I want to ask you some questions, because you've been accused of aborting Tekeya Mitchell's child. Now not only did you do it against her will, but you're not certified, at least not to my knowledge, to perform abortions."

"I didn't kill anyone's child. You have no proof I'm sure, so hurry up with your questions, because I have somewhere to be."

"Mr. Quinton, is it true that you had a lasagna dinner with Tekeya Mitchell about a month ago?"

"So?"

"I will take that as a yes. Ms. Mitchell claims that it was at that time that you poisoned her food, in hopes of killing the child that she was pregnant with."

"Why would I do that? I don't care about the children she has. I don't care about anything the bitch does."

"Would a Goldie Taylor have anything to do with that?" he slid me three pictures of Goldie and I walking hand in hand, kissing, and eating at some restaurant. I was getting angry but I needed to stay calm.

"Ms. Mitchell provided us with these photos."

"Neither one of us have anything to do with the fact that Tekeya lost her baby."

"See, I don't believe that. I believe that you got tired of Ms. Mitchell, and went out to find someone else, which happened to be Ms. Taylor here. Unfortunately for you though, you'd already gotten Ms. Mitchell pregnant, and that wouldn't go over so well with Ms. Taylor, so you got rid of your unborn. That sound about right, Mr. Quinton?"

"Alright, I don't wanna talk about this anymore."

This nigga had yet to show any evidence to me, and he never would be able to because the shit never happened. However, because I did switch Tekeya's and my plate, she did lose the baby. I was a bit worried that they would be able to pin the shit on me, despite the fact that if she hadn't tried to drug me for whatever reason, she would still have her child. *But didn't she say she fell?* I wondered to myself.

"Look, either you answer these fucking questions, or we can bring in that pretty, little bitch you have now, and rough her up a bit," Detective Jackson smirked. "And I like roughing up the pretty ones."

I stood up with force, making sure to tip the table in his direction. He shot up out of his chair, and Detective Campbell rushed over and placed the gun to my head. I wanted to go toe to toe with these niggas, even while cuffed, but I knew I would have my brains splattered in no time. We stood there in silence, grimacing at one another until there was a knock at the door.

"What!" Detective Jackson shouted, keeping his eyes locked on me. The gun was still pressed into my temple as I panted heavily to calm myself.

"Cooper said to let him go." Some pale-faced young guy peeked in. He was a little bitch, I could tell, because he was scared to even let Detective Jackson know the deal.

"What? For what?" Jackson hollered and turned to face him.

"Let him go!" A guy who I assumed to be Cooper walked up. I saw my dad standing behind him, staring into my soul it seemed. I swear I saw fire burning behind his blue eyes as he lowered at me.

Campbell removed the cuffs, and as soon as my hands were free, I sent his ass flying into the wall with a left hook for holding that gun to my head. I was gonna get that Jackson nigga too, but my dad called my name letting me know it was time to go. I glared at Jackson as the Cooper guy and pale face helped Campbell up before leaving with my dad.

"Did you get my car? They impounded it," I said to my father as we walked out of the police station.

"Get in the car, Britain." He hit his alarm before we both slid in. "What the hell is going on with you and your brothers?"

"What? This has nothing to do with anybody but Tekeya!"

"Tekeya," he chuckled. "No, it has a lot to do with that gold haired slut you've been bouncing around with and her slutty ass friends!"

"Just take me to get my car." It took every muscle in my frame for me to hold back from delivering his ass the same punch that I'd just given to that detective.

"Everything was running perfectly fine until you guys decided to turn into some little bitches! First TQ, then stupid ass Lendsey, and now you! I didn't expect this from you, Britain."

"So you'd rather me be with Key?"

"I don't care who the fuck you're with as long as it doesn't fuck with my reputation, my business, and the family."

"The family, that's all you care about," I scoffed and shook my head as he lit a cigarette at the red light.

"You're damn right! I worked my ass off to become who the fuck I am! I risked my life by betraying people who could have me killed, just to become who the fuck I am! I came from being a poor, little boy in Russia to being one of the biggest crime bosses on the East Coast, and I will not let you and your pussy ass siblings fuck it up for me! I will murder all of you and start again with new offspring!" He blew smoke out, prompting me to roll the window down. "I only have one damn daughter, but it seems like I have five! I will tell you this Britain, if those girls cause any more bullshit, I will kill them. And if you guys have a problem with it you can join their club." He pulled up to my condo.

"I told you to take me to the impound place."

"Your car is here already. Be thankful that Cooper and I are friends. If one of his people hadn't seen you and called me, you would've still been in there probably fucking something up like always."

"Fuck you." I opened the door to get out, but he grabbed my arm, which I snatched.

"Get them in line before I put them in the ground." He stared into my eyes. I just smacked my lips and got out of the car, slamming the door.

The thing about my father was that he was dead serious. Everything he said he was serious about. He would absolutely kill us all, including Goldie, Kimberlyn, and Matikah. Summer may be safe because she wasn't fucking with Rhys, but I was sure he would kill Indiya. That's just how Stony Quinton was; anything that came at him he shot it down. It could be his own mother, and he would still kill her ass dead and not have to think twice about it.

When I got into my condo, I pulled my iPhone out and went into my texts.

Me: Baby, have Dimitria bring you home and right now.

Baby Mama: *Why?*

Me: Goldie.

Baby Mama: *Okay.*

Jayce Lincoln

"For real, Jayce?" TQ frowned as I pressed the gun deeply into his forehead.

I was sweating profusely, so I grasped the gun tighter in my hands so that I wouldn't drop it. I was angry and I hated this nigga. He'd betrayed me in the worse way, and we were supposed to be best friends. I had his back and I thought he had mine, but clearly I was wrong. The only thing this nigga cared about was himself, and that little, wide mouthed bitch he called a girlfriend. To make matters worse, I didn't see any fear in his eyes. I wanted to see fear; I needed to see that he was afraid and that I had the upper hand. The only thing visible in his face was confusion and disappointment. I could tell he was wondering what he could have done to me for me to react this way, but he should've known. He knew every fucking thing else; he should know this, too.

"Shoot me, man." He stared into my eyes.

The only thing stopping me from killing him right now was the fact that I wasn't sure what I was gonna do after I did it. The initial plan was to kill him and then take my place in Gang's empire, but that nigga was dead. Tonight was just supposed to be a meeting. I had no idea that all of this would take place. Gang told me to stay close, so after I left the party, he told me to come through and make sure Burke didn't try to pull anything on him. I didn't know what he was meeting Burke for, but when I heard shots ring out, the first thing I thought to do was kill him. When the other shooter turned out to be TQ, I knew I would have no way of explaining why I was here with Gang, so I just put the gun to his head. I wanted him gone, but who would have my back against his brothers if I pulled the trigger? I wouldn't make it home before I was dead.

"I ain't want to have to do this but—"

WHAM!

Before I could finish, he twisted my wrist, removed the gun, and clocked me over the head with so much force I swore I heard Ricky Ricardo playing the bongos. My vision began to go in and out, before I finally blacked out altogether.

***

I opened my eyes and recognized the dirty ceiling of the warehouse. My head was throbbing like crazy, and my eyelids seemed to have ten-ton weights on them. I gained enough strength to look around, and spotted TQ sitting in a chair on the side of me. He was holding his gun, and my gun was sitting in his lap. I tried to get up, but I realized he had handcuffed one of my wrists to the plumbing pipes.

"TQ, man, get this shit off of me," I slurred and closed my eyes, hoping to relieve the headache I had.

He said nothing. He always did that shit and I'd hated it ever since we were little. It was so rude to just not respond to someone because you felt what they said didn't deserve a response. The more I thought about things, the more I hated this nigga. He was the reason my life was in shambles. Had he not got me into this fucking crime family, I wouldn't have been with all them bitches and gotten my wife killed. I would probably have some regular nine to five and a wife and kids at home.

"You were working for Gang," he nodded. The way he said it sounded more like a statement than a question, so I wasn't sure what to reply with.

"He was treating me right. Y'all niggas didn't want to give me what I was owed, so I went elsewhere."

"What did we owe you, Jayce? My father took you in when you had no one, and my mama damn near raised you. We didn't owe you shit, nigga. You owed it yourself to get better and do better, but you were too busy sulking and feeling sorry for yourself to accomplish anything!"

"My wife was killed!"

"Because of you! Everything that happened to you is because of you, nigga!"

"Y'all were the ones who were always around different women every damn chance y'all got! I was never the one looking to bring around females, that was you and your fucking brothers!"

"And how hard is it to look the other way, Jayce? You were a grown ass man then like you are now. Nobody told you to cheat on your wife, and if they did you didn't have to do it. None of us stuck a gun in your face and told you to fuck with Jennifer or anybody else. You chose to fuck around knowing you were married, and unfortunately you were met with the consequences."

"Fuck you, TQ." I began to tear up, thinking about my wife, Sadie.

"You're a little ass boy, Jayce, and you always have been. Yes, it's sad that your wife was murdered, but you needed to man up and take responsibility. Jennifer may have pulled the trigger, but you were the one who caused the whole shit. Stop always looking for someone to feel sorry for your ass and be a man about your shit! You're immature and you're stupid as hell. You're never gonna change."

"I am a man about mine! I could've killed myself, but I didn't!" I yelled. He just shook his head and raised his eyebrows as if he was saying I would never get it.

"And this shit with Gang. Did you honestly think he was gonna make you his partner?" he furrowed his eyebrows.

"He was." Before the words even left my lips he was laughing heartily.

"See what I mean? Dumb. That nigga was never going to make you his partner. He was using you for what you knew about me and your direct connection to me. You're way too seasoned in the game to let shit like that happen, Jayce."

"You don't know what the fuck you're talking about!"

"Then why was he here, huh?" he stood up and pointed to the nigga I'd shot earlier. I just stared at the body before regaining eye contact with TQ. "Exactly. He was here to take Peel's place. I know because I hired him to do just that so I could get Gang without his security." We stared at one another before he began smiling. "So stupid. You betrayed Tarenz Quinton, for Gang. That wasn't the smartest move, my nigga." He slipped his gun into his waist, and then cocked mine.

"Look, I'm gonna go to rehab and get myself together."

"Oh you think you have a chance?" he chuckled. "You honestly think that I'm not gonna kill yo' ass?"

"TQ, it's me, man."

Everything was starting to settle in, and I suddenly regretted my actions. I wasn't sure if I just didn't want to die, or if I actually felt bad for betraying him and Stony.

"I know who the fuck you are."

POP!

Kimberlyn Harrey

*G*oldie had just left the party using the family's assistant Dimitria for a ride because she said Britain had asked her to. I wasn't sure what the hell was going on, but I knew TQ hadn't come back through that front door yet. It'd been a while since he'd left, and I needed him to show up.

This was what I didn't like about the life he lived; you never knew when one would die. He told me himself that it wasn't strange for someone to burst into a restaurant and blow your head open. I always feared for his life when he ventured out, but right now I was about to have a nervous breakdown. And on top of that, Rhys and Lendsey were acting weird, Britain never came to the party, and then he was making Goldie leave. What was going on?

"Stony!" I saw TQ's mother racing behind his father as he stormed over to where Matikah, Summer, Indiya, and I were sitting with the boys.

"Get the fuck out! All of you!" he barked, but glared at me.

"What the fuck is wrong with you?" Lendsey moved Matikah behind him, frowning at his father. *Lord, whatever is about to happen, don't let it happen.*

"Ain't shit wrong with me! Get these bitches out of my fucking party right now before I send them home in body bags." His father removed his gun, and pressed something long up into the bottom.

"Stony!" Mrs. Quinton reached to touch the hand that the gun was holding.

"Daddy, stop!" Saya screeched.

"Move." Mr. Quinton looked at Mrs. Quinton with an evil expression, causing her to back up and pull Saya with her. "Out!" he hollered so loudly that I literally felt myself jump out of my skin.

"They ain't going nowhere." Rhys pulled his gun out as well as he stood to his feet.

"Ah!" Summer screamed when Mr. Quinton yanked her over to him and placed his gun to the side of her head, while hugging her neck from behind. She was crying so hard that I started to cry.

"Get out, or I will blow her head open right here and now."

I could see in Rhys' face that he didn't want to back down, but he also didn't want Summer getting killed. After staring at his father for an eternity it seemed, he placed his gun back into his waist and helped Indiya stand up. Lendsey escorted Matikah and I towards the exit, just as Mr. Quinton walked Summer to the door with the gun still to her head. Once we were all out of the house, he shoved Summer across the threshold and slammed the door.

What the hell just happened?

Matikah and Lendsey agreed to give me a ride home, Rhys and Indiya left together, and since Summer drove herself and Goldie, she was able to just go home. Although not her man anymore, I saw Rhys hugging her tightly as she cried, just before she got into the car. Indiya didn't seem to mind, and I guess it was because she understood why Summer was so shaken up; we all did. I would've had my baby if that gun were to my head like that. And Mr. Quinton would kill her ass for real if we didn't cooperate; we all knew that.

"Thanks," I whispered as I got out of the car.

"Let me walk you up. Come on, Matikah." Lendsey shut the engine off and climbed out of the car. Usually I would've decline, but I was scared that Mr. Quinton had someone up there waiting for me.

The three of us went inside of TQ's condo building, and got onto the elevator. Once we made it to the door, Lendsey had me unlock it before he went inside alone. After he checked the place thoroughly with his gun in hand, he came back to let me know I could come inside.

"I called TQ, but he hasn't answered. Just wait here for him," he said.

"Where is he? What if he's not okay?" I sobbed as I sat down on the couch. I could see tears in Matikah's eyes as well as she looked at me with sympathy.

"He is ma, don't think like that. TQ gon' always be alright." Lendsey half smiled, trying to make me feel better.

I just nodded before he and Matikah both gave me a hug. Once they were gone, I stared at the huge TV mounted on the wall for a bit. I then called TQ five times back to back, and he didn't answer one of them. I was gonna text him but for some reason I felt that wasn't a good idea. Getting up off of the couch, I made myself some hot chocolate, and downed it before passing out on the couch.

***

I woke up in the bed, and I could see through the curtains that it was still nighttime. Looking the other way, I saw TQ sitting in the La-Z-Boy across the room, drinking some brown liquor. When he saw me sitting up, he removed his gun from his lap and set it on the dresser. I got out of the bed, and that's when I realized I was in one of his white t-shirts.

"How are you feeling?" he questioned before taking another sip. As I got closer, he placed the glass next to the gun to welcome me into his lap.

"Your dad—"

"I know, I know shorty," he sighed. "I'm gonna have to get at him."

"What do you mean?" I kissed his forehead and changed my sitting position so that I was straddling him.

"I'm gonna have to kill him, Kimberlyn. What he did tonight was the last straw. The disrespect, and just the way he moves, I can't take it anymore."

"TQ, don't kill him. Maybe just meet with him first, and try to talk things out." I held his handsome face in my hands and searched his beautiful blue gray eyes.

He chuckled before asking, "What you think he's gonna kill me first?"

"No, of course not. I just don't want you and your father to be at odds because of me. We're supposed to be a family remember?"

"Shorty, listen, killing my father has nothing to do with you. For a long time he's been rubbing my brothers and I the wrong way. Since I was a little boy, he and I have always been at odds. When I was sixteen, I flew in a shipment and was missing *one* key of product. When he found out he put me in the hospital, he and his goons. They whooped my ass. I had broken ribs and everything," he explained, as he looked off a little bit. He chuckled lightly, but I knew he was still bothered by it.

"I don't know what a key is, but I'm sure it wasn't that serious. If you kill him for yourself I don't mind, but don't do it for me or for us girls."

"I ain't gon' lie, baby, part of the reason is because of y'all. I love you and I will take out anything that tries to harm you. That's just life. A man that isn't willing to lay his life on the line for you doesn't deserve you. I'm here to protect you."

"You're here to love me and make me happy."

"And a part of me loving you is making sure that no one touches you. I don't care who it is, family or not, I refuse to let someone come at you. I already fucked up with that Monica shit, but I'll be damned if I let it happen again."

"We could run away," I smiled.

"Your smile is so beautiful, shorty. And yes we could, but men don't run away from their problems, they face them."

"You love me that much?"

"Absolutely, you and him." He rubbed my belly and kissed my neck. "Have you told anyone what it is?"

"No, I'm gonna wait until the delivery date."

"I can't wait," he whispered.

Draping my arms around his neck, I hugged him tightly, and he did the same but hugged my torso. I caressed the back of his head before kissing his ear and pulling away. We made eye contact for a few seconds, before kissing hungrily, but gently. Whatever he wanted to do, I was gonna have his back because I loved him.

Lendsey Quinton

Two days later...

"Yes, she should be in tomorrow morning as requested. I just wanted to know if she would have her own room?"

I was at work, talking to one of the employers who worked with my father's unemployment agency. She'd hired one of our people to be her housekeeper, and since it was a live in situation, I wanted to make sure our party would have her own room. That was mandatory if you wanted one of ours to move in. Too many times people, mainly men, would try to take advantage of the Russian women we sent out, and I wasn't having that shit. That's why I made sure to keep in contact with them so they'd let me know if some shit popped off.

"Yes, she actually has her own living quarters, Mr. Quinton."

"Wow, okay great. Well, everything looks good, so look for her around 9am. She will be dropped off. Thanks." I hung up the line and exhaled with my eyes closed.

What happened the other night was still very fresh in my mind, and it was to the point where I could barely sleep. My father had always been a hot head, but he completely disrespected Rhys, our women, and me. I mean putting a gun to Summer's head was severely over the top, not to mention the fact that we had no idea why the nigga was even doing all of that. If I were to sweep that shit under the rug, I wouldn't be able to live with myself. He was my father, but if he didn't give a fuck about me, why should I care about his ass?

As I was thinking, I looked up to see Alyona standing in the doorway fidgeting. I hated that she did that instead of letting me know she was here. She would always wait for me to look at her before she said anything, and sometimes she would stay planted in my doorway for ten minutes straight. I was sure that when I took naps here she watched me, but that was another story for another day.

"Yes, Alyona?" I frowned, irritated by her.

"The-there is someone here to see you, Mr. Quinton." She smiled and glanced away for a bit.

"Close the door and come here," I stated sternly. "Close it and come here," I repeated since she was just staring at me like a deer in headlights.

She did as I asked, and then came over to me slowly. I just sat there for a bit, scanning her frame and taking her in. She was so weird to me, and I wanted her to open up some. I was a nice guy, so there was no need for her to be so damn shy when talking to me. I also wanted to make sure that once my father was 'gone' she'd still be down for the team, and not go run her mouth because of her loyalty to my father.

"Did you want me to ma-make you a drink, sir?" she questioned.

"No, I don't. Do you like me, Alyona?"

"Yes, you are very nice, Mr. Quinton," she nodded. I stood up, and she inhaled sharply as I circled her for a little bit.

"No, do you like me? Meaning you find me attractive."

"I'm, I... Yes."

"Is that why you're so shy all the time?" I stepped back from her, and she turned to face me. She tensed up at first, but finally relaxed her shoulders and nodded. "You need to chill out, Alyona. Don't you find me to be a pretty nice guy?"

"Yes."

"Then promise me you will relax."

I needed her to be comfortable with me, because that way we could develop a friendship, giving this loyalty a stronger foundation. If she was scared of me she would flip on my ass in a hot second.

"I will, yes I will relax."

"Thank you. Alyona, there may be some changes and I wanna make sure that if those changes go through, you will continue to have the family's back."

"Have the family's back?" she cocked her head. I hated when Russians didn't understand slang, especially because I used it frequently.

"Meaning that you will still work with us and be dedicated to the cause. We don't want the changes to affect the way you feel about QCF."

"Oh yes, I mean no. No sir, it won't change anything. I am appreciative of what has been done for me, and I plan to be around no matter what."

"Great, now who is out there waiting for me?" I sat down and turned my computer on. She hadn't responded, so I looked to her, snapping her out of her trance.

"Uh, she said her name was Rosie Huerta."

"Send her back, thanks, Alyona." I said, not really paying attention to who she said was out there.

"Of course, Mr. Quinton." She stood there for a few, and then turned to go and get my guest to bring them back here to me. When she returned, I was surprised by who I saw. *Lendsey, you need to start remembering these hoes' names.* I swear it was like I needed to see the person to recall.

"Rosie?" I frowned.

Rosie was Dania's cousin, or someone she liked to call her cousin. I wasn't friendly with everyone in Dania's family, but I could tell that she wasn't Dania's actual family member. Anyway, I'd let Rosie suck me off a few times, but it never went past that. I don't know, for some reason I wasn't interested in getting some pussy. She had some big ass juicy lips, and I only wanted her to suck my dick. After I busted I would be off her and that's just how our 'relationship' was.

"Hey, Len," she smirked. I looked at Alyona who was still standing there, so she finally left out, closing the door behind her.

"What are you doing here?"

"I came here because I need some help around the house, and I know you guys assist people in getting services like that."

I forgot her ass had six kids by four different men. That was why I never wanted to fuck her; she was way too damn fertile for my blood. Every nigga I knew that smashed, soon became her baby daddy. One nigga even said he wore a condom, and although I don't know how true that is, I believed you could nut on Rosie's knee and it would make its way inside of her. That's why I stayed up by the mouth, and even that was dangerous with a bitch like her, which is why I never busted in her mouth.

"Rosie, there is a process before we can send you someone. How soon did you need the help?" I began clicking on my computer.

"As soon as possible. Is there anything I can do to speed it up?" She rose to her feet.

She had six kids, but her body said otherwise. Rosie had a fat ass, big titties, a flat stomach, and sexy long legs. Trust me it was hard not to slide up in her, but I had been victorious in the past, and I would continue to succeed in turning her down. And only a fool would cheat on mean ass Matikah again.

"No, there isn't. Sit down please."

"Why, Lendsey? You don't like looking at me anymore?" I just glared at her, so she giggled and took a seat. "Now that Dania is gone, maybe we can chill sometime."

"When did Dania stop us from chilling in the past?"

"She didn't, but she was the reason you were stingy with the dick. And now that her ass is in the ground, bless her heart, I can finally get what I've been wanting for years."

"Ain't you fucking with some nigga named Carlo?"

"No," she lied. "Even if I was, you wouldn't care. I was never single in the past when I gave you head, daddy, so that shouldn't even be a concern."

"Yeah, well I was, and now I'm not so I'm gonna have to turn down the offer." Even if I didn't have Matikah, I wasn't sliding up in that baby factory.

"Was? So it's true, you have a girl? I thought Dania was bugging."

"Nah, she wasn't bugging. Ain't Dania your damn cousin? Why you be doing her dirty like that?" I frowned, a little bit disgusted by her disloyalty.

"Doing her like what? You didn't care about her when I gave you some head."

"But she ain't my family. And then on top of that you would be telling her shit so that she'd stop fucking with me. For one I wouldn't have cared, and two, I still wouldn't have fucked you. Get yo' ass up outta my office as a matter of fact."

"What? Lendsey, I didn't mean to make you mad, I was just stating facts."

I ignored her as I opened my drawer and removed my pistol. Once I slid my loaded magazine into it, she hopped up out of her chair and started backing away.

"Get out of here and don't even think about coming back. Spread the word to the rest of these hoes that I have a girlfriend, and if any of you try to shake that shit up I will put a bullet in you."

She just nodded with her eyes bucked before turning around and leaving. Once she was gone, I laughed to myself as I put the gun up.

These hoes man…

CHAPTER TWO

Goldie Taylor

My annoying ass sister hit me up the other day saying she had some news to tell me. I wasn't even sure how she'd gotten my number, but I was annoyed as fuck. I usually would have told her to go fly a kite, but a part of me wondered if it was important. I didn't want to wave her off and she be dying or some shit, because strangely enough I would feel bad. I didn't hate my sister; I just really disliked her fake ass.

I sat down at a table inside of this bar named Eastern Standard. I chose this place because they had some really good ass food, and some of the seating was outside. Now that I was pregnant, it seemed like I was always sick, but fresh air helped a lot. So food to feed my baby, and cool outside air sounded like a perfect combination. While waiting, a waitress came over, so I decided to put in my food order. I knew it was impolite to do so, but fuck Chenaye, I was hungry.

About five minutes after the waitress walked away, Chenaye came sashaying in wearing the tightest dress I'd ever seen. It was fairly cold outside in Boston, and also Chenaye never dressed like that. She was always in pants, and if she did wear shorts, skirts, or dresses, they were at her knees. As she got closer I saw that my mother was with her, and I almost wanted to get up and leave. More than I disliked Chenaye, I disliked my mother. I hated that she was so judgmental and always talking shit. Suddenly I wanted to cancel my food order and take my ass home.

"It's uncouth not to stand when your guests arrive to the table," my mother said before sitting down. I just stared at her for a few before turning my attention to Chenaye.

"Why am I here?"

"Well, first mama wants to talk and then you and I will have some sister chat when she leaves," Chenaye grinned.

"Well," I looked to my mom.

"Your father and I—"

"He's not my father."

"Roger and I are losing the home, Goldie. We put a lot of money into the church to keep it open, so we eventually had to dip into our bill money. I figured you could help us out, especially since our money is gone for a good cause," she finished, removing her leather Gucci gloves.

My mother was beautiful with her fair skin and dark hair, and she seemed to have stopped aging years ago. Her waistline however, expanded and seemed to never stop. She wasn't morbidly obese, but because she used to be so skinny, it was crazy to see her at the size she was. I used to think it was happy weight, but overtime I knew it was the exact opposite. She looked like an overweight version of Paula Patton, and I couldn't say that was a good thing.

"How would I help?" I furrowed my brows.

"Not you necessarily, but that man of yours. Chenaye tells me you've been able to benefit from all your premarital activities," she said, enunciating when she hit each of her T's. "Ask him for the money. He's sleeping with you; he should be able to give you some money."

"And what reason do I have to ask him? You have the nerve to come in here and insult me, all while asking for some money? Are you serious? Please tell me you're joking."

"I can't help that I speak the truth, Goldie. I'm not trying to insult you, I'm merely trying to get you to see that your ways will send you straight to hell. However, if you are going to gallivant around town like a jezebel, you might as well do some good. Roger and I have devoted our lives and money to the Lord, and the least you can do is have that man replenish it."

"No." I shot daggers at her.

"Well, Goldie, just know that God is watching you turn down your own mother. I have cared for you and done my best to make something more than a slut out of you."

"I'm pregnant by the way." I grinned at her as the waitress brought my food. It seemed like she did that shit right on time.

"No' honey, I'm fine." My mom smiled at the waitress after she took Chenaye's order. Speaking of Chenaye, she said nothing, and just watched with her eyes bucked as if this was reality TV. My mom waited until the waitress walked away, and then stood up. "Goldie, you are a huge disappointment. That man will never marry you, and you will be left alone with a baby, no money, no pride, and no dignity. You can never please a man who isn't close to God like that Quinton. He's going to ruin your life once he gets bored with you, and I can't wait." She grabbed her gloves and walked off.

"Neither of our fathers married you!" I yelled after her, but she ignored me. I didn't know my point in saying that, but it was the first thing that came to mind that I knew would hurt her.

I hated to admit it, but she'd successfully gotten under my skin. That's exactly why I avoided talking to my mother. She had the ability to make me feel like shit with just her words. She was so damn mean, and every thing that came out of her mouth dripped with venom. She could kill you with her words, and right now I was feeling like I had a huge sword in my back. A little part of me wanted to cry, but I refused to give her such satisfaction. She wasn't here, but I was sure her golden child would run back and tell her.

"You're pregnant?" Chenaye smiled.

"Tell me whatever you have to tell me so that I can go." I began scarfing down my fries like a nigga on death row.

"You have to promise not to tell mama." She nibbled on the corner of her lip, and I thought I saw a few sweat beads on her forehead despite the cool crisp air.

"I promise I won't say anything during our girls' night out," I stated sarcastically as I bit my burger.

"Okay. I have a boyfriend, and we're in love."

"That's great, Chenaye. So I guess Rhys is no longer someone you're interested in?" She cleared her throat, and then shook her head 'no'. "Good, he has a new girlfriend anyway."

"He does?" Her eyes became filled with sadness, odd for someone who wasn't interested in him.

"Yes, he does."

"Oh, who cares. We need to hang out more you know. We need to come together so that you will have some family and stuff."

"Maybe." I sipped my lemonade.

Chenaye and I continued lunch, and surprisingly she didn't annoy me that much. I would be lying if I said I didn't light up when I heard her say my mother was irritating her. Maybe it would be good to have my sister, especially if she wasn't gonna be conversing with my mom on the daily.

Once we finished our food, we promised to hang out again, before I went and got into my car. When I did, I immediately called Britain.

"Hey, beautiful," he answered, making me smile widely as hell.

"Britain, are you happy?"

"With certain things, why?"

"Certain things like what?"

"You, and the baby. That's about it right now until further notice."

"Oh okay, well I will see you later."

"Why did you ask me that?" I could tell he was frowning.

"Just wanted to know that was all. Are you coming over tonight?"

"Yes, but late."

"Okay." I nodded and quickly hung up.

And that's exactly why I stayed clear of my mom; she always

made sure to get in my head.

Chenaye Daugherty

I watched as Goldie drove away in her new G-wagon, courtesy of Britain. She thought she was the shit just because her pussy was able to finally come through for her. She'd been a skank for a while now, and it had finally paid off. Was I jealous? Absolutely. I'd done everything I was supposed to do, and the right way, yet here I was without a man and jealous of my scum of a sister. Well, I had a man, but not the one I wanted. You could definitely say I'd settled, but that was only for the time being.

Being jealous of Goldie was nothing new for me, and begun the day my mother and her father brought her home. My father, Walter Daugherty, was a crazy and abusive man who could never hold a job. One night he went to a bar, met a woman, and was about to take her home until her husband showed up and killed his trifling ass. Once he was gone, my mother began dating all kinds of men. I was only about four years old, but I remember distinctly. Every time I looked up she was bringing someone home, and having him buy us things. She had finally hit the jackpot when she met Johnathan Taylor. Mr. Taylor was a wealthy lawyer, nice looking, and was a great man to my mother. My mom was obsessed with him, and therefore she was obsessed with the child they produced, Goldie. She even named Goldie after her favorite color.

From then on everything was about Goldie, and it was almost as if I wasn't a part of the family. Johnathan tried to include me in things, but it seemed like my mother was the one who preferred that I stay an outcast. I was sure that if she could wish me away at that time, she would have done so.

My mom loved Mr. Taylor, a little too much, which eventually ran him off. He took back the engagement ring and left us, causing my mother to become depressed and gain weight. However, he did promise that if my mother kept Goldie from him, he would support us. He continued to do that until my mom got married to her current husband, Roger. When that happened, he assumed her new man could take care of home, and started only giving money to Goldie as long as she agreed to stay away from he and his wife.

So see, I've always had the bad end of the stick, and I refused to continue to let that happen. The only reason my mother liked me more now was because I put on this Christian hat for her and did whatever she told me. Goldie rebelled and therefore she no longer liked her.

I enjoyed things the way they were when shit was going bad for my little sister, but now that her life was looking up, I needed her to help me get mine going in the same direction. Only way that could happen would be to get me back with the love of my life, Rhys.

I made it to the apartment I shared with my boyfriend in Dorchester, and quickly climbed out of the car. I made it up to the door, and did my signature knock since I realized I'd forgotten my key. In no time, he was answering with a big ass smile on his face; a smile that I had seen over the years and still didn't love. He was simply dick and nothing more, he always had been. The only difference now was that I gave his desperate ass a title.

"So how did it go?" he questioned, letting me by.

"It went well. I can tell she is warming up to me which is good." I plopped down onto the couch.

"How long before you think she will start letting you come over to her crib and shit?"

"I'm not sure Ethan, and she doesn't even live with Britain. The goal is to get to Britain's money right?" I raised my brow and he nodded while sighing.

Ethan and I started fucking around years ago when he was still with Goldie. We were never anything, just simply fuck buddies. He would always beg me to be with him, and swore that he would leave Goldie if I just asked, but I wasn't going down that road. Unlike Goldie, I could see that Ethan wasn't shit from miles away. Dudes like Ethan were only good for one damn thing, some dick. I used to laugh at Goldie when I would see her crying over this trash ass nigga. I knew about every time he cheated on her ass, and I never told her. It made my pussy wet to see her in such despair.

Ethan just wasn't my type, but for now I would be with him because I couldn't be alone. I hated just being by myself with no boo at all. For as long as I could remember, I've always had some kind of homeboy that I could fuck on or something. I would only hit Ethan up if I felt bad for him, or if I only wanted my pussy ate and nothing more. The niggas I fucked with wouldn't go for that, but he would. Right now though, I was out of options, so I agreed to be with Ethan. He was just some bridge dick until I got the man that I really wanted.

Now we were both conspiring to get Britain's money from any safes he kept in his home. At least that's what Ethan thought our plan was. My only goal was to get close to Goldie so she could get me back closer to Rhys. I missed him and I knew I could have him. I was so close to getting him to be with me, but his girlfriend, Summer, fucked that up by diverting his attention elsewhere. I just wanted Rhys so fucking bad man, and Goldie could get him for me. Is that so terrible? I mean Kimberlyn did it for her, and now Britain has her hoe ass at the top of the food chain.

"Why are you so far away?" Ethan smiled and pulled on my arm.

"Stop, Ethan." I removed my arm from his grip.

"Fuck is wrong with you? I thought you said everything went well, Chenaye."

"It did I just—"

"I swear you better not be trying to get close with old boy. If I find out that you're out here trying to give the pussy to that nigga, it's a wrap for you."

"A wrap for me?"

"Yes, a wrap for you. I don't play them games and you know it, ma. The plan is to get in good with your hoe ass sister and get that damn money. I know the nigga got a safe somewhere up in his crib, and that's the only thing you need to be focused on getting."

"I swear, sometimes I think you love Goldie."

I think it was a simple case of 'you don't know what you've got 'till it's gone'. Ethan couldn't have cared less when he had Goldie, but now that she was gone, I kind of felt like he was realizing he wanted her more than he knew. Niggas always love you more when you start to love them less.

"Well I don't love her. You know I don't. I've always only loved you, but you stayed on that bullshit. Now that Goldie is with that nigga, you and I can finally be. Did you tell her anything?"

"I just said I had a boyfriend."

"So you didn't mention the baby?" he quizzed, and I almost slipped up and said what baby.

I was pregnant by him, and I initially wasn't gonna tell him, but he found the test. I went and got the abortion anyway because I knew I didn't want this nigga's baby. And to be honest, it may not have been his because I'd recently had a one-night stand with this guy from my church. Anyway, the only dude I was having a baby by was Rhys Quinton, and the closer I got to Goldie, the closer I would be to getting pregnant. I smiled as I thought about it. And whomever his new girlfriend was would either have to move over or get killed... her choice.

Summer Gillies

I was inside Trader Joes because I needed a few things from here. I was trying to slowly phase into a healthier lifestyle like Hakim, and this was somewhere that he frequently shopped. I wanted to go alone, but his ass just had to come with me. There weren't many places that we didn't go to together. The only time we were apart is if I had to drop Bryleigh off or pick her up from her father's condo. I think a part of him was a bit afraid that he would get his ass whooped again. I didn't care about his reasoning, I was just happy his ass didn't want to come.

As I was looking at the jars of salsa, I spotted a familiar side profile pushing a basket. I waited a bit to see if she would look my way so I could see her face. She finally did when she looked to her right side. I was gonna keep it pushing, but I just couldn't; I had to say something. I didn't like her ass, and I wanted her to know. My dislike for her was because of jealousy, but I would never admit it. I would also never admit that it was my fault she had me envious.

"Shopping." I cut her off when she was about to push her basket.

"Oh hi, Summer," she smiled as if she was really happy to see me. I hated that she pretended to be some goodie two shoes.

"Don't act happy to see me, Indiya."

"I never said I was happy to see you, but I'm not mad about it either."

I scowled at her for longer than intended, because I didn't know what to say. I wanted to jump on her and choke her to the ground, but not only would that cause a scene, but Hakim would think I was crazy. He was already suspicious that I wanted to be with Rhys still, and that would only add fuel the fire. I was even risking it by talking to her right now. Due to my thoughts, I looked to see if he was still across the store, and thank God he was.

"Well, I just wanted to talk to you and make sure that you're not influencing my child. She's a very impressionable little girl, and I don't want you convincing her to be a hoe or something."

"Is this about Bry, or is this about Rhys?" she grinned as if she was so sure that she was right.

"This is about *Bryleigh*, not Bry."

"Why would, or better yet, how would I convince her to be a hoe, Summer? Look I understand that you still love Rhys, and you're a little bothered by us being together, but over time you will get over it. And in case you need to update your database, I'm not an escort anymore."

"I don't give a fuck about you being with Rhys! I left him, did you forget?"

"You did, but I think deep down you're realizing what a big mistake you've made. I'm here to let you know that you will never have him back. I want him just as much as you do, and I'm not going down without a fight."

"I told you I don't want him, I have a man."

"A dumb man who can't even tell that his woman is still lusting after her ex," she chuckled. "Look, Summer I would love to sit here and go back and forth with you, but I need to finish shopping so I can go home and cook for my boyfriend."

"Home? You live there?" I thought the skank was just sleeping over a lot, not fucking living there. Rhys and I took ages to start living together.

"Yes, I do. Rhys and I live together, and do *everything* together."

"Well, I hope you know about his herpes," I lied and turned around to power walk away. She was getting me angry, telling me all that shit. I was not in love with Rhys Quinton, and they could both go suck a fat one for all I cared. "I wanna leave." I walked up to Hakim.

"Okay, let's just checkout."

"No, I want to leave right fucking now," I gritted, making him look at me with a confused expression.

He placed the bag of chips back on the shelf, and then we left out. Once we got in the car, we sat there for a little bit. I wanted him to hurry up and turn the fucking car on, but he was just staring straight ahead like he didn't know what to do next. Lately everything he did, including breathing, irritated my soul.

"Summer, why did we leave?" he quizzed, still looking straight ahead.

"Because I wanted to leave, I just told your ass that!"

"Did it have anything to do with what you and that girl were talking about? Who is she?"

"That's Rhys' girlfriend. I didn't like what she was saying to me, and I didn't want to be in the store with her any longer. It's really no big deal."

"Why did you approach her?"

"Who said I approached her huh? She could've come up to me!"

"Did she, Summer? Did she approach you? I find it hard to believe that she would come up to you when she's the one that has Rhys."

I folded my arms across my chest to lock in my hands so that I wouldn't punch this nigga. His words made my skin hot, because he knew nothing of what he was talking about. At least I tried to tell myself that.

"Leave it alone, Hakim, damn!"

"No! I'm not leaving shit alone! All you talk about is that nigga, and now his girlfriend has you up in arms? What did she say to piss you off, Summer? Because I'm starting to think that you wanna be back with that nigga!"

"Well I don't." *Do I really only talk about Rhys?*

"What did she say!" he barked.

"She was making up lies, telling me they live together and how I want her man. I didn't like her attitude, and I'm gonna make sure I tell Rhys to get her ass in check." I shook my head as he began laughing. "What?"

"Do you want to be with him?" He finally looked at me. His facial expression was no longer filled with anger, but with innocence. He really just wanted to know.

"No, Hakim, I don't want to be with him. If I wanted to be with him, trust me I could. He loves me, not her, so all I would have to do is snap my fingers and he would be back in my life like that."

"And that was supposed to make me feel better?"

"What is wrong with you? Are you jealous of him?" I furrowed my brows. I'd already told this nigga I wasn't interested in Rhys, yet he kept acting like I was. I was starting to think his ass wanted to be with Rhys.

"I mean I wasn't at first, but now I am a little. Can you blame me though? My girlfriend sits up and talks about another man so damn much that it has me wondering if she really even wants to be with me. So yes, there is a little bit of jealousy there."

"Hakim, I have love for Rhys, but I don't want to be with him. I want to be with you, I promise. Rhys can't do anything for me but cause me a headache, and I don't want that. I want an adult relationship with someone who will love me, and I believe that's you." I caressed his face, and then pecked his lips.

I wasn't sure if I even believed what I'd just said, but I would say anything to get him to shut up and drive me home.

Tarenz "TQ" Quinton

One week later...

For a while now, all day everyday I'd been trying to figure out how and when I'm gonna take my father out. I wasn't scared at all, but unlike him I had a conscience. He deserved to die, but a little part of me wanted to let him live because he was my father. He may have been a bad one for eighty percent of my life, but he was my dad nonetheless. In addition to that, I would have to take out anyone who was loyal to him, which was a lot of muthafuckas. Outside of his children, my dad had a whole team that killed and did all kinds of shit for him if we couldn't. Quinton crime family was full of muthafuckas, and we all answered to one nigga, Stony.

Pulling up to my condo, I quickly shut the engine off and got out. It was around 10pm, and hella cold outside. I brought my hoodie up over the back of my head, hit my alarm, and walked across the street after looking both ways. As soon as I stepped onto the curb, some nigga came up on the side of me. I reached for my gun, but was immediately stabbed in the back. I turned to see who it was, and once we made eye contact, he stabbed me again. Men started coming from everywhere, plunging knives into my mid section, arms, and anywhere else they could get to. I was trying to get my gun, but because I was losing so much blood, and constantly being struck, I couldn't get to it.

Finally I collapsed to the ground, bleeding out. I knew this was it for me, and all I could think about was my shorty and my son. I would never get to meet him, and that shit caused a tear to come out of my eye. The pain in my body wasn't enough to bring me to tears, only the fact that I wouldn't see my kid; my first and my only child.

Right before everything went black, one of the men said, "Stony said hello."

My own fucking father...

***

"Ah!" I woke up in a dimly lit room, and the pain in my abdomen caused me to wince. I immediately began looking around, before a light came on. It wasn't too bright, but it gave me more light than before.

"Good morning, Tarenz." My father walked over and sat down in the chair next to the bed I was in.

Touching under what looked like a hospital gown, I felt bandages all over my stomach. I knew what had happened wasn't a dream. The pain was still unbearable, and I was surprised that I was even alive. I just knew I was gonna die when it happened.

"Where am I?" I finally asked.

"My medical facility."

"Where is Kimberlyn? I need to go." I tried to sit all the way up, but my body was aching way too damn much. I kept trying, because I needed to get to my shorty. I didn't care about being in pain.

"She's fine, I'm guessing. Relax, no one has touched your little concubine. All my men did was take care of you and leave." He pulled a pack of cigarettes from inside of his suit jacket. "I'm sure she's looking for you though." He lit the cigarette.

"What do you want?" I stated calmly, in a low tone.

"I want you to show me some fucking respect. You and your brothers are getting out of control, and I would hate to have to kill all of you."

"Would you? Would you really hate to do that?" I glanced over at him angrily.

He burst into laughter as he blew some smoke out.

"Oh, well… Come on moy syn (my son). I made sure my guys didn't kill you, Tarenz. I could have, but I didn't because I want to give you a chance to get your shit in order."

"My shit is in order."

"Oh yeah? Then why don't I have a Boston distributor?" I said nothing in response. "Exactly. What the fuck were you thinking killing Gang! I didn't ask you to kill him, therefore you weren't supposed to! Now we have no funds coming in from Boston! And it is not even your job to kill, only Rhys unless I say otherwise!"

"I'm not explaining myself to you."

"Well you better if you wanna live, Tarenz. You are fucking with my money, and I don't play that shit. Now either you find me someone who can make as much money as Gang out here in Boston, or the next time you see my men it'll be the last."

"Fuck you, Stony."

"Oh have I lost the privilege of being called Dad? Pop? Anything?" he chuckled and took a pull on his cigarette. I wish I had the strength to kill his ass right here. "You know this did backfire a little bit. Your mother has decided that she wants to divorce me. I tell you, she treats you guys like some little ass babies." He stood to his feet. "I won't let her though. I'm sure she'll change her mind soon. I've always had your mother wrapped around my finger."

"Get someone in here so I can leave."

"First I need to know if we have a deal. As soon as you get out of here, you need to get right to work in finding me someone to move weight in Boston." He was now standing next to my bed with his hands in his pockets, and the cigarette hanging from his lips. His once blond hair was slowly turning white in some places.

"Fuck. You." I stared into his blue eyes, and he stared into mine.

He threw his cigarette down, and stepped on it while whistling. When he did that, two men came in and started fucking me up with bats, only hitting my torso and arm wounds. Every now and then he would tell them to stop and ask me to agree, but every time I declined. I was no bitch, and he would have to do better than this. Finally he realized that after they'd fucked my body up, so he told them to stop and began whispering to them. Once they left, he sat next to my bed as I fought to stay conscious. They didn't hit my head, but for some reason I was going in and out. The pain caused a tear to slide down my face.

"TQ, I love you a little bit, so it does bother me *somewhat* to do this. But if you don't agree you will regret it."

I said nothing and rested my head on the pillow. I looked down and saw my hospital top was soaked in blood around my midsection. My vision started to get blurry, and then everything went black.

***

"Wake up!" Son my way! one smacked my face, and when I opened my eyes I saw it was my father. My stomach felt tight, so I could tell that one of the medical professionals had come in and fixed me up again. I watched my father walk to the door and open it. Those same men came in, but this time they were holding Kimberlyn's arms.

"Let her go." I tried to get up, but the pain was even worse than last time.

"Do we have a deal?" my father asked as he slowly placed a .45 to Kimberlyn's temple. She was crying hysterically, and in turn that shit caused me to silently tear up. Her having to endure this shit was all my fault. I should've left her alone that first night I saw her.

After being quiet for a couple moments, I finally nodded and said, "We have a deal."

"Let the bitch go," he ordered before placing his gun in his jacket. "A doctor will be in here shortly," he added and then left the room.

The guys let Kimberlyn go, and she rushed over to me while crying. I waved her over so that she could get into the rather large hospital bed, and once she was next to me, I did my best to cuddle her against me as she sobbed.

My father's actions had me feeling ashamed, pitiful, weak, and embarrassed. But I swear on everything I love, that nigga was gonna pay dearly for it.

CHAPTER THREE

Matikah Jacobson

It seemed like things were slowly getting back to normal ever since that costume party mishap. But right when shit did become regular, I found out that Mr. Quinton had TQ shanked, kidnapped, and some other shit. I knew his ass was crazy, but I never expected him to be so cruel to his own children. It made me hate him even though I didn't want to.

I still had nightmares and trouble sleeping every now and then, because I was afraid that Lendsey's father would burst off into his condo and murk us. Lendsey claimed he and his brothers had a plan, but I just hoped they carried that shit out carefully and quickly. Because if he would put a gun to Kimberlyn's head while pregnant, I was sure he would have no problem actually pulling that trigger on me.

I walked into work, and immediately checked my schedule. I usually had the same people every week at the same times, but I still liked to look. While I was doing so, my co-worker Annalise walked to the front with one of her clients and began checking her out. Once the client left, she turned to me and smiled.

"Good morning," I said as I started towards the back.

"Hey, Matikah, have you heard from Isyss? She hasn't been to work in two weeks."

"Isyss and I weren't the best of friends, so I really didn't converse with her."

"I know it's just I saw you guys talking a couple of times, so I assumed that you two were friends and shit. She told me you were coming over a while ago."

"You assumed because we're black that we're good friends?" I folded my arms, trying to make her feel guilty because I was.

"No, Matikah, that's not what I meant. I'm black, too. I'm just saying that I thought you guys were cool since she mentioned that you were gonna come over." I didn't know her ass was black.

"Well no, Annalise, we weren't cool. She did invite me over, but I didn't get around to it. Isyss was kind of weird, so I'm not surprised she hasn't showed up in weeks."

"I do agree that she did have some strangeness to her, but she loved this job a lot. She hasn't missed a day since she started, but maybe you're right. Maybe she's out doing some weird shit," she chuckled lightly.

"Yep. Well, Annalise, I have to get my room ready, my client will be in, in about a fifteen minutes." I tied my hair up.

"Of course, do you wanna eat lunch together today?"

"Sure."

Once she left, I closed the door and began prepping my room. My client showed up about ten minutes later, and after her I was working nonstop. When I checked the computer, I'd made three hundred dollars in tips just this morning. I hadn't even had lunch yet, and I'd made all that damn money doing something that I loved. I began giggling as I looked over my weekly tip earnings because it was over two thousand dollars. Boy did it pay to work with affluent people.

"Look at my shorty," I heard a familiar voice say. When I picked my head up I saw my sexy ass boyfriend holding food from Tasty Burger.

"Baby, you brought me food?" I half smiled as I rounded the counter. He nodded and leaned down to kiss my lips a couple times. Forgetting I was at work, I hugged his neck tightly as our tongues came in contact.

"Well, who do we have here?" Isabetta's voice caused me to jump.

"What's up?" Lendsey nodded to her.

"Hi, Lendsey." She kept glancing back and forth between he and I. "When did you two start dating?" She tilted her head to the side, squinting her eyes.

"We've been dating for a while now, Isabetta. Come on, shorty." Lendsey took my hand into his and we left out. I looked over my shoulder as we exited, and Isabetta was still standing there watching us walk away.

Lendsey and I found somewhere to sit, and as he opened the food bag, my mind began to wander. I felt uneasy about what had just happened because I'd intentionally kept the fact that I was dating Lendsey from Isabetta once I found out Dania was her sister. I was a bit scared to go back in there, because I wasn't sure of what she'd say exactly, and how she would react.

"Thanks for the food, baby." I smiled and put a fry into my mouth. He didn't say anything, he just started texting on his phone. "Lendsey, seriously? You bring me food to sit here and text?" I reached for his phone, but he moved it in time.

"It's the only thing I can do to keep from wringing your fucking neck, ma," he grimaced.

"Wringing my neck for what? What the fuck did I do?" He really had my attention right now, because I was beyond confused.

"Why the fuck doesn't she know that you're my girl, Matikah?" he furrowed his brows, looking sexy as hell. I loved him so much.

"Because the topic never came up! I don't just go around letting people know who my man is!"

"Oh you don't? Because every time I look up yo' ass is telling someone that I'm your nigga, or giving a bitch a face if she's looking too hard. Were you ashamed to tell that hoe I'm yours? Because if so we can dead this shit!"

"No, I just didn't want her to know because of Dania."

"Matikah Jacobson, if you're gonna be my girl, you have to *really* be my girl. I need a rider, someone who will have my back and be down for the cause no matter what. I can find a scared little girl anywhere, and if that's the shit that you're on, we should just wrap this shit up." He stared into my eyes as his beautiful, blue ones darkened. "Cool." He rose to his feet and started off before I could get my mind right.

"Lendsey, stop!" I rushed after him and grabbed his hand. Placing his arms around my waist, I gripped the sides of his face, which was twisted all up. "I'm sorry I didn't tell her that you were my man. I won't act like that anymore, okay?" I raised my brow and he nodded begrudgingly. "I would never be ashamed to call you my man, if anything I would rather show you off. I was afraid, I admit, of what she would think, but all I care about is you and being with you. If that means it's just us until the end, against everyone else, that's okay."

He finally hugged my body tighter, before bringing his lips to mine. After kissing softly for a few moments, he pulled away and flashed me his smile.

"I love you, shorty."

"I love you, too."

We went and sat back down so I could eat. Once I was finished, we talked some more, kissed, groped, and then said our goodbyes.

"Hey, Matikah, Isabetta left early today and she said she will be back a week from today." Annalise approached me.

"Oh, did she say why?"

"No, but she said to give you the keys. You will be the opener and supervisor while she's gone away." She smiled and dropped the keys into my hand.

"Thanks." I looked down at the keys.

What the hell was going on?

Rhys Quinton

The next day...

I palmed the back of Indiya's head as she bobbed up and down on my dick. Her head game was crazy, and she gave the best blowjobs hands down. I've had my dick sucked by a lot of different bitches, but Indiya was phenomenal. She didn't try to look cute while doing it, which was most girls' problems, so I think that's what made her ass so great.

It seemed like the more time I spent with shorty, the more I liked her. I have to be honest and say that she does keep me calm. In certain situations where I found myself acting out in the past, she was somehow able to talk me out of getting irrational. I wasn't sure if it was her calming voice or the words she used, but I preferred it over Summer's screaming and crying about how much of a monster I was.

"Fuck," I groaned and pressed my head into the pillow as I spilled my seeds down her throat.

She licked me clean, and then got up to go brush her teeth. As soon as she came back, I pulled her ass back down onto the bed and kissed her hungrily. Pulling away, I pushed her hair behind her ears and just admired her beauty. She half smiled, but then her eyes darted downward, making it obvious that she was bothered by something.

"What's wrong?" I questioned, but she just shook her head. "Tell me."

"I saw Summer when I went to the store, and by the way she was coming at me, I could tell that she still loved you."

"So what?" I shrugged.

"You don't miss her? You don't think about her anymore? I don't want to invest in what we have for you to come back later and tell me you're going back to her."

"I won't, shorty, I promise."

Hearing Indiya tell me she thought Summer still loved me had me feeling some type of way. I was feeling guilty, and I shouldn't have been. I felt that way because upon hearing that she may be in love with me still, I realized that I didn't feel the same anymore. I used to get all warm and shit when I thought about Summer, but these days I didn't. She was just my child's mother, and the fact that I didn't love her like I used to made me feel bad. It was almost as if I felt obligated to still be in love with her because of our history.

I think what made my love for her dwindle was the constant rude comments she'd made since being with Hakim; like saying she was never in love, on top of how she acted while we were together. Granted I did shit to make her feel that way, but I was really trying. And even when I tried doing what she wanted, like coming home, she still found a way to bitch at me or treat me like I disgusted her. It's only so much a person can deal with before their feelings start to change. She wasn't the girl I fell in love with at all. The Summer I knew loved me like crazy, but this new Summer was only interested in making me feel like shit.

"I hope not. It's kind of scary because I have deep feelings for you, and if you leave me to go back to her I don't even think I will be able to function," she began tearing up.

"Are you in love with me?" I frowned and she shrugged one shoulder.

"I've never been in love so I wouldn't know. I just want you to be sure that you don't love her anymore. Because if you do, I want you to let me go now so I can salvage some of my feelings. I promise I won't be mad if you tell me that's where you want to be. You guys have a baby so it's not odd for you to have feelings still."

"Listen, shorty, I love Summer because of our history and the fact that she has my baby. Did I want to be with her when you and I first started, yes I did, and badly. But over time I had to accept the fact that she and I weren't meant to be. As badly as I wanted to believe that she was the one, I had to come to terms with the fact that she wasn't. It's like I was trying to force something that had been done with long ago. So don't stress over that shit aight, ma?" I pecked her and she nodded.

"She said she didn't want me convincing Bryleigh to be a whore," she giggled, but that shit immediately pissed me off.

"She said what?" I sat up.

"She was just upset Rhys, she didn't mean it I'm sure. She was just trying to ruffle my feathers!" She called after me since I'd left the room.

I went into the bathroom, brushed my teeth, and then got into the shower. As I was letting the water fall all over my body, I heard Indiya climb in behind me. I turned to face her, and then kissed her full lips gently and sensually.

"Don't be mad about what she said, it doesn't matter." She caressed my face.

"I don't want her thinking she can talk to you like that, shorty."

"It didn't bother me."

"It bothers me."

"Don't let it bother you, baby. It's really not that serious if you think about it. She's upset and unhappy right now, so don't let her words disturb what we have." She began washing my chest and abs. "You're too fine to sweat the small shit." She grinned with her pretty ass. "You're Rhys Quinton, you can't be bothered with things like that, especially when you have this stuff going on with your father."

"I know."

"You have bigger fish to fry, and I am the only woman that I want you getting worked up over. She will get out of her feelings soon enough, daddy." She continued washing me. "Uspokoysya (calm down; relax)."

"Come here." I pulled her closer, lifted her up, and brought her down onto my dick. "What would I do without you?"

"Be out there killing everything walking," she whimpered as I eased in and out of her.

I pulled her bottom lip into my mouth and sucked on it as I guided her up and down my rod. Seeing her body covered in water droplets was the sexiest shit ever. Her beautiful face was knotted up as she let out all kinds of whimpers and coos. Her body shivered as she released on my pole, so I held her small torso tighter in my hands before slamming into her wet center.

"Ahh, uuhh, Rhys!" she gripped my shoulders to hold on, as I slammed into her pussy with force. She looked deeply into my eyes, crying as I fucked the shit out of her, which caused me to bust all inside of her pretty ass.

While still inside, I brought her into me, and she hugged my neck tightly, trying to catch her breath. Once she did, she slipped her tongue into my mouth as we stood under the water.

See what I meant about her keeping me calm? I could never let her go, I needed her.

Tekeya Mitchell

*T*he day I went into Gang's office, he and I came up with a plan to pin the murder of my unborn on Britain. I spoke to my brother, who is a police officer, and he explained to me that there was a good chance because he was present when I took the drugs that killed my child. We immediately got to work, and after greasing some palms, my brother was able to have Britain arrested on feticide charges. Unfortunately for me, I had forgotten all about his father and his connections. Britain didn't even spend the damn night in jail before his father was making calls to have him let go. When I asked my brother to look into it, he told me the case was dropped completely, and he was also a bit shaken up because he claims Britain gave him a death stare.

Upon finding out about the case being dropped, I decided to go ahead and get out of town. Before Britain got arrested, I was already making plans to leave and head to Illinois with Angelica, but changed my mind since I was able to hook up with Gang. Initially I'd applied for a couple jobs in Illinois, and so did Angelica, but we had yet to find anything. Because my brother feared for my life, he bought us both plane tickets and put money into my account so that I could pay rent should I find an apartment. I agreed with him on leaving now, because my plan had gone completely south.

Gang was supposed to take care of TQ, but I hadn't heard from him since the night Britain got arrested. I was sure he was dead, but then again he had probably left town. All I knew was that I didn't have his protection, or Peel's, and I'd made an enemy out of a Quinton. The only thing left for me in Boston was a bullet.

"This is nice," I said as I walked into the hotel room.

Angelica and I were in Bolingbrook, Illinois, ready to start over. My brother was still working on getting us a condo through some friends he had out here, so we would be living in this hotel until then. I hated to admit it, but I really missed Boston already. I loved the atmosphere, and I was just used to my life out there.

In such a short time, everything had changed for me, and just the thought alone had me wanting to break down and cry. I'd lost my man, and now I'd lost my life. Out in Boston I was somebody. I was the prettiest bitch in the hoods, and I was the girlfriend of Britain Quinton. Now, I was just a regular bitch in Bolingbrook.

"Cheer up, Key. We're gonna be okay out here. This area is really nice." Angelica smiled as she looked around the hotel room.

She knew nothing about Illinois to be able to make such a comment. And it was clear that she didn't feel the same way I did about living out here. She was happy to move away, and I guess it was because she wasn't like me. She was known as being my sidekick and nothing more, so she really wasn't leaving anything behind. I'd tried getting her hooked up with one of the Quintons, but them picky niggas wouldn't even let her sniff the dick. Angelica wasn't ugly, she was just kind of whack if that makes sense. She had no swag or anything special about her. She had a pretty face, an okay body, but nothing else. You needed way more than that to get with a Quinton.

"I'm gonna take a shower and get ready for bed. I wanna wake up early tomorrow so I can apply for some jobs," I sighed, taking my bag with me into the bathroom.

I quickly undressed as tears began to roll down my cheeks, before hopping into the shower. When I was done, I brushed my teeth and dozed off as soon as my head touched the pillow. I could not get used to this.

An hour and a half later...

"Key, Key." I felt someone shake me.

I opened my eyes to see it was Angelica. The room was dark, and she was lying next to me in my bed. She better have had something important to say, because if she woke me up out of my sleep for some bullshit, she and I were gonna have a fucking problem.

"What, Ange?" I sat up.

"I just wanted to make sure you were okay."

"Yes, I'm fine." I nodded. I wanted to be mad, but I appreciated the fact that she cared enough about me. These days it seemed like no one did, and when I say 'no one' I mean Britain. She stared at me for a little bit, before pressing her lips against mine, catching me off guard. "Ange—"

"Just relax, Key." She pushed me onto my back, and dipped her head under the covers.

I pushed them off of her, and watched her tug my panties down my legs. Throwing them to the side, she buried her face into my center and got to work. Was my best friend really eating my pussy? And she was doing a good job at the shit, too.

"Ange," I whispered and ran my fingers through her short haircut.

She was sucking the life out of my clit, and it was the best feeling in the world. Pushing my pussy more into her mouth, I began grinding my hips against her tongue, fucking her face slowly.

"Oh my gosh, Ange!" I screeched as my legs began to tremble wildly. "Shit, keep doing it like that!" I hollered and threw my head back.

Angelica was a beast. She hadn't slowed up yet, and I'd already exploded three times. My body was getting weak, and in a minute I would be going into cardiac arrest. My body froze up before quivering, and I was finally able to push her face away.

"You taste so good, Key." She smiled as she kissed my inner thighs. I was too out of breath to respond to her ass, so I just caressed the side of her face while gazing up at the ceiling. "I was thinking maybe we could give us a try." That woke my ass up real quick.

"Give what a try?"

"Us."

"Like as in being a couple?" I frowned. Was she serious? She and I had been best friends for the longest, and she thought we could just be in a relationship? It was weird enough that she'd decided to eat my pussy.

"Yes, I mean we already love each other."

"I love you as my best friend, Ange, not as a girlfriend. Plus I'm not gay. Hello, the whole reason we're even in Illinois is because of Britain.

You know I'm still in love with him, otherwise I wouldn't be in this situation."

"How do you know you're not gay if you've never tried it?"

"I did just try it, and yes I liked it, but that doesn't mean I like women. A damn dog could've gotten down there and I would've liked it, that doesn't mean I wanna date dogs."

"Well you did a date a fucking dog! You dated a nigga who had you out here looking dumb as fuck on the daily! That's why bad shit happens to you, Tekeya, you don't know when you have a good thing in front of you." She climbed off of the bed and began rummaging through her purse for her cigarettes. Once she retrieved them, she took one out, lit it, and inhaled deeply.

I was perplexed at what was happening right now. We hadn't drank anything, nor had we smoked, so she couldn't have been under the influence. Maybe she had a little something while I was asleep. I wasn't sure, but I didn't like the way she was acting at all.

Angelica was supposed to be my best friend all of these years, but now I was starting to think that for the last couple she may have had an ulterior motive. Lately, but prior to Britain and I breaking up, she would always try to convince me to leave him. She would sometimes even bring chicks to me who would then tell me how they had slept with him. It backfired for them because I would always fuck the bitch up after. Then once I was finished breaking my foot off in their ass, she would ask, "So are you finally done with him?"

I watched Angelica continue to pace the room, taking pull after pull on the cigarette. It seemed to be burning away by the millisecond.

She looked enraged, and I was actually a bit afraid of what she'd do.

"Ange—" I cut the lamp on.

"Shut the fuck up!" she shouted through tears. Her eyes were puffy and red, and I could see how sad she was to find out that I wasn't gonna be with her. "I am tired of sitting back watching you chase other people!"

"Angelica, calm down! I am not gay, and even if I was gay I wouldn't be with you because we are best friends!"

What I said seemed to stir something up inside of her, because she smashed the cigarette into the writing desk next to her, and began panting heavily like some animal. As I looked into her eyes, it was almost as if she wasn't there. This was not Angelica, and once I realized that it only frightened me some more.

"You bitch!" she charged me, gritting her teeth.

POP!

I pulled my .45 that I'd stored in the drawer next to the Bible, and shot her ass in the neck. She fell back immediately, with her eyes wide open, staring at the ceiling.

"Ange?" I climbed out of the bed slowly. "Angelica! Angelica ,I'm sorry!" I began shaking her ferociously, hoping she'd wake up. "I only meant to harm you!" My brother had been begging to help me get my aim together, but as usual I thought I knew how to do everything already. And because of my stubbornness, my best friend was dead.

Could my life get any fucking worse?

Britain

A few days later…

*K*NOCK! KNOCK!

I stood outside of Tekeya's brother Stewart's house, banging on the door like I was the police. Stewart lived in Dorchester, a pretty shoddy neighborhood that I was very familiar with.

I was here for a couple of reasons, and none of them muthafuckas were positive. I knew that since he was in law enforcement, he'd definitely helped Tekeya file murder charges against me, and that had me heated. That wasn't my only clue, because I'd seen him hiding in the back as they brought me through, hoping I didn't see his ass. He was the first muthafucka I noticed, and from that night I knew he would meet his deadly fate at the hands of me.

"Open up this muthafucking door before I blow this got damn house up!" I barked, sounding like the wolf from the three little pigs story.

Finally I heard whispering as the doors were being unlocked. Cocking my gun, I pointed it at the door, and as soon as it opened, he and his wife held their hands up.

"Britain, hey man, what's good?" Stewart smiled, still holding his hands up in mock surrender.

"Move back," I grimaced, pointing the gun at he and his wife.

"Key—"

"Move back!" I hissed, and they both did as I asked.

Walking in, I closed the door behind me and then used my gun to gesture for them to sit down on the couch across from the door. Once they were seated, I plopped down on the couch across from them and just mugged the fuck out of their asses.

"Where is Tekeya?"

"She's here in Boston, Britain," Stewart shrugged and smiled.

"She's not here, she's in Illinois, but I need to know which part. The last thing she bought was some peanuts in the Chicago O'Hare airport, so I know she's close to Chicago."

Stewart was hesitating, but his wife was looking as if she wanted to give Tekeya's ass up. I wasn't leaving without some answers, and if I did, both of them would be dead when I was gone. I refused to give Tekeya's ass anymore passes. I didn't give a fuck if she moved and would be away from me. She immediately became a foe of mine once she decided to have charges brought against me. It's crazy because I thought she was smart enough to know not to fuck with a nigga like me.

"Promise not to hurt her." Stewart looked into my eyes.

"I won't." I smiled.

He couldn't be serious. He had to know that I was gonna kill that bitch, but hey, maybe he had no idea about what and who my family was, and why we had so many people in our pocket. If he didn't and felt comfortable telling me his sister's whereabouts, that was perfectly fine with me.

"She's in Bolingbrook, at the Holiday Inn on Remington," he responded, prompting a grin to appear on my face.

"Thank you," I stood to my feet, and turned on my heels.

"Britain, please don't kill her. Rough her up a bit, but let her go. She didn't mean anything she did, she just loves you man," he said to my back.

I looked over my shoulder with a smirk and said, "I promise I won't."

POP!

"Ahhh!!" Stewart's wife, Laila, screamed at the top of her lungs as her husband lay dead on the floor with a bullet in his forehead. I went back and removed his wallet from his jeans, before stuffing it into my pocket.

"Come on." I grabbed her arm. "You better come out of this house like you have some sense, and if you don't I will drop you like I did your husband. No one will tell either, ma, because the Quintons own Boston and you know that," I whispered into her ear and she nodded. I wanted her in case Stewart had lied about where Tekeya actually was.

We walked out of the home, and she was calm just like I had told her to be. It was late in the night, so no one was outside, but I wasn't worried either way. There wasn't a muthafucka that was dumb enough to tell on a Quinton, and if they did, not only would they die, but it would be for nothing since we had ninety percent of law enforcement on our payroll. We even had a couple of judges. I mean look at what snitching got Tekeya.

Once we both were in the car, I peeled out and headed to the warehouse. She was quiet the whole time, looking scared out of her mind.

"Wipe that fucking look off your face," I stated calmly as I lit a blunt at the red light.

She wiped her face down with the back of her hands, and then took a deep breath. As we drove through the dark streets, only lit up with streetlights, there was silence in the car. I had nothing to say and she damn sure better not have had anything to say. But suddenly, I felt her hands in my lap, and when I looked over she was lowering her head to try and suck my dick.

SCURRRR!

I slammed on the breaks and immediately lifted her head from my lap with my gun.

"Don't touch me, ma, just sit there and ride like I fucking told you too, aight?"

"Yes, I'm sorry I just—" I put my hand up and she stopped talking.

I pulled up to the warehouse, and threw the Oldsmobile in park. I tugged her across the seat by the arm so that she could get out of the car on my side, and then I brought her around by the trunk. Opening the trunk, I took out a sack, and covered her head with it. She began moving wildly until I shoved my gun into her spine, calming that ass right back down. I placed her weeping ass into the trunk, and then drove to my condo to get a few things.

When I got inside of my condo, I saw Goldie on the couch wearing just a bra and some of my boxers. My dick sprang up, but I didn't have time for that.

"Baby, where are you going?" she hollered after me as I power walked to my bedroom.

"I have to go to Illinois, shorty. I will be back as soon as I handle some business."

"I want to come."

"No, Goldie, I'm going alone. What do you need to come for? Don't you have work at that little magazine place?"

"They're not operating for the next three days because of some religious holiday my boss has to take. That's why I'm here right now. Please let me come, Britain, think about me and the baby being here all alone. There will be no one here to—"

"Alright, come on but you can't pack nothing. Anything you need we will stop somewhere and get it."

The only reason I was allowing her to come was because my dad was on some bullshit, and I feared he would try something. He was acting like everything was cool, but I had a feeling that if he got word that I left Goldie and went out of town, he would make sure something happened to her. Yes, I would murder his ass in front of a crowd of people, but that wouldn't bring my baby and girl back, so I wanted to prevent it altogether.

"Yay!" she jumped up and down, but I put my hand on her shoulder to stop her.

She grabbed her shoes, a t-shirt, her purse, phone, snacks, and some magazines before we went down to the car.

"Why are we riding in this?" she frowned.

"Get yo' ass in the car, ma." I opened the door for her and she slid into the passenger seat. "What are we going to Illinois for?"

"Shorty, stop asking me so many damn questions. Do you wanna come or not?"

"Okay, I'm quiet now!" she giggled. I couldn't help but smile because she was adorable.

"Come here," I gripped her chin lightly and kissed her a good couple times before pulling away from the curb.

I drove to TQ's port, because I needed his pilot to fly me to Illinois. I usually would have used my father's people, but since I really wasn't trying to fuck with him like that, I decided against it. When I made it there, I had TQ's co-pilot Primo help me remove Laila's body from the trunk, after taking the sack off of her head.

"Who is this bitch?" Goldie turned her lip up.

"Baby, get on the plane." I kissed her face as she kept her eyes locked onto Laila.

The three of us got on, and once everyone was situated, Primo flew us to Bolingbrook.

***

"Do you know what room number?" I asked Laila as we walked into the hotel. She shook her head no.

"He just paid for the room, he didn't get the number."

We'd just come from the suite that Goldie and I were gonna be sleeping in for the night, and we were now at the hotel Tekeya was in.

"Welcome to the Holiday Inn," the clerk smiled.

"Hey, I need another key for my room. I've had a long day and I'm not sure where I misplaced it." I was holding Laila's hand, squeezing the living daylights out of it to let her know not to try any fly shit.

"Absolutely, what room number?"

"Umm, shit, I can't even remember. Can you look me up?" I frowned, making sure to strategically shield my face from the three cameras I spotted. My dreads were pulled back and stuffed into my hoodie, so that helped too.

"Sure, can I see some I.D?"

"Of course." I removed Stewart's wallet from my pocket, and slid his I.D. across the counter to her. She glanced down at it, looked back up at me, and then looked down at it again. I looked nothing like him, but we had similar skin colors, he was just a tad bit lighter.

"Thank you, Mr. Mitchell." She nodded and began clicking around. Thank God. "There is your I.D., and your room key. Was there anything else I could help out with?"

"Nope, you've been perfect." I winked, making her blush and smile.

Laila and I walked to the elevator hand in hand, and just in case they had cameras on that bitch, too, I kept my head down towards my shoes. I wasn't too worried about getting caught, but I still liked to be somewhat careful. I didn't kill niggas on the daily like Rhys, but when

I did I wanted to keep it clean. Finally we made it to Tekeya's floor, and tread down the hallway until I got to the room listed on the little, white card holder the clerk gave me. Upon arriving, I put my gloves on.

Slipping the key into the door, I entered and saw Tekeya watching TV and eating. The room smelled foul, and I was sure it was a dead body in here. The smell was very distinct, and I knew what it was every time I came in contact with it. If not, Tekeya needed to have a couple hundred showers and a check up.

"Britain!" She dropped her food onto the floor as I slid my gloves on.

As soon as the door closed behind me, I pulled my silenced gun from my waist and popped Laila between the eyes.

"Ah!" Tekeya jumped at the sight of Laila's body dropping.

"What's good, Key?" I smirked as I moved closer to her. When I looked to my left, I saw someone in the other bed faced down.

"She's dead already," Tekeya cried when I aimed my gun at the person in the bed.

Turning them over, I almost threw up when I saw Angelica's decomposing body.

"Yo, how the fuck are you chilling and eating in here with a dead fucking body?" I frowned at Tekeya's silly ass. This bitch got crazier and crazier as time went on.

"I don't know! I was scared! I didn't mean to kill her, just like I didn't mean to get you arrested! Britain please!" she sobbed.

"Why couldn't you just move on? Why couldn't you just be with the guy who got you pregnant, Key?"

"Because your brother killed him! And I didn't want him, I wanted you!"

"My brother? Bitch, who got you pregnant?" I placed my gun to her forehead.

"Peel."

PHEW!

I sent the bullet through her head.

I couldn't believe that hoe. And all the fucking guilt trips she sent me on about fucking around on her with different women, yet here was she was doing the same thing, only worse because she was doing it with a business affiliate and getting knocked up. Anything that I may have felt for her ass was completely gone, and for once I didn't feel bad about it.

CHAPTER FOUR

Kimberlyn

"Ms. Harrey, it's time!" the doctor yelled to me as I laid on the hospital bed sweating. I was about to have a baby, and I was excited, yet scared. It seemed like everything was happening back to back because I'd just graduated from college, and a week later I'm giving birth.

"Where is TQ?!" I hollered as my grandmother rubbed my head.

"He's coming, honey. They just had to get him in the right attire so that he can come in," my grandma answered as I continued to cry.

"He's here!" the nurse shouted over the room, and I almost broke my neck trying to look around her. He finally made his way through, wearing that gorgeous smile of his. "Okay, it's time to push," the nurse added, before going to stand by the doctor.

"Give me one nice push, Ms. Harrey," the doctor instructed. I clenched my teeth and tried to push, but I didn't do well I guess. "That was good, Ms. Harrey, but I need you to push a little harder for me okay?"

"I can't do it!" I cried and gripped TQ's hand tightly.

"Yes you can, Ms. Harrey, just be a little bit tougher, honey," the nurse replied.

"I can't do it!" I repeated.

"Can y'all give me like twenty seconds?" TQ asked, and everyone looked at him like he was crazy. "Just twenty seconds, maybe even less."

The doctor and nurse made eye contact, before getting up to leave out. My grandmother followed, and once the room was clear, he turned to look at me.

"I can't do it, TQ, I'm sorry," I panted and cried.

He leaned down and began caressing my face gently, calming me down a little bit.

"Kimberlyn, this is our baby, you have to bring him here so we can be a family. Don't you want that?" he asked and I nodded. "Okay, so just try a little harder for our baby, shorty." He kissed me softly a couple times, before going to open the door and letting the doctor, nurse, and my grandmother in.

The doctor got back in position, and although painful and difficult I was able to deliver. All I kept thinking about was how badly I wanted my baby, how happy TQ would be, and how much I wanted to make our family complete. My thoughts alone gave me the ability to woman up and do what I had to do. Seeing him be held up in the air was surreal, because I couldn't believe this was happening to me. Not long ago I was an old virgin looking for love, and now I was a mother. I couldn't wait until they brought him back in so that I could hold him and kiss him.

"Good job, shorty. Thank you." TQ grinned and pressed his full lips against mine as the nurse began to clean me.

I was just happy the hardest part of delivery seemed to be over.

**

One month later...

I was sitting in bed, holding my son, Tarenz Quinton II. He was so cute and small, but I wished he didn't sleep so much. I enjoyed seeing him look around with his beautiful, blue eyes, and seeing him give me little smiles. I loved when he held my thumb in his small hand, or moved his little legs. However, right now, like always, he was knocked out.

"Are you hungry?" TQ walked into the bedroom and sat on the edge of the bed.

"Yes, even though I probably shouldn't be eating."

These days I stayed in shorts and crop tops. My stomach wasn't too fat anymore, I could actually show it, but I had more thighs and butt than usual. I thought it would go down with my stomach, but my grandmother said it probably wouldn't.

"What? You look good shorty." TQ frowned, biting his lip as he looked my body up and down.

I just smiled at him, and laid my son on the little pallet I'd made for him. He had a crib, actually a whole room full of shit, but I wanted to keep him close while I worked on some jobs, just in case he woke up. I didn't wanna miss seeing him awake and moving around.

"What did you make to eat?"

"Just cereal, you want some?" he chuckled, showing his beautiful smile. He was such a handsome man, and I never got tired of looking at him. The more I saw him, the better looking he seemed to be.

"Actually I do want some, can you bring it to me?"

"Nope!" He scooped me up and carried me out of the room.

"TQ, I have to watch—" he cut me off by pressing his lips against mine a couple times.

"That little nigga will be fine. Your other baby needs some attention." He put me down in Baby Tarenz's room which had a bed and started kissing on my neck. "Walking around here in these little ass shorts and shit, got a nigga hard as a rock," he said in a low tone as he sucked on my neck and squeezed my ass.

Kissing me hungrily, he led me to the bed while unbuttoning my shorts. He then tugged them off right along with my panties, and laid me down gently. He stared at me lustfully as he removed all of his damn clothes, and then climbed in between my legs with his monster swinging. Feeling his head caused me to tense up a bit, because we hadn't had sex yet.

"You want to?" He stopped himself.

"Yes, just don't be rough."

He nodded and pushed my tube top up and off to reveal my breasts. Suddenly I felt him pushing at my opening, and I began to pant heavily. It was already super painful, and he wasn't even in yet. I heard him mumble *damn*, before spreading my legs a little more and pushing into me with all of his might. Once he was inside, he went back to being gentle, and held my face to tongue me down.

"Yo, Kimberlyn, fuck shorty," he grunted into my mouth as he went in and out of me slowly. It hurt, but I could also feel the underlying pleasure as he wound his hips into me. "Damn, a nigga wanna cry because it feels so good."

"Uuuh, mmm." I gripped his torso as his long, thick dick invaded my body constantly.

"I wanna marry you, shorty," he growled in between kisses and thrusts. By now I was dripping wet, and I could hear him entering me. Hugging his torso, I kissed him harder as I released on his pole. My pussy throbbed around his dick as he continued to make love to me like he was on the job. "Tell me you'll marry me, Kimberlyn." He gazed into my eyes, pulverizing my center.

"I'll marry you," I whimpered as he pounded between my legs.

"Ahh fuck, ahh!" he called out the sexiest moan I'd ever heard, just as we came together. He immediately kissed me, and when he pulled away I just stared into his blue eyes.

"You really wanna get married?"

"Of course, shorty. I love you."

"I love you, too," I cheesed because I couldn't help it.

We laid there kissing, talking, and fucking, until Baby Tarenz woke up. But after I fed him, we showered together, turned on some low music, and cooked a Russian dinner together. I was for real obsessed with this nigga, but could you blame me?

Lendsey

I walked into the Quinton Workforce building, and on the way to my office, I spotted Isabetta and Rosie chilling in the front waiting area. Stopping in my tracks, I looked to Alyona, and she just shrugged her shoulders. I made my way over to the ladies, and once Rosie spotted me, she gave me that seductive smile she always wore. I couldn't stand these bitches.

"Is there something I can help you ladies out with?" I furrowed my brows.

"Yes, but can we come to your office?" Isabetta replied as Rosie licked her lips at me. I swear I hated her ass, and wished I could take back all the times I allowed her to suck me up.

I hesitated at first, but then waved for them to follow me back to my office. Once inside, I closed the door behind them, and then made myself a drink. I declined to offer them one, because they wouldn't be here that long. A part of me wanted to give their asses the boot before even speaking their piece, but I was a bit interested.

"Talk," I said before sipping my drink.

"Lendsey, we talked before about you helping me out with finding the person who murdered my sister. And before you told me you couldn't help me, but I believe you can," Isabetta smiled.

"I can't."

"Oh but you can. See your little brother was just arrested. I know because… well everyone knows. But a little birdie told me that your father pulled some strings and got the charges dropped."

"I don't know anything about that, but what's your point?" I shifted in my seat.

"My point is that you lied about having the connections to law enforcement to help me, Lendsey."

"I didn't lie. You said my father got him off, not me right? So again, why the fuck are you in my office begging me for some shit that I've so nicely told you I couldn't help you with."

"Lendsey let me tell you something—"

"No, let me tell you something, Isabetta. Regardless of whether I have connections or not, which I don't, I am not obligated to help you in finding out who murdered your sister. I don't owe you anything at all. And you think because I stuck my dick in her that it's my job to hit the pavement to bring her justice? Is it sad? Yes, it is. Am I sorry for your loss? Absolutely, but don't come up in my shit acting like me helping you is something that I need to do because I don't. I didn't even have to let your ass come back here."

"I didn't say you were obligated to help me, I just thought since you and my sister had a relationship that you'd want to find out who took her away. But I guess since now you have someone new to sleep with and throw to the side, my sister is no longer your concern."

"She stopped being my concern long before she died."

"I used to tell Dania to leave him alone." Rosie sucked her teeth and shook her head like she wasn't just in here begging to take Dania's place.

"Oh you're mad because you sucking my dick didn't get you the same treatment it got Dania?" I raised a brow, causing her jaw to drop, and Isabetta to snap her head in her direction.

"You've slept with him?" Isabetta asked her, pointing to me.

"Correction, she sucked my dick and nothing more. Now, ladies, if you don't mind, I do have some things to take care of, and I can't sit here all day discussing nonsense with you." I stood up.

"Rosie, go wait for me in the lobby," Isabetta said, and watched until her 'cousin' was out of my office before turning to me. "Lendsey, I tried to be nice. And I thought that because of you and my sister's bond, you would have been more than willing to help my family and me. But since you won't, I refuse to help you."

"I don't need yo' fucking help," I frowned.

"No, *you* don't, but Matikah does. If you don't agree to assist me, I will have to let her go and it will be effective immediately," she smiled.

"You can't just fire her for no fucking reason. You can get sued for that shit!" I seethed. She had hit a nerve trying to fuck over my shorty. I was about ready to wring her damn neck like a sponge.

"Oh but I can, and I can ruin her reputation forever, too. She won't be able to get another job unless she leaves Massachusetts, and even then she may not be able to work." She shrugged one shoulder. "I will give you forty-eight hours to think about it, Lendsey. But if I don't hear from you, or get the answer I want, Matikah will be let go." She nodded with a smile, before getting her purse and jacket to leave.

Plopping down in my chair, I massaged my temples because I was stuck. I didn't want to help this bitch, but I knew she would follow through and fire my shorty. I wasn't sure how the beauty industry worked, and I would hate for Matikah to not be able to work in her field of choice because of my deceased fuck buddy. She loved that fucking job, and not only would she not be able to work at Isabetta's, but she may not be able to work in the state.

Could I kill Isabetta? Of course I could, but that may make shit worse, especially since I'm sure she's told her family that she was seeking my help. If she disappeared, that may cause more harm than anything. This was some bullshit.

After working for ten hours, I finally decided to go home. When I got into my condo, I saw Matikah sitting on the couch, curled up watching TV. I tried to see if she was angry or sad at the moment, but I couldn't tell right away. I know Isabetta said I had forty-eight hours, but I didn't know if she had made her move already. When Matikah noticed me, she looked to me wearing a smile, so I let out a sigh of relief.

"Hey, baby, come here." She grinned and patted the couch cushion next to her. I plopped down, and she straddled my lap. "I missed you today. I had so many clients, but all I could think about was you." She pulled my hoodie over my head along with my t-shirt.

"Oh yeah?" I questioned as she unbuckled my jeans, releasing the beast.

"Yes," she smirked right before removing the dress she had on.

"Mmm." She tucked her bottom lip in as she sat down on my dick.

"Fuck," I grunted as I held her torso in my hands, while moving her up and down on my dick. "You are so damn wet, shorty," I licked my lips as I watched my dick disappear inside of her repeatedly.

I began groping her breasts, before taking one of her nipples into my mouth as she continued to bounce in my lap. I switched back and forth between nipples, while squeezing her ass roughly, giving her a smack every now and then.

"Lendseeeeeyy," she whined as she exploded right on me.

I leaned her back, placing her legs on top of my arms, and then gripped her ribs so I could beat the pussy up. The way she looked at me with her pretty twisted face as I demolished her middle made me cum so hard that my toes curled up.

"Fuck!" I shouted as we both tried to come back from that orgasm.

She removed her legs from being on top of my arms, and then pressed her body into mine so we could kiss.

I guess I didn't need to say anything just yet.

Goldie

"Do you feel bad?" I asked Britain as we laid in bed at my condo.

He was finally telling me what Bolingbrook was all about, so I was wondering if he felt any remorse for having to get rid of Tekeya. I mean I was happy that she wouldn't be popping up anymore, but I just wish that she had moved on instead of having to die. So if I felt that way, I was sure he must have as well, because I hated the bitch's guts.

"No, I really don't." He shook his head while caressing my thigh.

"Not even a little bit? You guys spent a lot of time together."

"She wasn't the same girl I spent time with, she was someone else. I told you she killed her best friend and was just letting her body rot in the fucking room."

"Oh yeah, that's not only weird, it's nasty."

My phone began ringing, but when I reached for it, Britain snatched that shit up with the quickness. His face was balled the fuck up, and I just chuckled because I knew I was innocent. No niggas had my number because he made sure of it.

"Who the fuck is calling you at 11pm, Goldie?"

"I don't know, Britain!" I turned my lip up as he tapped the green button to answer it.

"Who the fuck is this?" he spat into the phone.

"Where is Goldie?" I heard a female crying, so I snatched it from him.

"Hello?"

"Goldie, can you please come get me? This nigga is crazy and he's about to fuck me up! Please hurry up and come!" Chenaye screamed. I could hear a man going off in the background, and throwing shit into the wall. This must have been her new nigga.

"Chenaye, what the fuck? Text your address."

"Okay, and the door will be open," she whispered before hanging up.

"Where are you going?" Britain asked when I got off the bed.

"My sister, she needs me to come get her. I'm just gonna run over there before some nigga she's messing with kicks her ass."

"Okay." He got up, pulled his jeans on, and locked his 9mm in his waist.

"Britain, I'm just going over there—"

"*We're* going over there. And just in case that nigga gets froggy with you, I will be there to pop his ass. Come on." He stormed out after pulling his shirt over his head.

We left out to get into his car, and in no time he was speeding down my street. I plugged Chenaye's address into his GPS, and he followed it until we ended up in front of her building. Britain got out first, and then came around to open the door for me, before escorting me into her building as if I was some princess and he were my security. After checking my phone for the right unit number, we landed in front of Chenaye's. I should have been able to guess which one was hers because there were loud voices coming from inside.

KNOCK! KNOCK!

Britain banged on the door, but since it was open like Chenaye said it would be, it just slowly swung back. Britain entered first, and made sure I stayed behind him as we followed the loud voices to the back. He kicked open the bedroom door, and there Chenaye was, getting choked by some nigga on the bed. Britain immediately yanked him off, and when he did I thought I would pass the fuck out.

"Ethan?" I frowned. He just stared at me angrily while panting.

"Calm yo' ass down," Britain gritted as he held a gun to Ethan's head. That nigga shaped up quickly as fuck.

"Oh my gosh, Goldie!" Chenaye rushed over to me and tried to hug me, but I shoved the shit out of her. She must have lost her muthafucking mind thinking she could embrace me after what I'd just walked in on.

"Ethan, bitch? Really?"

"This bitch aborted my baby!" Ethan hollered out.

"Yo is this yo' ex?" Britain quizzed, staring hard at me with his bluish gray eyes. I simply nodded my head before turning my attention back to Chenaye.

POP!

"Ah!" Chenaye and I screamed in unison once Ethan's body

thumped against the floor.

"Britain! Why did you do that?" I stared in disbelief as he stepped over Ethan's body and walked over to me.

"You said the nigga hit you one time!" He looked at me like I was out of my mind for even questioning his crazy ass. I just touched the side of his face and kissed his psycho lips.

After gazing at a dead Ethan for a few moments longer, Chenaye said, "Goldie, he and I had been messing around for a long time. This isn't new, and I never wanted him like that! Forgive me," she tried to touch my arm, but I moved it.

"No, Britain," I grasped his arm when he pulled his gun out on her. "It's fine, let's just go."

"Wait, Goldie, can I come spend the night with you? I know I shouldn't be asking, but I need somewhere to stay tonight. I can't sleep in here with him dead on the floor, and plus we were going half on this place. Please, it'll just be temporary, I can't go live with mama."

I looked at her for a while, wondering if I should or not. I didn't give two shits about Ethan honestly, and only remembered him when I saw him. Niggas fucked each other's girls all the time and still remained friends, so why should I let my sister hang out to dry over a nigga, especially one I didn't care about. Now if this were Britain, that bitch would have been dead on the floor already.

"Fine," I said before slipping my hand into Britain's.

"Really?" she cocked her head.

"Yes, really, I don't give a fuck about that nigga. You're a damn fool for even getting pregnant by him. I can pretend to be mad, but honestly I don't even care when I really think about it. But this one," I pointed to Britain. "That will get you gutted like a fish, bitch, so don't even dream about it."

She just nodded her head as Britain and I continued to the living room.

We waited as she gathered some stuff, and once we left some crew came in to clean the house for Britain. On the way home we stopped for some Raising Cane's, and then took it to my condo to eat it. Once we finished I helped Chenaye get settled in.

"You can sleep in here." I showed Chenaye my extra bedroom. "But you need to start looking for some place else starting tomorrow, because this is not permanent."

"Of course not, Goldie. But I am excited about becoming closer with you," she smiled. "Your condo is beautiful."

"Right."

"I need you." Britain walked into the bedroom and hugged my body from behind.

"Okay, just give me a second."

"Nah, now." He picked me up from behind and carried me out.

I looked over his shoulder as he kissed on my neck, and I saw Chenaye watching with a devious smile. She could play games if she wanted to, but it would only send her to the same place Ethan had gone.

As soon as Britain and I got into the bedroom, he placed me on my feet and began removing my clothes so quickly that it seemed like it was being done in one motion. Once I got ass naked, I helped him get the same way, before rushing to close and lock the bedroom door.

"Get back over here." He yanked me back to him, and laid me down on the bed.

He then roughly pressed my legs into my stomach, and latched his mouth onto my clit. Massaging his dreads, I threw my head back to enjoy the area that he was so talented in. I knew exactly why Tekeya was going dumb for this nigga, because his dick and head game were out of this fucking universe.

"Brit— uuuh, uuuh," I couldn't even finish what I as saying as I moaned loudly, totally forgetting that Chenaye's ass was even here. I didn't care though, this shit was feeling too bomb. "Shit, oh my— fuck!" I called out as I released for the second time.

He cleaned me with his tongue, and then stood up. Like a good girl, I sat up and took his dick into my mouth. I let my spit do its own thing as I switched back and forth between sucking fast and slow. Looking up at him, I saw that his head was hanging back as he called out sexily in that deep voice of his. That only gave me more motivation, so I began putting in more work as if I were performing a show.

"Goldie, shit, baby. Tell me this is the only dick you suck like this, shorty," he panted so heavily that his muscular tatted chest rose and fell rapidly. "Tell me." He gripped my hair, pulling my mouth from his dick.

"It's the only one," I responded sweetly, before he slipped himself back into my mouth.

A few more nasty slurps and sucks, and he was cumming hard. I stroked him for about a damn second, and he was right back up. I got on my knees because that was usually how he liked it when he wanted to be freaky.

"I wanna see your face, baby," he grunted, flipping me onto my back.

I laid there, watching as he spread my legs a little. His eyes wandered all over my body, as his teeth dug into his bottom lip lustfully. Bending down, he kissed the small bulge I was getting, and then made his way up to my lips before tonguing me down. Suddenly I felt his head at my hole, so I grasped the sheets as he entered me slowly. Our fingers intertwined as he placed them behind my head, and worked in and out of me.

"Baby," I whimpered while we sucked each other's lips.

He was so fine, and I just loved his lips. As I released, I pulled his bottom one into my mouth to bite down on it gently. Placing my legs on his shoulders, he started slow, but soon enough he was going in. Hearing his moans mixed with mine was enough to have me shaking and cumming all night. After pounding my center to a pulp, he finally shot off inside of me, and growled so sexily that I couldn't help but kiss him.

"You're the shit, shorty," he exhaled.

"No, you're the shit," I giggled.

He finally let my hands go, so I wrapped them around his neck to French him good.

Summer

The next afternoon…

*N*ia and I were out to lunch at this new place named Melon, and boy did I have a lot to talk with her about. Lately we couldn't really say much on the job because Hakim worked with us, and he was always finding time to come by and talk to me. I really didn't see how women only talked to and hung with their man, because you always needed someone to talk about his ass to. I could complain to Kimberlyn, Matikah, or Goldie, but I was a bit embarrassed to say what I had to say, because I feared they would shake their heads at me. I wanted them to continue to think Hakim was my prince charming.

"So how is the love life?" Nia asked once the waiter set down our chicken salads. Damn, she was getting right to it, but I guess since we worked together she had no reason to ask about my work life.

"It's umm, it's okay."

"Okay? Bitch you're still in the honeymoon stage. I remember when you first got with Rhys, that's all your little ass could talk about."

"I was a freshman in high school that's why. But Hakim is great, it's just sometimes I feel like he's smothering me. He's always calling me and shit, and I just don't like that. I need space sometimes and I just hate that he always wants to be together. And then it's not like I can get a break when we're at work."

"I'm glad I dodged that bullet, girl." She stuffed some salad into her mouth. "But damn, you went from not getting enough time with Rhys, to getting too much time from this nigga."

"I know and I feel like I'm being punished for not giving my relationship with Rhys a chance. It's like I love Rhys with all of my heart, but I cannot get over him cheating on me. I have tried Nia, but I can't."

"It is understandable, Summer. It takes a strong person to be able to brush something like that under the rug. I'm like that too, my pride just won't let me move on."

"So it's not just me then. I know I sound insecure but the trust was lost when I found out he was unfaithful, and no matter how much Rhys tried, I couldn't bring it back."

When I found out Rhys cheated on me, it felt like I was hit by a fucking eighteen-wheeler. Rhys was the perfect man; always there for me, the sex was great, he was gorgeous, and a lot of fun. He got angry like he always did, but it was rarely around me because we always got along. There was never a time where I called him and he didn't answer, and there was never a time where I found out he was somewhere that he shouldn't have been. That's what was so scary about the shit; he'd hid it so damn well.

I never even had a gut feeling that he was cheating on me, because he showed no damn signs. There were no late nights, no dead phone excuses, and I never saw a girl calling or anything, so how the hell was I supposed to suspect it? I don't even know how and when he was able to cheat! The only reason I found out was because his friend Jayce's wife got killed by Jayce's side chick, and Rhys felt the need to come clean to me about his. My heart literally stopped when he disclosed that information, and I suddenly felt like I didn't know him anymore. He promised he would leave her alone, and like clockwork Lisa started acting a fool. She stayed calling his damn phone, harassing me on social media, texting him, just all kinds of things. It all led to her running up and shooting me.

So see, because Rhys cheated so damn well, it made it harder for me to trust him. Had he been a messy ass cheater, maybe I would feel better because I would be able to watch out for the signs. But he could be cheating on me again and I would never fucking know. That was frightening to even think about. So no matter what he said to me, I just couldn't move past it enough to rekindle what we had. But did I love the nigga? More than anything in this world, which is what made it so hard.

"I know you've tried to forgive him, Summer, but if you can't you need to move on. And if you're not feeling what you have with Hakim, then you need to let him go, too."

"Then I will be alone." I stabbed my food.

"Ain't nothing wrong with being alone, Summer, it may help you even."

"And Rhys' girlfriend, I ran into her at the store. She's so damn pretty, I hate her," I chuckled and so did Nia.

"Is she?"

"Yes, very. And I can tell she's in love with him. I saw the way she looked at him when she was at Bryleigh's grandmother's house. She looked at him the same way I used to, and sometimes still do."

"What does he think of her?"

"I don't know. Sometimes I want him to not even like the bitch, but then again I don't want him to miss out on a girl who can trust him. I love him, so I want him to be happy, but I want him to be happy with me. Some days I believe I can force myself to get over the past so we can be together, but then some days I know it's not true."

"I feel you, girl." She shook her head, and then looked behind me. "Ooh shit, it's some sexy ass nigga in a suit on his way over here. Don't look!"

I stiffened up and then dug into my salad to act natural.

"Good afternoon, ladies, my name is Romeo. I'm the owner of Melon and I just wanted to see how the food was," he smiled.

He was dressed in a navy blue Brooks Brothers suit, with an iced out watch, and smelling so damn good. He had a low cut fade, and trimmed facial hair, which surrounded his sexy lips. He reminded me of a younger version of Laz Alonzo. Everything about him was so well put together and classy, and I was immediately smitten.

"Romeo, my name is Nia. You look too young to own a restaurant," she flirted.

"I guess so, I'm thirty-four." He smiled at her. "And what's your name?" He diverted his attention to me, licking his lips.

"Summer." I nodded before sipping my water.

"Summer, that's the perfect name for you. I don't mean to be fresh, but are you seeing someone at the moment?"

"No, she isn't," Nia answered and I bucked my eyes at her.

"Today must be my lucky day then," he chuckled. The way he laughed, and even his mannerisms were sexy, but I had a boyfriend. "Take my number." He wrote it down. "I mean I would like yours, but you seem like the type to make me work for it."

"Maybe." I half smiled and took the napkin with his number on it.

"Fine with me, I'm a hard worker." He stared into my eyes, making me temporarily look away. "Well, ladies, enjoy your lunch and the bill will be taken care of. I hope to see you back soon." He winked and then walked away. There was silence at the table for a bit as both Nia and I watched that fine specimen walk off. He even walked sexy.

"Bitch!" Nia burst into laughter. "If that wasn't God sending you a blessing, then I don't know what is! You better call!"

"Nia, I have Hakim remember?"

"Who?"

"Nia!" I giggled.

"Fine, miss out if you want to, *shawty*, but Mr. Romeo is where it's at. Only other nigga as fine as him is Rhys Quinton, remember that. Unless you wanna fuck TQ, Lendsey, or Britain," she smirked.

As Nia talked, I watched Romeo converse with one of his employees. He was extremely good looking, but I wasn't sure if I was ready for all of that. Plus, I was with Hakim. I was with… Hakim.

CHAPTER FIVE

"You wanna hold him, daddy?" Kimberlyn walked into the bedroom holding our son. I nodded and she placed him in my lap. This little nigga seemed to grow every damn day, but he was still hella small. His face just looked more like a person now, and he looked exactly like me.

"Man we gon' have to get you in the gym with this belly." I stood him up in my lap and bounced him, making him chuckle.

"No, he's cute like that." Kimberlyn climbed into the bed and rubbed his stomach before kissing his fat cheek. "I love you," she cooed to him with her big smile. She was so pretty.

Staring at him shove his small hand into his mouth, I wondered how my father could do the shit he'd done to me. I could never see myself treating my son that way, ever. He was my kid, and someone I was supposed to love and protect, not subject to danger and harm. I kissed his cheek lightly as Kimberlyn watched with a smile. He yawned, so she took him and began rocking him so that he'd fall asleep.

I observed her for a little while as she made sure he was comfortable before covering herself to breastfeed him. She was so good at this, and it was strange because she didn't have any kids. I loved everything about my shorty, and it sometimes made me wonder what I'd done to get someone like her.

I was never the best nigga, especially when it came to women, so I wonder why God decided to give me someone so special. She was so selfless, caring, loving, and not to mention beautiful, and I didn't deserve her, but I needed her. I didn't even like to think about my life before her, and I won't ever have a life without her. It may sound selfish, but I hope that I go before she does, because I wouldn't know what to do with myself.

"Let's get married, shorty."

"Okay, when? Next summer?" she looked to me.

"No, like right now. Let's go to Vegas or something and get married. I can fly us this evening. Primo should be okay with it."

"Tarenz, are you sure?"

"I'm one hundred percent sure. What you don't want to get married?"

"No, I do. I just wanted to be sure that you did."

"I know everybody won't be there and shit, but I want to do it now. I don't want you being my girlfriend anymore. I wanna call you my wife."

She smiled and began blushing, so she looked away out of embarrassment, making me laugh.

"Okay let's go. I need to pack."

"No, we can get you new stuff out in Vegas. You can pick out a dress and all that stuff okay?" I leaned over to kiss her full lips a couple times before getting out of the bed. "Once he's asleep, get your jacket and shoes. I'm gonna call Primo since it's a night flight."

"Okay, I love you, Tarenz."

"I love you more."

***

Some hours later...

Kimberlyn I made it to Vegas about thirty minutes ago, and checked into our suite inside of the Caesar's Palace hotel. Our suite had two floors, with a living room, a huge bedroom, and a bathroom with double sinks like at my condo. We were both pretty amazed by it, and I couldn't wait to sex her fine ass on the pool table in here.

"How much was this?" she asked.

"I'm not even sure. I had Dimitria, the family's assistant book it. I just told her to get the best and gave her my information. I'm gonna check my statement though," I responded.

"This is so beautiful, baby." She smiled up at me, so I planted a kiss on her lips.

Taking my son from her, I began showing him the colorful stuff because I'd noticed that's what he liked. Whenever he would get fussy, all you had to do was shove some shit with colors in it, in his face and he would relax.

Once I was done showing him around, Kimberlyn gave him a

bath and then put him to sleep. We then ran a bath for ourselves, and once I got in, I helped her straddle my lap.

"Tomorrow I will be Mrs. Quinton," she smiled.

"You deserve it, too. Thank you for my baby, and agreeing to my wife, shorty. You don't know how much I love you, like for real. I've never met anybody like you, that really cares for me just because, and not because I'm TQ." She was tearing up by this time, making me snicker lightly.

"Thank you for making me the happiest girl in the world," she sniffled and pushed her body into mine, making us even closer than before.

Tomorrow couldn't get here fast enough.

The next afternoon...

I stood at the alter holding my son as the wedding music played for Kimberlyn. We had two random people as witnesses, sitting in the pews smiling as if they were really happy for us. Shit maybe they were, but that would be weird as fuck considering they didn't know our asses. We had one of them agree to record everything, and they had better not fuck it up or I might murk their asses. No, I *would* murk their asses.

Kimberlyn finally appeared, wearing a tight fitting white dress and a veil. She was holding a bouquet of flowers that cost me a pretty penny, which she'd picked out earlier when we went to get the required documentation, dress, and ring. I told her the ring she chose would be temporary because I wanted to get her something customized down the line. She didn't care, but I did. She could wear the shit she got today on a necklace or something.

"Isn't your mama beautiful?" I whispered to my son, and he just stared at me with his big, blue eyes.

She made it down the aisle to me, and the music finally stopped as the pastor prepared to say his speech. My shorty was smiling widely like she always did, and it made me feel good to see her so happy, especially after the way my father and his people had traumatized her. Don't think I've forgotten about that shit.

"We are gathered here today to join Mr. Tarenz Quinton and Ms. Kimberlyn Harrey in holy matrimony. The couple would like to say some short personal vowels, before we proceed with the ceremony. Go right ahead, Ms. Harrey."

"Tarenz, I just want to say that I love you more than anything in this world; you and Baby Tarenz," she smiled. "You came into my life like a tornado, but the good kind. Everything changed for me from the moment I met you, and I knew I wanted to be with you forever. I am blessed that you felt the same, and I couldn't have asked for a better partner in this life. I can't even imagine having a life without you, and frankly I don't even know how I was happy before I met you. I don't care to know either. I want you to know that I will always have your back and stick by you no matter who is against you, even if it's the world. Nothing or no one could ever convince me to turn my back on you, because I'm here for you through the good and the bad. No matter what you go through, I want you to know that I will always love you the same. Not only do I want you, but I need you and badly." *Damn,* I thought.

"Mr. Quinton."

"Kimberlyn, the night I met you I never would have imagined that we'd be standing here today. From the moment I laid eyes on you, I was drawn to you. Your beauty, your demeanor, your warm smile, and your loving personality was something I'd never encountered before. Everything about you was so genuine, and it kept me intrigued and eventually made me fall in love. Shit with you is so simple, and so pure, and it's relaxing to the mind. Every time I look at you, it's so calming. I love everything about you, and I feel so blessed to have you, that I have begun to thank God for you every night just to be sure he doesn't take you away. I don't ever want him to think that I'm ungrateful for such a precious gift in the form of you and my kid. For as long as I live Kimberlyn, I promise to love you, respect you, protect you, and provide for you. You will never have to look elsewhere for anything, because I will always make sure you're happy. I love you and my son more than my own life, and don't you ever forget it." I reached under her veil to wipe the tears she had racing down her smooth cheeks. I glanced to my left, and frowned at the lady who was crying like she was one of our mothers or something.

"Beautiful. Okay, Kimberlyn, do you take Tarenz Quinton to be your lawfully wedded husband? For richer or poorer, in sickness and health, until death do you part?"

"I do." She nodded, and I slid the wedding band on.

"Tarenz, do you take Kimberlyn Harrey to be your—"

"I do," I cut his ass off, prompting him to chuckle. She pushed the wedding band down my finger, and then waited for him to finish.

"By the power vested in me, I now pronounce you man and wife. You may kiss the bride." He nodded towards us.

With my free hand, I lifted her veil, and planted a kiss on her lips.

We had the few people in the room take pictures of us, then we went to dinner to celebrate. After scarfing that damn food down with the quickness and the swiftness, we drove straight back to the hotel. Kimberlyn got our son right and put him to sleep, then we got into the shower together to wash off the days grime, even though it was only around 5pm. Once we finished, she lit a few candles, and then removed her towel to lie across the bed on her stomach, naked.

"Look at my wife." I grinned as I walked the flute of non-alcoholic champagne over to her.

"It's Mrs. Quinton." She took the glass from me and sipped it.

Running my fingers down her small back, I planted kisses down her spine while inhaling the scent of her body wash. I was obsessed with this woman, but it was cool because the feeling was mutual. I spotted her looking over her shoulder at me, so I began sucking on her lips a bit before our tongues came in contact. Keeping my lips against hers, I climbed on top of her, and entered her slowly from behind, making her whimper lowly into my mouth.

"Mm, uhhh," she began moaning in her sweet soft voice. I swear her moans were enough to make me nut in a fucking jiffy.

I held her small waist as I humped her from behind, while kissing her lips. No pussy was better than pussy that you knew was yours. The way her shit pulled me in, letting me know it belonged to me was indescribable. And the feeling of her delicate skin under my hands as I let them roam and wander over her perfect body only intensified shit for me.

"Uuuh," her voice trembled, as well as her body when she released on my rod.

I sped up, watching her small, round ass jiggle a little bit every time I slammed into her. Her hands gripped the comforter, and her face twisted all up every time she hit the base of my dick. I kept my eyes fixated on her beautiful face, watching it go through the motions from when she came to when she got aroused again. I never slowed up no matter how many times she spilled her nectar, getting wetter and wetter every time. It was so good that I never wanted it to end. Winding my hips into her opening as I listened to her whimper and cry, was an experience I would pay to have over and over. The candles, the low light, that big rock on her finger; the atmosphere was just perfect, assuring me that this nut would be one of the top fives I've ever had. Grasping her waist firmly, I slowed down tremendously, savoring the moment of being inside of her.

"Oh fuck," I groaned, knowing that my dick couldn't hold out much longer.

She was too tight, too wet, and too perfect for me to keep ahold on my stamina. Biting down on her soft shoulder, we both cried out together as we exploded. I pushed into her some more, making sure I got all of it out, and then gripped her chin to make her look back at me so I could kiss her.

"I love you so much, Tarenz," she whispered before I slid my tongue into her mouth, while groping her breasts in my hands.

Now that my personal life was where I wanted it, it was time for a whole lot of muthafucking blood to be shed. These niggas better be ready, because I was about to take anybody out who wasn't with me against my father. No woman, child, or man was safe, because a sleeping bear had been awakened.

Matikah

"I literally walked in on him with the bitch!" my client, Wylie, exclaimed as she laid in my workroom getting waxed. She was telling me how she caught her drug-dealing boyfriend named Marcus cheating on her.

"And then what happened?" I raised my brows as I spread more hard wax on the area I wanted. I loved working with people like Wylie, because they always kept up good conversation. It was also better for them because they wouldn't pay as much attention to the pain of the waxing.

"I rushed out before he could see, went to get my bat, and then came back in that bitch swinging! Girl, tell me why she hopped from the bed and out the window?"

"She didn't even get dressed?" We laughed in unison.

"Nope, left all of her clothes. I broke his fucking leg though. He's mad, but he'll get over that shit. He deserved more, so he should be happy he's alive."

"You're gonna stay with him?" I pulled a patch of hair off.

"Yeah," she sighed. "I mean we have two babies and I wanna try to work it out. It's only the second time, and he swears he won't do it again. I believe him, especially since I broke his leg this time," she chuckled lightly, but I could tell this wasn't a laughing matter for her.

"I hope he's telling the truth, because if not he doesn't deserve you, Wylie."

"That's what everyone says. I can't think about that though. No one has to live my life but me, so I can't listen to anyone else."

"True." I nodded as I spread some ingrown hair serum all over her vagina. "Alright you're done. I'm gonna go to the front, and you can just get dressed and meet me out there."

"Okay." She smiled and sat up.

After I washed my hands, I left out of the room. As I was walking I got light headed, something that had been happening a lot. My stomach had been feeling queasy all day too, so by now I just wanted to lie down. I had a doctor's appointment on my lunch break though, so hopefully they'd prescribe me something so that I could get back to work.

Wylie came out a few minutes later, and after checking her out and collecting payment, I clocked out and went to the back to get my things for the doctor.

***

"Good morning, Ms. Jacobson." My doctor walked into the room.

"Good morning." I smiled.

"So you said you were feeling queasy and light headed right?" He looked at the paper on his clipboard, before a frown covered his face.

"Yes, that's right."

"Ms. Jacobson, it says here that you're six weeks pregnant, did you know that?"

My heart stopped in its tracks, and it seemed as if the world was suddenly frozen. Pregnant? Me? He had to be mistaken because I was on birth control, and I didn't slip up with it. I knew when they had me pee in that cup they were checking, but I thought it would be negative. It was negative!

"I'm on birth control though."

"Do you have unprotected sex?" He raised one of his bushy eyebrows.

"Sometimes, but not all the time," I lied. "Most of the time it's protected, but there have been one or two times without," I continued to fabricate my story. I couldn't even remember the last time Lendsey pulled a condom out.

"And do you take the pill the same time everyday?"

"Around the same time. I work so sometimes it's an hour or two off, but still within the same vicinity."

"Ms. Jacobson it must be taken at the same time everyday, not just in the same *vicinity*. Now if you just don't believe it, we can give you another test, but it's right here on my sheet."

"No, it's fine," I sighed.

"I see that you're a bit distressed. Are you financially stable?" he asked and I nodded. "And is the father around? Or better yet, will he stick around?"

"Of course he would! What is that supposed to mean?"

"Nothing, that's just something we have to ask. So if you have the money, and a willing partner, I guess I should say congratulations."

"Thanks."

He left the room, so I could get undressed, and then came back in with some nurse. While she stood to the side, he shoved some stick into me and moved it around for a little bit while we stared at some small, out of date screen. Once he made sure my baby was alright, the nurse cleaned me before they both left so I could put my clothes back on. Walking back in, he wrote on a piece of paper, and then ripped it off before handing it to me.

"Go downstairs, and give this paper to Sheila so you can get some prenatal pills okay? And again, congratulations Ms. Jacobson."

I just nodded and watched him leave. Hey at least I had a good job with a nice income.

Once he was gone, I stuffed the paper into my back pocket, before going down a floor to get my pills. Thankfully it was fast, because I still needed to get some food and get back to work. After going to Raising Cane's, I sped to my job, and made it there with fifteen minutes to spare. I usually complained about having an hour-long lunch, but this time I was happy about it.

As I was eating in the break room, Isabetta walked in wearing a smile. She came closer to me as I scarfed down my food, so I stopped, wondering what was up.

"When you finish, please come see me, Matikah."

"Okay."

I ended up eating all of my damn food, and I knew right then that the doctor was right, I was pregnant. I'd eaten this same meal hundreds of times and I could never finish. But today, I ate every damn scrap and was still hungry for some sort of dessert. After throwing my trash away, I went to Isabetta's office.

"Sit down for me, Matikah." I did as she asked, and she removed some papers from a folder. "Matikah, I really enjoy your work, your energy, and just you as a person, but unfortunately I'm gonna have to let you go."

Closing my eyes tightly I asked, "Wait what?"

"Yes, it's been great, but it's time we part ways. Now I need you to sign this paperwork here so I can go ahead and hand over this check."

"You already have a paper check ready? How long have you been planning to fire me?"

"That doesn't really matter, Matikah, just please sign the documents."

"Isabetta, I don't understand why I'm being let go. Did I do something wrong?"

"Sign the papers or I will have to call the authorities to escort you out, Matikah."

I stared at her, astonished for a few moments before getting up. I wasn't signing shit, even though I had no idea what the fuck it was. This bitch had me fucked up, and the only reason I wasn't going across her fucking face was because I didn't want her blackballing me in the beauty industry.

"No signature, no check!" she called after me as I left the room.

I quickly went to the back to gather my things, as well as some other shit of mine in my workroom. As I was walking out Annalise spoke to me, but I was in utter shock and just couldn't respond right then. When I made it to my car, I threw the shit inside, and then hopped in before speeding the fuck out. This day had been a fucking rollercoaster for me, and all I wanted to do was lie in bed and cry.

I picked up a carton of ice cream, and then went straight to Lendsey's condo because I wanted to watch his big screen and sulk on his plush ass couch. I loved his place, which is why I'd damn near moved in. That's how my ass ended up pregnant.

I shook my head at my thoughts as I opened his front door. Tossing my purse onto the couch, I set the ice cream down, and went to his bedroom to change into some pajama shorts and a crop top. I then went back to the front, got a spoon, popped open the ice cream, and cut on Netflix.

Me: *I got fired.*

Kim: *What the fuck? Why?*

Goldie: *Are you serious? Who did you curse out?*

I chuckled at Goldie's text, and as I was about to respond to them, Lendsey walked in wearing his beautiful smile.

"Look at my shorty, relaxing and shit. You must be off tomorrow." He walked over and kissed me before sitting down.

"I'm gonna be off for a long time," I began to tear up.

"What? What are you talking about?"

"Isabetta fired me today, and she wouldn't tell me why." The tears began cascading down my cheeks as I stabbed the ice cream with the spoon. He didn't say anything, so I looked over at him and he was staring at the TV angrily. "Lendsey, did you hear me?"

"Ye-yeah, and she didn't give you a reason? She can't do that, shorty. You need to go back and demand a reason, and if she can't give you one, tell her ass you're gonna report her."

"I don't want her to ruin me, Lendsey."

"Fuck that bitch! She can't go around firing muthafuckas for no got damn reason! Go ask that bitch why she fired you before I go down there and smoke her hoe ass!" he seethed. He was way madder than I had expected, but his crazy ass was getting me pumped.

"Okay, baby," I smiled at him. His angry face was so sexy.

"Fuck you smiling for? That bitch is this close to getting her wig split, ma." He held his pointing finger to his thumb to show me how close she was.

"I know. And guess what else happened today?"

"Aww shit, what?" he turned his lip up.

"I found out that you got me pregnant," I grinned and rubbed his soft kinky hair as he gaped at me with his beautiful eyes.

"Me and you are gonna be somebody's parents?"

"I know right," I scoffed.

"That's gon' be the dopest fucking kid in Boston, I mean besides Bryleigh and Baby Tarenz." He smiled as he stared down at the floor, before turning his attention to me. "Come closer."

I moved closer into his body after he removed his jacket, and he wrapped his arm around me before kissing my lips. Caressing the side of his handsome face, I admired his smooth brown skin and how well they complemented his beautiful, blue eyes. We kissed again, and then started eating the ice cream as he looked for something for us to watch. He could always make me feel better.

111

Rhys

I was helping my daughter make up her bed, and put up her toys since her mother was coming to get her. Summer was slowly becoming less difficult, and now agreed to just pick our daughter up from me instead of her mother's and vice versa. It felt good to see her not be so spiteful, but you never knew how long some shit like that would last with Summer. She would be cool for a short period of time, and then after a while she'd go back to her crazy ass ways. But I was gonna enjoy her new attitude for now.

"Going home already, Bry?" Indiya walked into Bryleigh's bedroom, looking good as fuck. My dick immediately came to life upon seeing her.

She was in a simple dress with no straps, but that's just how beautiful shorty was, she didn't need much to be pleasing to the eye. Her beautiful, caramel skin glistened, and her alluring smile lit up the room. Her shapely, but small, physique was something I would never get tired of, and her long hair swept her sexy back enticingly. Shit.

"Yes, I will be back soon though!" Bryleigh giggled and walked over to her.

I liked that she and my daughter got along, because my baby girl came before anybody, and I could never be with a bitch who couldn't get shit right with my shorty.

"Okay, well don't have me waiting too long, I need you to do my hair," Indiya chuckled. My daughter loved doing hair, and she loved Indiya because Indiya let her braid her hair up and shit. "I'm gonna go to the nail shop, and when I get back we can go to the movies and dinner." She looked to me.

Pulling her closer, I kissed her neck while inhaling her sweet perfume. Pressing my lips against her soft skin, I made sure she felt my dick hardening as I hugged her tightly.

"Rhys!" she snickered and nudged me off. After gazing down into her eyes for a little bit, I kissed her lips and then let her go.

The three of us walked into the living room, and when Indiya opened the door, Summer was walking up. She ignored Indiya and came right in with her eyes on Bryleigh.

"Okay, I will be back," Indiya said before closing the front door behind her. I just nodded in response, before sitting down on the couch. Bryleigh climbed right into my lap.

"Is she always here?" Summer folded her arms.

"You know she lives here, Summer. Don't start."

"You don't even know her that well, yet she already lives here and is around your daughter? I didn't let Hakim meet Bryleigh that soon."

"That's why you're Summer and I'm Rhys. Plus she and I have been together for a while now, shorty, and it's pretty serious. I don't have to explain shit to you, I'm a grown ass man."

"Bryleigh, go to your room and let mommy talk to your daddy, okay?"

"Okay," she climbed off of my lap and ran to her room.

I didn't know what the fuck Summer had to talk to me about, but I wasn't in the mood for her bullshit. Sometimes it was hard for me to even recall the good days when I was in love with her. Don't get me wrong, I would always love Summer until I was being lowered into the grave, but I wasn't in love with her ass anymore. She was a different person, even different from whom she'd become just some months back.

"Rhys, I've been doing a lot of thinking, and I wanted to know how you felt about possibly being back together, or trying at the least."

"Where is this coming from?" I asked as she sat down next to me.

"I've just been doing some thinking you know. Being apart gave me some time to get my thoughts together."

"What happened to Hakim helping you realize that you were never in love?"

"Oh my gosh, Rhys, really?"

"Yes really what the fuck? Do you know how that shit felt when you said that? We were together for almost ten years and here I was thinking that we were in love, just for you to shit on it because you had a new nigga."

"I didn't know what I was saying."

"No you *did* know what the fuck you were saying, and you know why you said it. I don't know if it was the truth, or if you were just trying to hurt me, but either one is a fucked up reason."

"You knew it wasn't true, so why is it even a big fucking deal?" She frowned her pretty face. Summer was one of the prettiest women in Boston, but her insides were rotten sometimes.

"It's a big deal because for the last fucking year and a half I have been going above and fucking beyond to try to prove to you that I was being faithful! I was trying to show you that I loved you and nobody else! There were times where I could have slept with women and you would have never found out, but did I? No! My whole fucking family was telling me to drop your ass, but I refused! I loved your ass, and I dealt with your insecure bullshit for the longest because I loved you! I didn't care about anything or anyone else and how they felt about the shit, and for you to diss me because of one little ass picture that meant nothing was low! And not only that, you felt the need to try and break me down by saying you were never in love with me. And the worst part about that was even *after* you said that shit, I still tried. I still fucking tried because I loved you. But you know what, I had to realize that you didn't love me the same. Yeah you care for me, and you love me, but you don't love me the way I need to be loved, Summer."

"Tell me how, Rhys," she began tearing up. "How?" she scooted closer to me.

"You needed to trust me, Summer. I understand that I fucked shit up by creeping around, but when you agreed to forgive me, you should have done that. No one was asking you to forget, just to forgive."

When I met Lisa, I was hesitant to start fucking with her because like I said, that shit wasn't me. But Lisa was pretty, and she had a somewhat cool personality so we started being friends. One thing led to another, and next thing I knew I was fucking her here and there. I would usually only smash either right before a job, or right after, because I didn't want to look suspicious to Summer. I never spent the night, never took her out, I never did anything but drop by her house and beat her guts out.

After a while I found myself simply smashing her because I knew that she liked me and if I cut her off I would hurt her feelings. I didn't care too much about her feelings, but I knew it would be fucked up for me to curve her like that. Women take everything personally, and I was sure I would possibly scar her ass for life if I just quit her. So by saying that I kept fucking until I could figure out a way to let her down easy.

I started dropping by less and less, but I was still dropping by. Then when Jayce's wife, Sadie, got murked by his side bitch, I felt like it was God telling me to quit my bullshit, so I did. As I suspected, that shit fucked Lisa's head up and the bitch went coo coo for coco puffs. If I could go back in time, I would have went with my first mind and never even engaged in conversation with Lisa, because that shit had fucked my family up. I have been paying for that damn mistake ever since.

Did I blame Summer for not trusting me? Of course not, I cheated on her. But she agreed to be with me, and she promised she would be able to see past it, but she never made good on that promise. I thought as time went on she would eventually get less insecure, but it only seemed to get worse. And as a wise person once said, a man gets tired.

"Okay, I'm ready to forgive, baby." She straddled my lap, and cupped the sides of my face.

"Summer stop." I turned away when she tried to kiss me.

"Rhys, it's me. Don't do this, I promise I'm ready now. Don't tell me that you're really serious about this girl, I mean she's a fucking hooker."

"I'm very serious," I stated calmly, even though I wanted to put her in her place for disrespecting Indiya. "And she hasn't done that shit for months."

"I forgot my phone—" Indiya came in, stopping in her tracks when she saw Summer straddling my lap and holding my face. She quickly turned around and darted out of the door.

"Move ." I placed Summer to the side of me and got up.

"Really, Rhys? I fucking hate you! You whack ass nigga!" Summer screamed after me as I ran out after Indiya.

Rushing down the hallway, I quickly slipped into the side door and took the stairs since it appeared Indiya had already taken the damn elevator. *Fuck, fuck, fuck,* I kept saying in my head. I finally made it to the parking garage, and saw her walking towards the vehicle I'd purchased for her. When I finally caught up, I grabbed her wrist, but she snatched it from me.

"Indiya—"

"Take these fucking keys, I don't want the car." She threw them to me after unlocking it. She reached into the passenger seat to get her purse and jacket, bit I pulled her away before she could get it, and pinned her up against the vehicle.

"Indiya, what you saw was not even like that. She—"

"I told you to fucking tell me if you were gonna go back to her!"

she hollered loudly and shoved me. She continued pushing me with all of her might, as tears rolled down out of her eyes in abundance. "You're a fucking liar!" She tried to push me off of her as I grabbed her waist.

Removing her hands from pressing into my chest, I quickly hugged her tightly before she could put them back. I'd never seen someone cry this hard in all of my life, and I wasn't sure what the fuck to do about it.

"Baby, calm down, aight? She was just speaking her mind, and she got the wrong idea. She climbed into my lap, but before I could move her you walked in," I half lied.

I mean Summer had been in my lap for a few moments, and I was going to move her, but got caught up in the conversation she and I were having. By the time it had even crossed my mind again, Indiya was walking in.

"I hate you, Rhys," she sobbed.

"I love you, though." I kissed the side of her face as I hugged her small frame.

She pulled her face away to look up into mine while still sniffling. She was so fucking pretty it was almost unreal.

"You love me?" she quizzed, wiping her eyes with the back of her hand.

"Yeah, I fucking love you, why do you think a nigga came running down here and shit like a bitch? If I didn't I would've let your ass think whatever the fuck you wanted. After all that shit I've told you, do you honestly believe I would leave you?"

"No," she whispered.

"Aight then. Now come on so we can get your phone and I can get my wallet." I took her hand into mine.

"You're coming with me to the nail shop?"

"Hell yeah, make sure yo' ass don't try to leave or some shit."

She giggled before saying, "I would never leave you."

Wrapping my arms around her shoulders, I kissed her smooth lips as she embraced my torso. We stood there kissing for a little bit, before I finally pulled away.

"Promise?"

"I promise," she nodded. "I love you, Rhys."

When we made it back upstairs, Summer's ass was gone, but she made sure to cut up my fucking sofa with a knife. I still had love for her though.

Britain

*C*urrently my brothers, sister, and I were in my dad's office waiting for him. He said he wanted to discuss some shit, and I don't think any of us were interested. Over a short period of time our family had begun to crumble. All of us were at odds with my father, maybe excluding Saya, and my mom had filed for divorce because of what my dad did to TQ. As much as I wanted my parents to stay together, I couldn't blame my mother. TQ may have been a grown ass man, but he was her kid and she always said she would choose us before anything and anyone. I guess she was proving herself. And right now I wasn't that nigga's biggest cheerleader anyway.

"Should we talk to Saya—" Lendsey was cut off when TQ put his hand up and shook his head 'no'.

"Not here, we can discuss that later and I will let you know when," TQ said.

"Talk to me about what?" Saya frowned, but softened her face when TQ gave her a look. We all went back to being quiet as we waited for my father.

"Sorry to keep you waiting guys, but look who's back." My dad walked in with Pharaoh right on his heels, smiling widely as fuck. His eyes were locked on Saya, and she was blushing and shit.

"What's good? When did you get out?" Rhys stood up to dap Pharaoh up, and we all followed suit.

"Last week. I've been staying low-key, working with your father on some things. But I'm ready to work and shit." Pharaoh nodded, glancing from us to Saya.

"Oh yeah, what will he have you doing?" TQ asked, making my father look over at him.

"I ain't really sure yet, but he said that's what we would find out today." He sat down. Once he did, everyone turned their attention to my father, waiting on his bitch ass to speak.

"So, Rhys I need you to take care of Solomon because he fucked up the weapon order. Bring me his hand for confirmation, preferably the one with his wedding band," my dad chuckled.

"Aight," Rhys sighed, glancing at TQ who just gave him a nod.

"Alright, and since Solomon's job is open, Pharaoh, you can take over that area. I will go over the details with you tonight. Umm, we can go out since my wife isn't up to cooking tonight." I guess he didn't want Pharaoh knowing my mom chucked the deuces up.

"That's cool," Pharaoh nodded. "So I'm gonna have my own area within QCF? That's dope." He looked around at us and we gave him half smiles. Not that we weren't happy for the nigga, we were, its just that shit wasn't the same no more, and soon enough this shit would be somewhat disbanded.

"Well, everyone is dismissed, I just wanted you all to find out at the same time about Pharaoh being out, and what he will be doing. TQ, don't forget about the cat you have to meet in Youngstown." TQ just stood up and walked out without another word.

Everyone else got up, preparing to leave, but when I did, my dad walked over to me and put his hand on my shoulder. I paused to let everyone leave his office, and once they did he closed the door behind them and turned to me. In all my years of being his son, I'd never seen him look so stressed or worried. Stony Quinton never worried about shit, so I was floored to say the least.

"Your mother, have you seen her or talked to her?" He squinted his eyes.

"Yeah, I have."

"So she's serious, huh?"

"About the divorce? Yeah, she's very serious. The lawyer was in the hotel room when I went to visit her. You fucked up, dad, you know that. I don't even know why you did that shit thinking she wouldn't trip."

"Tarenz is a grown ass man! That's y'alls muthafuckin' problem now! She treats you guys like some fucking toddlers! This is business, and when you fuck up you have to pay the price. She's lucky I didn't kill his ass."

"And what did he do exactly to deserve to be stabbed, beaten, and have his wife kidnapped?"

"He murdered Gang and Peel, Britain. Don't act dumb, it doesn't suit you." He poured himself a drink. "He murdered them for nothing!"

"He was protecting his wife, Pop."

"His wife," he chuckled angrily and sat behind his desk with his drink. "I can't believe he married that bitch. I mean she comes into the family, fucks his head up, gets pregnant, and then convinces him to marry her. I mean honestly I expected him to do better for himself; I expected that from all of you. First Rhys has a child with a broken woman, just to break up with her and get with a whore. Then TQ marries a wounded dog he got from the pound, and now you've gotten some Boston hood rat pregnant." He took a sip. "Sadly, the only one who hasn't chosen as badly is Lendsey, but he needs to keep her in check. She doesn't know her place as a woman."

"Dad, I'm not gonna ask you again to stop being disrespectful to Goldie," I stated calmly, while staring into his eyes. I was dead serious, and I wanted him to know that and feel that.

He just laughed before taking another sip.

"You know, to be such little bitches, you and your brothers sure try to stand up for these girls." He rose to his feet, swishing his drink around. "What does your brother have planned?"

"Huh?"

"TQ. What the fuck does he have planned? He came from my nut sack, I know him. He's acting strangely, and I want you to tell me what the fuck he has planned."

"He don't have shit planned. And if he does, which I doubt, he ain't told me. He just ain't fucking with you, nothing more nothing less. He wants to do his job and go home to his family."

"I feel like you're lying to me."

"I can't tell you how to feel, Pop. TQ isn't thinking about you, and you should stop being so fucking paranoid. His mood has changed because you had him shanked, fucked up, and then put a gun to his girl's head while she was pregnant. What you thought he was gonna be coming over for drinks?" I frowned. He was really losing his mind. Yeah TQ definitely had something up his sleeve, but even if he didn't, how could my father expect them to be cool again?

Scratching his ear, he stared at the floor in deep thought, before gulping his drink.

"I know. Look, the next time you see your mother, tell her that I want to talk to her. Tell her that I'm sorry, and I may have gotten a little bit carried away."

"You tell her."

"I've tried, but she doesn't answer my calls." He pleaded with his eyes.

"Okay, but under one condition. Send a flower arrangement to my shorty's job, with a card and a written apology. If it's not delivered by this afternoon, you can forget about me talking to mom."

"Britain—"

"That's the deal."

"What does she like?" he sighed. I'd finally found a weak spot on this nigga. Nothing scared him, not even death, but losing my mom seemed to be the sweet spot that we'd all been searching for, for years.

"Roses, white *and* red. She's pregnant, so get her some chocolates, too."

"Shake on it." He reached his free hand out, while sipping his liquor.

I shook his hand, gave him a fake smile, and then turned on my heels. Bitch ass nigga.

CHAPTER SIX

Saya Quinton

I was finally home from that awkward ass meeting with my brothers, dad, and how could I forget… Pharaoh. He was looking so good dressed in that all black Gucci suit, and he smelled just as good too. I don't know, it could've been my brothers' cologne, but I'd like to think it was him. I could barely look at his ass without wetting my panties, so after getting one good look, I quickly turned away and kept it that way. He and I had never slept together, and I would be lying if I said it didn't cross my mind earlier.

I smiled when I walked into my living room because I saw Aries wasn't here. For the past few weeks, every time I got home I was walking in on him chilling with Jamie and smoking. Not only was I annoyed by his bum presence, unless he had his tongue out, but I didn't feel like being interrogated on why he hadn't been brought into the family yet.

I was gonna ask and see if he could somehow help out, but when I got ready to, I came to my senses. No way was my father gonna give him access, and honestly I couldn't blame him. What the fuck did the family need Aries for? And then, even if he did get on he wouldn't be getting much because you only got money when you worked for it.

Not only that, but now that my mom was looking to separate from my dad, I wasn't sure about how our escort business was gonna run. My dad got a cut from that, and I highly doubt he would just let my mom and me have it. I had bigger problems and no time to be worried about helping Aries. I shook my head at my thoughts as a loud knock was heard throughout my living room.

"Who is it?" I called out as I pulled my gun from the secret drawer in the kitchen. As I pushed the loaded magazine up into it, I looked through the peephole to see Pharaoh's fine ass smiling. He knew I was looking. "Did you follow me?" I opened the door, cocking my head sexily. At least I hoped it was sexy.

"Yeah, I did. Can I come in?"

"How do you just pop up on people, Pharaoh? What if Aries was here?"

"So what if that broke ass nigga was here. He had no business pushing up on you when I got knocked anyways. He deserves an ass whooping." He barged in with his rude ass, hitting me in the face with his cologne. I closed the door behind him once I came out of my trance.

Pharaoh was a muthafucking twenty out of ten, especially since he'd bulked up a bit behind bars. He had smooth, light skin, luminous, curly hair, a scruffy beard, tattoos, a banging body, and the best feature of all, he got to the money. He was the total opposite of Aries in the sense that he would never be chilling in my condo on the daily not doing shit, and begging for a handout. Yeah, Pharaoh had the luxury of being in the family, but that's because he proved himself to my father, and showed him that he was needed. Pharaoh wasn't some trap star like Aries, he was a for real criminal.

"I wasn't your girl," I finally replied as I walked my gun back to the kitchen.

"You were about to be. And if anybody knew how I felt about you, he did. I know he ain't hitting that shit right." He ran his tongue across his full bottom lip. Damn.

"You don't know what he's doing," I smirked and so did he. "Would you like something to drink? I have wine, dark liquor, clear liquor, champagne, pretty much anything you can think of."

"I will take some Bourbon if you have it."

"I do." Pulling two glasses down, I filled them both with Bourbon and then walked them to the couch where he was sitting.

"Don't sit so fucking far away, Saya."

"Pharaoh, don't. You know I have a man, so stop acting like that. I'm not a cheater aight?" I frowned.

Throwing his glass back, he set it on the coffee table and then yanked me into his lap. Pushing my dress up past my thighs roughly, he began moving his fingers across my pussy slowly, while staring me in the eyes. Good Lord this nigga was handsome as fuck.

"Robert, stop," I moaned his government name, while grinding against his fingers.

"You want me to?" he moved my panties to the side, and slipped his fingers inside of me.

I began moving slowly, riding his fingers like they were a dick.

Why was his finger game better than Aries' dick game? I kept moving slowly as he plunged his fingers in and out of me feverishly. Moments later, I was spilling all over his hand. He immediately removed his dick, and then pulled a condom from his wallet.

"This is how you want the first time to be, Pharaoh? Really?" I furrowed my brows at him.

"You're right," he sighed. "I haven't had any pussy in a while, shorty, so please forgive me."

"You haven't had anything since you've been out? Not even from Kat?" I smirked, referring to this bird he used to fuck with.

Smiling, he rubbed his beard and said, "Yeah I fucked Kat, but only a few times since I've been out. I haven't had the pussy that I've been craving for years."

"Well I think you know how to go about getting it. I just don't know about this, Pharaoh. I've been with Aries for years and I just can't leave like that. And why would I leave him without even knowing if you're serious?" I moved from his lap and stood up so I could go to the bathroom. He followed me, and as I wiped myself up, he washed his hands.

"Saya, I've been serious since before you got with this nigga. I'm the one who needs to be worried and shit. You like to play games, ma."

"No I don't." I turned the faucet back on to wash my hands.

"You're telling me that you're happy with that nigga? You can't be, look at your fucking collarbone, it has a damn bruise on it. You're lucky I haven't killed his ass yet."

"It's not like that. He gets mad and he will get a little rough with me, but it's not like he slaps or punches me," I shrugged, a little embarrassed.

"Do your brothers know that he just gets a little rough with you?"

"Fuck no! And you better not tell them, not one of them. They're all a little off in the head you know."

I shuddered as I thought about their reaction. Not one of my brothers had a sane bone in their body, so if they found out some nigga was hitting me, especially Aries, they'd kill his ass.

"Agree to give me a chance and I won't say shit." He raised his brow as he stared down into my face. "You are so pretty, Saya." He thumbed my cheek as I pondered.

"Fine, I will give you a chance. A low key one, but a chance nonetheless," I smiled because he was smiling. I was also a little happy that he was out and still on me.

Tugging me close, he pressed his lips against mine as his big hands rubbed my ass. This was gonna be interesting, but I couldn't wait.

Kimberlyn

One week later...

$\mathcal{S}$aya invited me over to her condo because she wanted to see the baby, and she was gonna cook for me. I was excited to come because I wanted to get closer to my husband's family. Because his father didn't care for me, I felt a little bit of a disconnection from his people, despite his mother adoring me. For some reason I really wanted Stony to like me, but that was before he tried to kill TQ, before his people kidnapped me from the damn bed, and before he put a gun to my head. That nigga was crazy, and I wanted no parts of him any more.

"He is so cute, Kimberlyn." Saya took Baby Tarenz from me and kissed his fat cheeks. Like always, he grabbed some of her hair, clutching it tightly in his chunky hands, before shoving it into his mouth.

"Don't do that," I chuckled and tried to gently pry her hair from his hands.

"It's fine." She kissed him again and then handed him back to me.

"You are gonna love women with long hair, huh?" I smiled at him as I stood him up in my lap. He was the cutest little thing in the world, and so well behaved. He had his moments where he would cry for the longest and couldn't be consoled, but it was rare.

I played with my baby as Saya made her way around the kitchen, and I couldn't wait to see what she was making. I was sure it was some Russian food, and since being with TQ, I had come to love it. I absolutely loved having Russian food for dinner, not only because it was scrumptious, but also because TQ and I usually cooked it together. Any time I got to spend with him was always bliss. I didn't know I could love someone that much.

"Fuck you making?" Aries walked into the condo frowning. That frown immediately turned into a smile when he saw Baby Tarenz and I sitting on the couch. *Why did I wear a tube top and skirt?* I thought. "What's good, shorty?" he strolled over to me, dragging his corduroy slippers across Saya's laminate flooring.

"Hi," I said in a low tone, before adjusting my son in my lap.

"Damn, when did you have him?" He looked at my body.

"Just four months ago."

"Shit, and you're already looking like that? I know that nigga TQ is happy yo' ass didn't blow the fuck up and stay that way. These bitches these days stay fat for years after their kids." He fired up his blunt.

"Having children does a lot to a woman's body. You shouldn't speak on things that you've never experienced, and I would appreciate it if you didn't smoke that while my baby is right here."

Grinning, he paused for a second before putting it out. Thank God, because I would've had to leave. If my own husband couldn't smoke around my baby, I damn sure wasn't about to let this trash ass nigga do it.

"So I heard you just graduated from college."

"Yes I did. It was about a week before I had him," I chuckled and kissed Baby Tarenz's cheek.

"Cool, cool. So umm, is that nigga treating you right? I know he has a reputation for being a bit of a ladies man, and I'm just wondering if he's changed up for you."

"We're married."

"Being married doesn't mean shit these days, especially to niggas like TQ. And y'all only have been married for like a month. Anyway, shorty, I'm just asking because if not I wanna take care of you." He got up and sat next to me.

"Take care of me? Are you crazy?" I already knew his ass was broke, so he was crazy to make such a comment for more reasons than one.

"Nah I'm not crazy. I don't give a fuck about what Saya has to say. That bitch is fucking around on me anyways. And I damn sure don't give a fuck about what that nigga, TQ, thinks. I've been dreaming about eating your pussy for months, even while you were pregnant." He touched my thigh and bit his lip.

"Uh, Saya, I'm gonna go." I rose to my feet, and when Aries grabbed my wrist, I yanked it away.

"What? Why?" She came running into her living room.

"Baby Tarenz isn't feeling well, so I'm gonna take him home. I'm so sorry, maybe we can do this another time okay?"

Before she could answer I just darted out. I didn't want to say anything to her in front of Aries, because I wasn't even sure if she would believe me or get mad as fuck. I'm just glad I got out of there before he pounced on me.

***

I was staring up at the ceiling, lying in bed, when TQ walked in from his shower. My son and I had just taken a bath together, and although I was in the comfort of my own bed, I couldn't get what Aries had done off of my mind. I no longer wanted to be around him, and I had a feeling that would be hard to do since he was Saya's man. A part of me wanted to say something to someone, but the other part of me felt like it wasn't even that serious. All he did was touch my leg and flirt a little bit.

"You should've known better than to put something on." TQ got into the bed and began pushing my little nightgown up until it was off. "So sexy and beautiful," he whispered as he kissed on my neck and then took his lips to my nipples.

Once he got his fix, he made his way down my stomach and spread my legs so that he could suck on my clit. Throwing my head back, my breathing became heavy as he groped my thighs while eating my pussy. His face was pressed into my center as he sucked gently on my button. I loved that when he ate pussy he moaned very subtly here and there, letting me know how much he enjoyed it. Flicking his tongue over my bud, he let it travel to my hole and stuck it in for a little bit before bringing it back up.

"Tarenz," I whimpered while I caressed his fresh fade.

"Give it to me," he growled, seemingly pulling the orgasm out of me.

"Ahh, uhh, mmm." My body trembled as I called out loudly, brushing my toes against his strong back.

He French kissed my pussy very slowly as I let it all out, sniveling a little bit. He made eye contact with me as he swiped his soft tongue over my clit, causing me to shiver violently for some reason. Trailing his lips up my body, he positioned his head at my opening, and pushed into me gently. It was a little painful, I guess because my body hadn't come all the way back yet. Stroking me slowly, he gripped the sides of my face and kissed me hungrily yet softly. He hugged my body as he wound his hips into me, hitting my spot and delivering pain and pleasure every time.

"You okay?" He stopped.

"Yes, why?"

"Your body isn't relaxed."

"I am relaxed."

"No, shorty, you're not. I'm inside of you, I can feel how tense you are." He pulled out of me.

"No, Tarenz, I'm fine. Just keep going I don't mind." I shook my head 'no'.

"I mind. I ain't trying to be fucking you if you're not enjoying it, shorty," he scoffed and laid on the side of me. Rubbing his hands down his face, he reached over for his phone to check it.

"I'm sorry, let's try again." I pecked his lips. I didn't want it to be like this. He was my husband and I wanted to make sure we stayed married.

As I was kissing down his chiseled abs, he gripped my bicep and yanked me up and off of him.

"Fuck is wrong with you, Kimberlyn? Tell me right now. Did somebody do something to you?" he grimaced, staring into my soul it seemed with those deep blue eyes.

"He umm—"

"Who the fuck is he?" He sat up, and I'd never seen him so angry.

"Aries, he just touched my leg and he told me that he wanted to take care of me earlier today. That was all, nothing else. It wasn't that bad."

"It wasn't that bad, yet you can't even fuck your husband because of it."

"I can, I told you let's try again." I moved towards him but he stopped me, and then got out of the bed to pull on his boxers. "Tarenz, don't leave! We can still do it!"

"I'm just going to get some water, stop acting like that. What you think I'm only with you for sex? I can go out and fuck anybody, Kimberlyn. I married you and I'm with you because I love you. Yes the sex is a bonus, but that's all it is, shorty." He held my face in his hands and kissed me deeply. "Come on, we can go chill in the living room for a little bit." He picked me up off the bed once I pulled my gown over my head.

I smiled once he placed me to my feet, so he pecked me again.

"I love when you smile, shorty. I swear it's more contagious than Ebola."

I just chuckled before slipping my hand into his, as we made our way to the bathroom so I could clean up and he could brush his teeth. We then went into the kitchen to shop. While we gathered our snacks, he was quiet and in deep thought, so I knew it was over for Aries. I didn't feel bad either.

Aries Jenkins

I pulled up to the curb in Saya's Maserati, before hitting the unlock button. One of these little shorties I was messing with named Melina gave me a sweet smile as she took her seatbelt off. And if you're wondering, hell yeah she thought this was my whip, and that's the way I preferred the shit.

"You're coming back to see me tonight?" she smiled.

"I might, why? What incentive would I have to come back and see you?"

"Good food, sex, and conversation. I'm sure Saya is gonna be working late like always, instead of tending to her man like she should be."

Melina was right as fuck. Saya had been working extra late, and all fucking day lately. Now don't get me wrong, she always had late hours and long days, but recently shit had been different. Usually during the day she would have little breaks and shit where we would converse or go eat. Now, she was too busy to have a break. Then the last three nights, she didn't even come to her condo. I woke up at 8am and her ass still wasn't there, talking about she did come home, she just left before I woke up. I wanted to believe her ass for the sake of my ego, but damn if it wasn't fucking with me.

"Alright, I will text you if I'm gonna come, ma."

"Okay, bye, baby." She leaned over and pecked my lips, before climbing her sexy ass out of the whip. Damn, I couldn't wait to slide up in that shit again.

Once baby girl was inside, I sped off, headed to meet Jamie at the barbershop. I'd gotten some cash from Saya after speaking with her ass on the phone this morning. She felt guilty I guess for not giving me her time, so she sent me some paper through this little cash app. That definitely made me happy and shut my ass up.

When I hit the corner of the street that the shop was on, I turned my music up loudly and rolled the windows down. A gang of people were outside talking, chilling, smoking, and just hanging out, and I wanted to show the fuck off. Bobbing my head to "I'm That Nigga Now" by Lil Snupe, I fired up a blunt and slowed down by a group of ladies eyeing my whip. Giving them a quick wink, I gunned it into the parking lot and swooped into a park, letting my music continue to play. Taking the blunt to the head, I ashed it before shutting the engine off and getting out.

"Hey, Aries." one of the girls standing outside of the hair salon next to the barbershop smiled at me.

"Sup, ma, I'ma holla at you when I come out aight?" I bit my lip and she just nodded her head 'yes'. Shorty's ass was fat as fuck, and all I could think about was hitting it from the back. Her face on the other hand… let's just say she'd be great for radio.

Girls stayed being on my dick, especially when I was driving one of Saya's cars. I didn't like having to floss using my girl's shit, but since

I didn't have my own money like that, I had to do what I had to do. I sold weed here and there, but selling weed only made it so I could buy the newest Jordans, and maybe two or three pairs of Robin jeans, and that would only be if I saved up over a couple weeks.

Walking into the barbershop, I dapped up a few of the homies, before going to sit next to where Jamie was getting lined up. He put his hand up to say what's up, and I did the same. The barbershop was full of niggas, some getting their haircut, and some just chilling and shooting the shit.

"Aye you fuck shorty yet?" he looked to me, using his peripheral vision.

"Who?" I had so many bitches I really didn't know who he was talking about.

"Kimberlyn's fine ass."

"Shit, nah, but I will. She was acting all shy and scared and shit when I touched her, but I know the real. Every bitch is a hoe, some just hide it better than others. Saya's bro got that pussy too quick for her to be this good girl she claims to be."

"You're talking about TQ's girl?" My barber walked up and threw the cape around me.

"Indeed."

"Nigga, you're crazy as fuck. That's a death sentence if you ask me."

"Well ain't nobody ask yo' ass shit. Plus she wouldn't tell if I fucked, because that would get her in trouble too. But anyway, I was looking at her body and how that shit has snapped back. Man I know TQ is tearing that pussy up and I can't wait to try it." I cheesed thinking about it. I was gonna fuck her hard as hell just because she was TQ's bitch.

I've always thought Kimberlyn was fine, from the first time I saw her ass. I knew I was gonna fuck too, and by the time I was gonna make a move I found out she was pregnant. I didn't mind eating her pussy at that time, but I wasn't fucking a pregnant bitch. Just the thought of poking a baby, another man's baby at that, with my dick kept me on soft. But I would've sucked on her pussy all night though. I licked my lips as visions of her breathing heavily with my head between her legs invaded my mind.

"Speaking of getting at other nigga's girls, what's up with you and Saya?" this dude named Carlo asked.

He was fucking with the biggest hoe in Boston named Rosie. Bitch had six kids, with four fathers, and was still busting it open for other dudes. But somehow she got Carlo's ass to claim her. He was out here looking dumb than a muthafucka. Yeah all women were hoes, but I damn sure wasn't wifing one who didn't keep it a secret.

"Saya and I are good," I responded.

"Oh word? Because I saw her out with another nigga, and he looked like Pharaoh." Everyone in the shop made some kind of a noise in response.

When he said that shit I swear my heart dropped into my nut sack. I knew that nigga was out, and when I asked her she acted as if she didn't know and didn't care. But even though that shit just hit me in the chest like a stack of encyclopedias, I wasn't about to show it to these hating ass niggas. Every nigga in Boston wanted a piece of Saya, and I enjoyed that shit.

"Man, yeah right." Jamie tried to help me save face.

"Nah, nigga, I'm serious. Looks like you ain't got a hold on her like you thought. Should've let a real man fuck with her, she about her shit and she fine as fuck."

"Aye nigga watch yo' muthafucking mouth!" I hopped out of my chair and so did Carlo. "I am a real man, partner, you better believe that! Worry about yo' bitch and her busted open ass pussy!"

"Real man, but you whipping her car and spending her money." He looked me up and down with disgust. "You don't get nice cars from selling dime sacks, you bitch ass nigga."

Before he could finish I had lunged over on him. We began tussling all over the barbershop, as women screamed, men cheered, and the barbers hollered for us to stop. Finally we were broken apart, and as I panted angrily, Carlo was laughing.

"That's why Rosie sucked my dick!" I lied. I wouldn't let that hoe touch me.

"And Saya is sucking Pharaoh's!" he smirked. I tried to get at him again, but the barber was holding me too tightly.

"Fuck off me!" I snatched away and rushed out, ignoring Jamie calling me. I no longer wanted to get my haircut, because to be totally honest, Carlo had embarrassed me. I was supposed to be *that* nigga, and he put all of my business out on the fucking table.

I slid into the Maserati, and immediately dialed Saya.

"Hey, babe," she sang.

"Where the fuck are you?"

"I'm working, I will be home in like an hour."

"Yeah you make sure you get there in an hour so we can fucking talk about you gallivanting around Boston with Pharaoh's bitch ass!" I seethed, and the line went silent.

"Aries, whatever you heard, it isn't true."

"Right, one muthafucking hour, Saya!" I hung up.

I looked down at my phone once I was done, and saw my mother had called me. I hit the number to call her back, but she didn't answer. After she didn't pick up the second time, I decided to just drop by since I didn't want to go to Saya's and twiddle my fucking thumbs for an hour. I got to my mom's in less than ten minutes since I was driving like a bat out of hell, and pulled into her driveway.

"Saya gon' have to put some more gas in this bitch," I mumbled as I got out.

Hitting the alarm, I walked up my mother's porch steps and used my key to get in. As soon as I opened the door I smelled food, so I knew she had just cooked. If she called me to come home and eat, I wouldn't even be mad because I was starved.

"Mama! What did you call me for?" I hollered out as I peeked at the food. "Mama!" I left out of the kitchen and went to her bedroom. Opening the door, my eyes almost rolled out of my head as I stared at my mother lying on a blood soaked comforter. "Mama! Wake up!" I shook her violently even though I saw a big hole in her fucking head. I wiped my eyes, and when I glanced to the left I saw TQ leaning up against the wall in an all black outfit, smiling. If this nigga had have been a snake he would've bit me.

"I just touched her leg man, I ain't even do shit!" I began sobbing. I already knew why he was here. *Tattle tale ass bitch.* He just stared at me, so I turned to run out, but he shot me in the back of the thigh. He walked over to me as I collapsed to the ground in agony. "Shit!" I cried out from the burning pain.

"Kimberlyn Quinton is off limits, especially to peasants like yourself, Aries. She isn't to be touched, talked to, or even looked at by niggas like you. Touching Mrs. Quinton, is punishable by death," he stated calmly. *This nigga is looney as fuck.* "Tell ya, mama, I didn't mean it. Collateral."

POP! POP!

Lendsey

"*W*hat is the plan exactly? Don't you think I deserve to know that?" one of my dad's men, Andrei, said. He was good at what he did, and we wanted to have him help us once my father was gone.

"Can't tell you the plan, but it will be successful. We need to know if you're down or not, Andrei."

"I umm, I don't know. Stony is almost unbeatable, and what if he finds out?"

"He won't find out, now are you with me? You and him," I looked to Andrei's right hand man, Yegor. They weren't best friends or anything, but they worked together a lot.

"I don't think so, man. You guys need to make up with Stony before this gets ugly. He will kill all of you. Andrei, I can't even believe you brought me here." Yegor stood up from his chair.

POP!

I shot his ass right in the head. I looked away before he even fell to the ground good because I didn't care.

"We can't afford that. Whoever doesn't wanna be down, will go down. Now are you in?" I looked Andrei in the eyes. I could tell he was floored by the fact that I'd just killed Yegor.

"Yeah, yeah, man, count me in."

"Don't try to play me, Andrei. I'm telling you right now you will regret it. My brothers and I will be victorious, and will remember anyone who wasn't with us." He just nodded. "I will be in touch. Call someone to clean his ass up out of here."

I slipped the gun into my waist and left the warehouse to head home. When I got there, I went straight to the bathroom to pee, and before I could even finish, Matikah was walking her ass into the restroom.

"Tikah, damn! Boundaries!"

"I've seen that little thing before." She waved me off.

"Little?" I raised a brow. "That's not what them gag reflexes be saying when I'm fucking ya face, shorty."

"Must you be so nasty?" she turned her lip up.

"I'm just trying to get clarification." I shook my dick before putting it away. "You be crying and shit when I'm stroking that pussy so I was confused." I began washing my hands as she chuckled.

"Hurry up, baby daddy, we have to go."

"What? Shorty I have to shower I ain't going nowhere. I planned to clean up, eat, fuck, and then sleep. I have a lot of shit to do tomor—" I stopped my self when she gave me those sad eyes. "Where are we even going?"

"My stupid mother is in town and she wants to see me."

"Why she ain't come here?"

"I told her that you said she couldn't," she giggled and wrapped her arms around my body.

"So because you didn't want her here, you blamed that shit on me?"

"I always do that. Whenever I don't want to do something or deal with it, I just blame it on you and say you don't want to."

"Yo' muthafucking ass," I laughed as I thought about her confession. "You got people thinking I'm mean as fuck when it's really yo' ass."

"Nothing wrong with that. And because you love me you won't tell her the truth right?"

"Nah I won't. But let me shower, I will be quick."

"Okay."

She left out so I got right in. Quickly cleaning my body, I went ahead and washed my hair as well with some shit Matikah had left in the shower. I smelled it first to make sure it wasn't too fruity and shit though. Once I was done, I dried off and got dressed in some jeans, a crisp blue polo, and some Adidas. After pulling my hat down on my head, and snapping my watch and chain on, I put on some cologne.

"Aight let's be out." I took her hand into mine.

Matikah and I got to her grandmother's home in Roxbury in about thirty minutes since there was a little bit of traffic coming from my place in Brighton. There was a bad ass accident, closing up some of the lanes and shit.

"What is your mom like? Is she young and hip? Or stuck up and old and shit?" I opened the passenger door of my car to help Matikah out.

"She's a hoe, so keep your eyes on me."

"Oh shit, okay." I trailed her up her grandmother's porch stairs, and waited as she rung the doorbell.

"She's already been drinking," her grandmother answered and then bucked her eyes at us, making us chuckle.

"Matikah! Baby!" the woman shot up off the couch and rushed over. She pulled Matikah into an embrace, before stepping back and smiling at her.

"Hey, Ma. This is my boyfriend, Lendsey."

"Lendsey," she moaned. "Damn, where the hell did you find him, Tikah? They didn't make men like him back in my day." She licked her lips and stared deeply into my eyes. "And blue eyes? Your mother must be white?"

"No, my father is Russian though."

"Russian is white, darling."

"Didn't say it wasn't." I fake smiled.

"Okay! Why don't you guys have a seat? Janine, help me in the kitchen please," Matikah's grandmother chimed in, sensing the room's mood going left.

"You know I'm not good in the kitchen, mother, take Matikah."

Matikah's grandmother stared at her for a few, before waving Matikah into the kitchen with her. I just took a seat, and looked at everything but Janine.

"So, how long have you been with Matikah?"

"About a year and some change now."

"Really? Are you guys having sex or is she still holding out? I told that girl that sex is what keeps a man, but she won't listen." She bit her lip, and crossed her legs slowly so that I could see between them. Wow, her mama really is a hoe.

"No actually, we aren't having sex. I'm willing to wait until marriage, and so is she," I lied, just to burst her bubble.

"You must be getting something on the side then, Lendsey."

"No, Matikah is all I need."

"No, you need someone that can satisfy you until she's ready. And once she is, you can act like you never cheated. I would be willing to find someone who can keep a secret for you."

"I understand that maybe you've never been blessed enough to find a man that wants more than what's below your waist, but your daughter has. My relationship with Matikah is not based on sex, because as you've shown me, I can get that from any hoe. If you want to sleep around, I couldn't care less, but don't bring that shit this way aight?"

"Matikah, bring me a beer, honey!" she called out.

"No," Matikah responded, so she got up to get it herself.

"How long is she gonna be here?" I asked Matikah once she returned to the living room and sat next to me.

"Why? You wanna fuck her?" she grinned, but there wasn't a smile anywhere on my face.

"I told you don't play like that."

"If I can joke about it, why can't you? If I don't get mad, you shouldn't."

"Well I don't like when you do that shit."

"I'm sorry, honey," she tried to kiss me but I moved my face. I didn't like when she joked about me cheating for some reason. "Don't turn your face." She climbed into my lap, and held my face tightly before kissing my lips repeatedly. "I'm sorry Len, I won't play like that anymore."

"Better not." I rubbed up and down her back.

"There won't be any of that. How many damn babies are you trying to put in her?" Hear grandmother walked out with a fresh fruit platter, as Matikah got out of my lap.

"Baby? You're pregnant, Tikah?" Hear mother raised a brow. Fuck, my lie was ruined.

"Yes, I am." She reached for a strawberry.

"How nice." Her mother looked to me with an evil smirk.

Wherever this bitch came from, she needed to go back ASAP.

CHAPTER SEVEN

Goldie

Funny thing is they swore when I get rich, I would turn my back on 'em, but I'm still up in the mix huh? God damn, ain't that some shit. Can't a young pull up in a six gettin' his dick sucked?

As Britain opened the door for me to get out of the car, I could hear Nipsey Hussle's "Where Ya Money At?" blasting from inside of the club. Tonight we were out celebrating Rhys' new girlfriend's birthday party. I tried not to like her just because I felt I owed it to Summer not to, but she was really nice. She was one of those people that if you didn't like them, people would know it was for a petty ass reason. I honestly felt she was better for Rhys, because he was such a hot head and her calmness balanced them out. Summer could get crazy, too, which I think added fuel to Rhys' already burning fire. I wasn't sure how that triangle would end, or should I say square since Summer had Hakim.

I rolled my eyes as my *half* sister Chenaye climbed out of the car smiling. She was so fucking annoying, and a part of me felt like her plan all along had been to get close to me so she could be close to the Quintons. Britain told me shit like this would happen, but I didn't expect it from Chenaye.

But these days she seemed to be shedding her fraud ass shell, because she had finally admitted that she'd lost her virginity at seventeen. At first she tried to lie and say she lost it to Ethan a few years back when he was *my* nigga, but eventually she came clean.

"I am so excited, Goldie. I have never been in VIP before," she chuckled, making me fake smile.

I slipped my hand into Britain's, which he gripped tightly. I prayed that tonight I would be able to enjoy myself, because this baby was kicking my ass. When I went to my internship every morning, I would have to keep a brown paper bag at the little desk I had. It was so hard to stay focused while feeling like you were gonna throw up everything.

"You look beautiful, baby," Britain whispered as we were being escorted into the club by QCF security.

Going up the winding stairs, we finally made it to the big ass VIP section that all the brothers and their women were in. We all spoke to one another, and when Indiya stood up to hug me I couldn't turn her down. I saw Chenaye staring hard at Rhys, but he wasn't paying her ass any attention. His eyes were fixated on his woman, as they should be.

We both sat down, on the plush ass couch like everyone else, and Chenaye started making herself a drink right away. I tasted what was in Kimberlyn's cup since she said it was a bomb ass nonalcoholic cocktail, and then I ordered one for myself and Matikah. When the hostess left, I looked to see Chenaye staring again.

"Don't even think about it."

"Think about what?"

"Trying to rekindle whatever you had with Rhys."

"Who said I wanted to do that? I'm just living life right now, I'm not worried about a man, especially after my last break up."

"Oh with my ex that I didn't know you were fucking the whole time?"

"I said I was sorry, Goldie, and I thought you didn't care."

"I don't care as far as him. I care because you're supposed to be my fucking sister, Chenaye. I don't get why out of all the men in Boston, you chose him."

"Because I hated you then, you know that, Goldie. And plus, he claimed he'd always liked me and I believed him."

She did have a point as far as her not liking me back then. There wasn't a time where we got along; this would be the first. And even now I felt like this was only temporary because she had an ulterior motive. So why was I allowing her to sleep in my guest bedroom and come out with me? Who knows. I think it was because for the first time in my life I was really happy, so it was hard for shit to bother me. My career was going great, I had a man who loved me, a baby coming, great friends, a great internship, and a beautiful condo. It would be hard to disturb me at this point, so Chenaye would have to try harder.

"Well, just don't try anything with Rhys. He's not the cheating type, so you'll be wasting your time."

"I don't think so. He was more than willing to hang out with me when he was with that other bitch, Sabrina."

"It's Summer."

"Whatever. He always came over and chilled with me when he was with her. So what's different now?"

"The difference is that he has a happy home." I hated to admit it, but his demeanor was different. Rhys was usually quiet and in deep thought, but nowadays he was smiling and upbeat. Britain said he was happy for his brother, and even though I tried to disagree, Stevie Wonder could see the difference.

"Well, we will just have to see won't we?"

"Chenaye, if you're gonna be causing problems, I'm not gonna let you come out with me anymore. I'm not trying to deal with your shit. And if she whoops your ass, don't look for me to stand up for you."

Indiya got up to go to the bathroom, so Chenaye waited until she was out of earshot to speak up.

"Hey, Rhys!" she called out over the music.

"Sup," he nodded nonchalantly, before turning away to talk to Lendsey and TQ.

"Happy Birthday!" she called to him again.

"It's not my birthday, it's my girlfriend's birthday."

"Oh yeah, my bad. So what are you guys gonna do after the party? Dinner? Or probably not because stuff will be closed." She looked and sounded so stupid right now.

"Chenaye cut the bullshit and enjoy the fucking party. You being in my grill is the reason I lost my last girl, but if you try some shit with this I will cut your fucking tongue out, shorty. I don't give a fuck whose sister you are. Be happy I'm allowing your ass to chill up here without sending a slug through your dome."

Everyone was frozen in place after processing his death threat to her. I hoped they weren't expecting me to take up for her ass, because we were not those kinds of sisters. I mean I didn't want her to die or anything, but I wasn't about to be taking up for her, especially when she was wrong and thirsty.

Indiya came back a few moments later, and slid into his lap before they engaged in a passionate kiss. I planted one on Britain, and then looked to a pouting Chenaye with a smile.

"Told you," I whispered, and she just shook her head in response.

I hoped she took Rhys' advice, because I was sure that if she kept treading on such thin ice, her ass would crack it and drown.

Summer

*E*ver since I left Rhys' condo that day I'd been feeling down. I hated to think about him with Indiya, and what made it even worse was that I knew he was done for sure. The look in his eyes when he was telling me how much he had tried for us, showed me that he was tired. And deep down I knew that I would never be able to fully trust him no matter what he said or did. I just couldn't do it. There was no point in me subjecting him to a life like that, when he had the chance to be with someone who trusted him. So, by saying that I was gonna let him go. I would always have him around because of Bryleigh, and that part made me happy. I loved Rhys, we were like best friends, so to know he would be in my life one way or the other was somewhat relaxing to think about.

The only thing that made me completely sick at this point was my relationship with Hakim. Some days I wanted to be with him because he was everything Rhys wasn't. He didn't stay out late working, women weren't falling over themselves every time we went somewhere, and he had never been unfaithful to me, at least not that I know of. Hakim was handsome, had a good job, and he wasn't out of his damn mind. Rhys only had two of those. But as much as I hated to admit it, Hakim was boring.

I didn't like saying it aloud because of how much I complained about Rhys being so unpredictable all the time. I was sure everyone who knew me would think I was bipolar. But not only was Hakim a drag sometimes, I also didn't like all the name calling in the bedroom. I didn't mind talking dirty, but being called bitches and hoes was not my thing. And the last time we had sex, he was so rough that I had a tear when I went to the gynecologist. They tried to pull out a rape kit and everything because they thought I'd been assaulted. On paper, Hakim was the perfect man, but in the flesh he wasn't what I wanted.

I shook my head as I stabbed a few pieces of my salad. I was back at that new place, Melon, because their food was so damn good. As I reached for my lemonade, I spotted the owner Romeo conversing with someone. I had completely forgotten about his sexy ass. I immediately began looking around for my waitress, because I wanted to get the check and leave before he saw me. As I was doing so, I realized he was already making his fine ass way over.

"Summer right?" he grinned and I nodded.

"May I?"

"It's your restaurant, you shouldn't have to ask."

"It is, but this is currently *your* table. I'm a polite person so excuse me." He licked his lips, making my lower ones salivate. "So I didn't hear from you."

"Yes, I was busy. And I have a boyfriend, Romeo, so I can't exactly entertain whatever you're trying to do. I'm not even interested."

"Really? Then why do you look at me like that?" He finally sat down.

"Like what?" I smiled because he was smiling. He had deep

dimples like Rhys.

"Like you wanna come over here and suck my dick," he replied, catching me off guard. I could've sworn he was straight laced, but I guess I was wrong.

"Trust me, boo, the last thing I wanna put in my mouth is your dick okay? Why would I wanna give you head when I don't even know you?" I had yet to even give it to Hakim.

"I wanna give you head and I don't know you."

"That's nasty. Head is a very intimate thing, so the fact that you go around eating all these bitches' boxes is disgusting. I expected better from you."

"I don't go around eating all kinds of bitches out, but I wanna eat you out."

"But you don't know me."

"But I can imagine how sexy you look, moaning and shit while sitting on my face. I'm a very visual person as you may have noticed," he smirked, making me smirk. This nigga was getting me hot.

"Yes I have noticed that Mr..."

"Smith, but just call me Romeo aight?"

"I see the way you *really* talk is coming out. Do you change your voice back polite when you go around talking to the other patrons?" I ate some more salad.

"Of course. I thought all black people did that."

"We do I guess," I chuckled.

"So where are you going after this, shorty?"

"I just got off work, and I was supposed to go home to meet my boyfriend, but I don't feel like doing that, so I don't really know."

"Problems in paradise?"

"No, not at all," I lied. "I just don't feel like going home at the moment. My daughter is with her father, and she keeps me entertained. So since she's not there..." I shrugged.

"Your man doesn't keep you entertained?"

"He... does." I nodded and we both burst into laughter.

"Yo, you're lying like hell right now. Why can't he keep you entertained? As beautiful as you are I can think of many ways to do such a thing."

"I don't think it's right to discuss my relationship with another man, do you?" I'd already made that mistake with Hakim.

"There is an unwritten code saying not to discuss your relationship problems with the opposite sex, so I guess you're right. But take my number down."

"Romeo I already have—"

"No, give me your number. I promise I won't bug you, I will just check up on you sometimes, as a friend."

"If I was your girl, would you want me giving my number to a man who came right out and said he wanted to give me head?"

"Hell yeah! I'd be like you better get that head, woman!" he joked, and we both chortled a little loudly. "Nah I feel you, ma, but the difference is that I can see in your eyes how unhappy you are. If you were mine, that wouldn't be the case."

"How cliché."

"It is, very, but it's the truth. And if you were unhappy, which you wouldn't be, then I would have to let you go so that someone else can give you that."

"Really?" I cocked my head and rolled my eyes.

"Really. Sometimes you're not the one who can make that person happy. You may love them, but that doesn't mean you're the one," he explained, and Rhys entered my mind.

"That makes sense."

"So can I have your number? And maybe I can take you out sometime."

"I'd like that." I nodded.

Hakim Murray

A couple days later…

Summer had been acting real standoffish lately, and the shit was starting to irk me. I wasn't sure if she was back fucking with her ex or what, but I wasn't having that shit. I'd done a lot for her ass, and she wasn't about to play me like that. I'd endured too much to be with her, and it seemed like she didn't appreciate it. I got my ass whooped, embarrassed, and I almost lost my career for good, all in the name in love, yet she still felt the need to be shady with me. Summer was making me an angry person, and I didn't like it one bit.

From the first time I laid eyes on her smooth, brown skin, perfect body, and long, beautiful dreads, I knew I had to have her. I didn't care that she was with someone; I was determined. It took a lot, but I was finally able to call her mine, which was all the more reason why I wasn't about to lose out on her. I deserved her, and I would have her.

I called in sick today because I wanted to do some deep digging. I wanted to follow Summer around, and see exactly what she was up to, cheaters' style. I swear if I saw her meeting up with her daughter's father, I would no longer be able to control my actions. I couldn't stand that nigga, so for her to be back with him would be the ultimate blow. As mad as I would be, I wouldn't even care about him fucking me up again.

It was finally around 4:38pm, so I watched as she walked out of work with her bag. She was clearly off early today, and I was about to find out why. Not to mention she was dressed as if she was going out, not wearing something she would usually wear to work. I waited as she threw her belongings into her G-Wagon purchased by Rhys, and sucked my teeth. I tried to get her to give it back, but all she did was curse me out and tell me to get over it.

That was another thing we needed to get in check, that mouth. I don't see how Rhys kept his hands to himself with her. Strangely, I have never felt the urge to hit my woman in past relationships, but Summer had awakened that trait I guess.

She pulled out of the parking lot, and I followed behind her closely until we ended up at the Beacon Hotel. *What the fuck*, I thought.

I gave her a little time after she got out of the car, before I did the same. We both entered the hotel, and I watched as she made her way to Mooo, an expensive ass steakhouse inside of the hotel. As I moved in closer to watch her better, I almost passed out when I saw her embrace some big, tall ass light skinned nigga in a suit. I could tell the shit was expensive all the way from where I was. His watch blinded me as he walked around to pull her chair out. *This bitch.*

"Are you lost, sir?" one of the hotel employees quizzed.

"No. Thanks."

I stood there like an idiot, and watched her laugh and talk with him. She had never laughed that much with me, and I'd never seen her so damn happy. She was enjoying herself so much, that I was sure that if I walked up she would need some time to remember me. My heart literally ached seeing the love of my life enjoy the company of another man. Not only that, I could tell that he was nothing like me. I stayed in the same spot for hours, watching them eat, talk, and drink wine, and when I saw the check come, I decided to go to her condo and wait for her. It was about to be some fucking problems when she walked through that door.

An hour later...

I was sitting on Summer's couch when I heard Bryleigh's voice in the hallway. I quickly downed the drink in my hand, and waited for her to open the door. She walked in with Bryleigh, but when she saw me her smile faded. Damn, like that?

"Hi, Hakim," Bryleigh smiled and then rushed to her bedroom. I ignored her little ass.

"Umm, I didn't know you were coming over this evening. Did we make plans? If so I'm sorry. I asked to leave early for a dentist appointment, that's why I'm here now."

"How was your steak?" I asked, making her pause before putting her coat into the closet. "Yeah, I saw yo' ass out to dinner with some white collar nigga."

"Hakim look, I can explain alright."

"Yeah explain, please. I would love to hear why my woman was out with another man. And don't say you're not fucking him, because I saw him touch your hand and shit. Oh and my favorite part was when he pulled his chair around to your side so he could sit next to you."

"Well first of all I'm not fucking him okay? Secondly, yes I went out with him and I enjoyed myself. Hakim, I think we've both sensed that this didn't turn out the way that we'd planned. I think we rushed into this thing, thinking that it was what we both wanted, but it's not."

"I'm sorry what? I'm fine. I'm happy and as far as I knew, so were you!"

"Well I'm not, Hakim." She fidgeted.

"I got my ass whooped for you, and I almost ended my career for you, and you think that you can just be done with me like that?" I snapped my fingers as I neared her. "Nah, baby girl, you got the game fucked up if you think you can just move on after all I've lost over you. You might as well call yo' little friend right now and tell him thanks, but no thanks."

"I'm not doing that. I like him and I wanna keep hanging out with him. You need to go. I don't like the way you're acting right now." She opened her front door.

WHAM!

I slapped her ass to the floor with as much strength that I could muster up.

"You fucking, bitch!"

"Mommy!" Bryleigh screamed.

"You get the fuck back!" I turned to Bryleigh, who was hugging that same fucking doll she always held onto.

"Don't talk to her like that! Sweetie, go to your room, Mommy is okay."

"I'm gonna call daddy! Where is my daddy?" Bryleigh sobbed, angering me even more because she was crying for her father.

"Baby, go to your room okay?" Summer walked to her daughter and kissed her forehead. Bryleigh glared at me as if she could whoop my ass, before doing as she was told. She looked just like Rhys sometimes. "Get out, Hakim."

"I ain't going nowhere."

"Get out before I call Rhys." She raised a brow, because she knew I didn't want that damn fade again. I mean I could fight, but that nigga was psycho. I know I talked shit earlier, but now that some flashbacks from last time were hitting me, I didn't want that shit right now.

"You know what, Summer, fuck you! You ain't nothing but a damaged ass bitch anyway! I'm happy to let the next nigga deal with yo' baggage, you bitch!" I barked before snatching the bottle of Hennessy I brought and bounced.

Fuck her. I was over trying to make her stupid ass love me. If she wanted to be alone and broken forever, then by all means. No one was gonna love her damaged ass but me, and she would realize that one day.

"If it isn't the infamous TQ. You didn't invite me here to kill a nigga did you?" Pharaoh walked into the warehouse buttoning his suit jacket.

"Nah man, of course not. Have a seat." I stood up to shake his hand, before gesturing for him to sit down across from me.

"Is that a Dolce and Gabbana suit?" he furrowed his brows, before nodding in approval.

"Yeah, man, it's old though," I replied as we chuckled. "But umm, I wanted to talk to you because there are gonna be some changes within QCF."

"Changes? Already?"

"Yeah, my father won't be in charge anymore, and I wanted to give you a heads up so that you wouldn't be blindsided by anything."

"Wait Stony is getting out of the game?"

"Yeah, he is," I smiled.

"Damn, he didn't say shit about leaving when he talked to me. I would think that he would tell me something like that you know?"

"He probably would have if he knew." Pharaoh stared at me wearing a confused expression. "Stony will no longer be a part of QCF.

This will be by force, not by choice."

"TQ, man, even speaking that shit is dangerous." He looked around the dark warehouse for a few moments before turning his attention back to me.

"Don't trip, this isn't a setup or a test of your loyalty to my father. I'm simply telling you what's about to go down. If you want to be a part of the new QCF, you can keep your position. If you don't, that's on you, but if you become a problem we'll have to eliminate you."

"I understand, shit," he sighed. "Who is gonna be in charge now? You?"

"Not just me, it'll be my brothers, sister, and you. All of us will have our same departments within the family. We're gonna work together, not for just one person like it is now."

"To be honest TQ, that sounds all good, but how do you plan to get at Stony? And what about the people that will ride or die for him?"

"I don't need you to worry about that Pharaoh."

"But how can I not? You know how dangerous your father is. He has an army backing him, and I mean you will only have us."

"Well, Andrei has agreed to fuck with us, but Pharaoh what you need to realize is that I'm like a king. I may be just one person, but I hold the power. When I tell you not to worry about my father, I mean it. All I need you to do is to be ready to work."

"I'm ready, I've been ready."

"Good. I have another meeting, so I have to go, but I will be in touch soon." I checked my watch before rising to my feet. He did the same, and we shook hands before exiting.

I was glad he was on board, because I would've hated to have to kill his ass right then and there. I'm sure my sister, Saya, would have a lot to say about that. I laughed at my thoughts as I remembered how calm and lethargic she was when I told her I'd bodied Aries. I think she may have wanted to thank me, but that would have been cruel on her part. I knew my sister though, so her silence was thank you enough.

After driving for what seemed like a century, I finally made it to my destination. Pulling into the huge ass driveway, I shut the engine off and exited calmly. Using my key to enter, I went straight through the foyer and to the back to see my dad. When I walked into his office, he was staring out of his bay window from afar, while sipping his drink.

"Tarenz, would you like something?" he smiled.

"No, I'm good. What do you have for me?" I sat down.

"I have this guy in Delaware that I need you to go meet. He's doing really well for himself, and he wants us to supply him." He handed me a folder of information.

"Alright, cool."

"Do you have an update on a Boston distributor, Tarenz? Gang's been dead for months, and the streets are drying up. I need someone quickly."

"Oh yeah, I've been meaning to talk to you about that. I met this guy named Geoff, and he's ready to work. I meet with him later this week to discuss some details. He claims that he can push just as much as Gang, and maybe even more since he's more well connected with the hoods."

"Really?" My dad grinned. "Damn, so it's a possibility that we could be making more money than we were making with Gang."

"Big possibility. He's a humble dude, too, so we won't have many problems with him. He ain't no bitch either, so he won't be crying over a girl he's never even smashed."

"Was that a dig at Gang? How do you know he never fucked the girl? Because she told you?" he scoffed and shook his head as he took another sip.

"I'm the only one who knows her like that, Stony."

"Oooh we're still calling me Stony?" he chuckled. "I guess it's better than what your mother has been calling me these days. If you see her, tell her there is nothing she can do to convince me to sign those papers."

"Will do."

"You know, Tarenz, I had a friend once, a female friend, and she told me she'd been a virgin five times. She said each time, the guy could never tell. You hear that, five damn times, and no man was able to tell." He wore a smug expression.

"Kimberlyn was a real virgin."

"She gave it up pretty quickly, you don't think that's alarming?" He raised a brow and laughed.

"I'm not with her because she was a virgin aight? And why are we talking about this shit? Why do you care about whether she was one or not?"

"Oh I don't. I just want you to pull your fucking head out of the clouds, and realize that the little act she puts on is fake. What woman is a virgin at her age, and then just gives it away to a man she's only known for about what? A week? Probably less if I remember correctly." He slurped his drink.

"And on that note, I'm gonna leave before this conversation gets out of hand. The only woman you need to worry about is my mother, because I can see how much of a toll the divorce is taking on you."

"She'll be back." He refilled and gulped his drink.

"You don't even believe that," I chuckled. "I used to always look up to you, and I admired how cold you were. I thought it was dope to see you go in on people, and smoke muthafuckas when they came at you incorrectly. But as I got older, I've realized that it's sad. You don't know how to turn that shit off, and that's your problem. It's one thing to fuck niggas up in the streets for fronting on you, but to treat your wife and kids like shit is a sign of being a weak ass nigga. You may be scary, intimidating, and strong to these niggas in the outside world, but all I see is an incapacitated, foolish, miserable old man with a fragile mind."

He stared up into my eyes, as he stayed seated behind his desk. I could see how much he hated me for speaking those words, but it was honestly how I felt.

"You're dismissed," he gritted.

"But even though you're a despicable piece of shit who isn't man enough to be a good father, I still love you." We stared at one another for a few, before I turned around and left out.

Closing his door behind me, I tread down the narrow hallway until I got to the winding staircase. Making my way up, I went down the hall to my old bedroom and entered. I went into my closet, which was pretty much empty, and pulled out a big white box. Taking out its contents, I inspected it before leaving out.

I was about to leave, but I stopped in my tracks and made my way back to my dad's office. When I opened the door, he was standing a little bit closer to the bay window, but not up against it. He was swishing around his drink, and I could tell he was in deep thought. I walked up behind him slowly, not wanting to disturb his peaceful mind state just yet.

"Dad," I said in a low tone.

He turned around slowly, now face to face with a loaded double barrel shotgun.

BOOM!

His brains splattered everywhere, and his body slumped onto the nearby couch. I then left the office, and went on about my day.

CHAPTER EIGHT

Robert "Pharaoh" Johannson

A week later...

I heard Saya knocking at my front door, so I paused the movie I was watching and went to answer it. We'd been chilling heavy since I got out of jail, especially now that her nigga had gotten killed. I felt some type of way about her getting with him when I got locked up, but honestly I couldn't say too much about it because we weren't really anything at that time. She knew I liked her but that was it, so I couldn't expect much. But once Stony let me know that he was getting me out, I set my mind on getting her back. Aries wasn't gonna be a problem whether he was dead or alive, but I will say that him being in the ground made it much easier for Saya to open up.

"I brought alcohol," she cheesed and held up a big ass bottle of Grey Goose.

"You know I don't like that clear shit, but it'll work for now." I took it from her and closed the door. "Would you like me to mix yours with something?"

"Yes, what juices do you have?"

"I have pineapple just for you."

"Nigga stop trying to get some pussy. You probably bought that shit for Kat." She sucked her teeth and rolled her eyes before making her way back to my bedroom.

I finished our drinks, and then took the glasses, juice, and liquor to my bedroom where I found her maxing and relaxing on my bed.

"I ain't bought shit for Kat," I replied to her previous statement as I handed her drink over.

"Whatever." She sipped it. "Why are you still living here? You didn't get paid from my dad before he checked out?"

"If you must know, yes I did, but I have someone looking for a place for me right now. I know this shit is shabby, but it's cool for right now."

"I guess. I prefer my condo, but this will do until you step your game up." She made a face before cheesing.

Saya was sexy as fuck, with pretty ass chocolate skin and perfect features. I couldn't wait to see that beautiful face twisted all up from me banging her out. I was backed up like crazy, and ready to let all of me go into her. The way she smiled, licked her lips, just everything about her was sexy as hell. She could flip her hair and my dick would get hard.

"How are you feeling about your dad and Aries?"

"My dad, I knew it was coming because that's part of the game.

I just didn't think TQ would do it. But I can't blame him. If my father had disrespected me like that I would murk his ass, too."

"I agree. If TQ didn't retaliate I don't think I could respect him. You don't fuck with a man's wife."

"Nope. And as far as Aries, this sounds bad but I'm not really sad. It's just like damn, why him? But then when I think about why he got killed, the sadness goes away. He had everything in me, yet he felt the need to push up on Kimberlyn." She shook her head and put her glass out for me to refill. "Straight please."

"Aww shit," I said, making her laugh. "I didn't like that he put his hands on you, shorty, you're better than that. You have way too much shit going for you to be allowing some bum to hit you."

"I know, don't remind me."

"So before a nigga gets locked up again, God forbid, I need you to know that I fuck with you and that I want you on some real shit."

"What do you mean?" she gave me that innocent face that I loved.

"I mean that I ain't playing no fucking games this go round. You and I are gonna be something, and I want to make that very clear. I didn't do that last time, and look what happened."

"True. I missed you, if that helps."

"Not really since I got no letters or anything. I wrote your ass, too, but you never said nothing back." I shook my head as I gulped some of the alcohol.

"I didn't know what to say. I'm sorry." She reached her hand into my sweats and began playing with my dick. It took absolutely no time for him to wake up and start hardening.

"Fuck, Saya," I moaned. Just the feeling of her soft hands stroking me was enough to make me bust. Pulling my shirt over my head, I went right to unzipping her dress.

She climbed off of the bed, and let the dress fall to her ankles. She knew she was bad, so she gave me some time to admire what was before me, and damn was it a sight to see. I watched her intently as she removed her bra and panties, then let her hair down. I stood up to get naked as well, and then made my way over to her, kissing her soft lips as soon as I got close enough.

"Lay back," I growled in her ear.

She laid her sexy ass across my bed horizontally, and I got down to bury my face into her center. I'd been dreaming of eating this pussy for years, and it was finally happening. I had jacked off at the mere thought while in the pen many times. Yeah I know a nigga sounded thirsty, but if you saw shorty you would be, too. Listening to her moans gave me more motivation to eat the shit out of this pussy, and before I knew it she was crying out and exploding.

Rising to my feet, I yanked her arm to sit her up so she could show me how sorry she was with that mouth work. She knew what was up, because as soon she came face to face with my third leg, she had her lips wrapped around it. Seeing Saya Quinton slurp me up like a professional was the shit. I wasn't even surprised that she was so good at it because there wasn't much she couldn't do.

"Fuck, ma." I threw my head back as I massaged her scalp. "Suck that shit, fuck." I began slowly humping her face, and she took each thrust like a seasoned dick sucker. Gripping her hair, I sped up just a little, but then pulled away before I busted. "Shit," I panted.

She pulled me down onto the bed, and after I put the condom on, she mounted me. Sliding down, her face knotted up just like I had imagined it would. Her pussy was wet and warm, making my toes want to curl. I reached up to squeeze her perky round breasts, and play with her nipples as she bounced on my dick.

"Mmm, uhh, shit," she hollered in a high-pitched voice right before her body quivered. "Shit, oh my gosh!" she screamed again as I humped upward feverishly, ramming her spot like a maniac. "Aaah, uuuh!" she called out, spilling her nectar.

She was spent, but I wasn't done yet. I flipped her onto her stomach, and then entered her from behind. Holding onto the headboard, I began pounding the shit out of her as we both yelled and yowled. Her pussy was even better than I'd assumed it was, and I was not complaining. Seeing her smooth chocolate ass bouncing up against my pelvis every time I slammed into her was too much to handle, so I was filling the condom up in no time.

"That was long overdue," she exhaled as I fell to the side of her.

"It was. I'm gonna be ready to do that shit again in a little bit, so be prepared." I reached for the blunt I'd rolled earlier and lit it.

"I will be."

"You hoe ass bitch!" I heard a voice yell, and looked up to see Jamie in the doorway of my bedroom holding a gun. He was trembling and shit like the little bitch that he was.

"Aye man, put the fucking gun down!" I hollered, while trying to remember if I had some heat close by.

"I knew we should've went to my house!" Saya shouted in a fearful tone.

POP! POP! POP!

I jumped in front of Saya, and clenched my teeth as each bullet ripped through my body. I saw Jsmile about to shoot again, but his gun jammed, thank the Lord. When it did, he turned to leave so I hopped out of the bed ass-naked, and pulled my gun from the dresser by the door. I made it into the living room to see him pulling on my door handle, so I lit his ass up with five shots.

POP! POP! POP! POP! POP!

Watching him drop to floor, I ignored the pain in my shoulder, rib, and arm. I was bleeding profusely, but I didn't give a fuck right now.

"Robert, I called my brother so the medical team can come get you. Oh my gosh!" Saya ran into the living room crying. "The clean up is coming for Jamie."

I collapsed to the floor, while trying to keep my eyes open, but the shit was hard as fuck. Damn, a nigga just got out and was already getting blazed.

Matikah

I'd finally gotten the courage to find out why Isabetta had fired me. I'd been practicing what I was gonna say, and even some possible responses to what she may say. I chose this day to speak with her, because I think if Lendsey found out I still hadn't said anything, he was gonna blow a fucking fuse. And honestly I wanted to know why she had let me go. She gave me no explanation and I felt I deserved that.

I walked into her spa, and once Annalise and I made eye contact, she came from around the counter and hugged me. It was unexpected so I kind of just stood there while she squeezed the life out of me.

"Matikah, what happened? I tried texting you!" she exclaimed.

"That's why I'm here. I wanna know why she fired me. Is she here?" I pointed to the back and Annalise nodded.

"Maybe she was having a bad day. I hope she let's you come back!" she called after me. I ignored her as I made my way to Isabetta's office.

KNOCK! KNOCK!

"Yes," she called out, so I opened her door and walked in. "Matikah, can I help you?" She raised her brow and folded her arms across her chest.

"Isabetta, I need to know why you fired me. Not the bullshit you

181

told me, I want specifics. If you don't give them to me, I will call my lawyer." I closed her door and sat down.

"You have a lawyer, Matikah?" She pouted playfully. When did she develop this sudden hate for me? I was sure it had something to do with the fact that I was dating Lendsey.

"I'm waiting."

"I didn't want to have to tell you this, Matikah, but since you insist upon knowing, I will oblige. On one of your days off, Lendsey came in here. My cousin, Rosie, was here, and he propositioned her. Now he didn't do this in front of me, but she told me. When I asked him about it, he admitted to it, and said he wasn't leaving unless she came with him. Now I know they've had sex before, but that was a bit much. And now knowing that you're his girlfriend, I think it's best that we go our separate ways. I don't want you bringing him to my place of work." She cocked her head and waited.

"You're lying."

"Am I? We both know Lendsey, Matikah, so it's not odd that he would be out trying to sleep with other women while you *think* he's busy working or something. Now granted Rosie is a bit promiscuous, but that still didn't give Lendsey the right to approach her in that way."

"Why would he try to sleep with your cousin, if he was sleeping with your sister?"

"I wish I knew. Honey, you know exactly what type of man you have at home, so stop acting like you're dating Mike Brady okay? A man like Lendsey has a large appetite for sex, especially with other women. You can't tell me that it's not believable that he'd sleep with one woman and her cousin, too."

"Isabetta, what if I convince him not to come up here." I needed this fucking job until I found somewhere else. Yes, Lendsey kept my bank account full, but I loved what I did, it wasn't only about the money.

"No, honey, I can't. Now if you don't leave, I will file a report of sexual harassment against him. I know despite what I told you that you still love him and don't want him in jail, so it's best you go."

"You're gonna regret this."

"Is that a threat, Matikah? Because I can press charges against you and him if you'd like. You do know that you'll go to separate jails right?" she giggled.

"Isabetta, I'm pregnant, I need the job."

"Wow, I feel sorry for you, being pregnant by a man like Lendsey Quinton. You better hope he's not fucking your cousin, too."

Before she could finish, I cleared her desk of all the shit that was on it as she screamed.

"You have fucked with the wrong person, Isabetta. You're gonna wish that you'd kept your mouth shut and gave me my job back." I panted before quickly leaving her office.

"Get out! And if you come back I will call the police!" she shouted after me.

"What happened, Matikah?" Annalise quizzed on my way out, but I just ignored her ass.

I quickly got to my car, hopped in, and peeled out of the parking lot. I wasn't gonna wait for Lendsey to come home, I was going straight to his workplace. I knew I was supposed to trust him, but I had to look him in the eye and ask him about it. My heart began to beat fast just thinking about if what Isabetta said was true. I loved Lendsey like a muthafucka, but if he had cheated on me again with Dania's cousin, I may haul off and butcher his ass. The only problem with killing him though, was that I would be the saddest one at his funeral.

I parked horribly once I got to Quinton Workforce, and slipped out in a hurry. Storming in, I bypassed his little timid assistant, and went right back to his office. He was typing on his computer when I entered, but stopped when he saw me.

"Baby, you okay?" he furrowed his brows.

"No, I'm not. Who the fuck is Rosie?" I dropped my purse on his couch before sitting down.

"Dania's cousin." He walked over and sat next to me.

"Did you fuck her?"

"Nah, I let her suck me up a couple times, but that was way before I even knew you, shorty, I swear." He looked into my eyes. I stared into his blue ones, before a smile appeared on my face. He was being honest.

"Isabetta claims you asked Rosie for sex while in the spa, and that's her reasoning for firing me." I closed my eyes and ran my fingers through my hair.

"What do you wanna do?"

"What should I do?"

"I say you let me take care of it, ma. Rest up and make sure my baby is good, it doesn't need you to be stressed right now."

"Don't kill her, Len."

"I'm crazy, but a nigga ain't stupid. Just know I got you, and you don't have to worry about anything else okay?"

"But what about a job? I liked working there."

"Open up your own shit."

"With what money, Lendsey?"

"My money." He palmed his chest.

"I don't want you to give me your money, and you know that already."

"I'm not giving you shit. I will loan you the money, and you will have to pay me back. Now it can be in the form cash or a check. If you give me head or pussy, that's $1,000 for each, both at the same time are $2,000."

"Damn, just for some head?" I giggled.

"That's how much it's worth."

"Aww, baby." I poked my bottom lip out and caressed his face. "You are so sweet." I planted a kiss on his full lips.

"I try." He grinned, showing his perfect smile.

Whatever he had planned for Isabetta wasn't gonna be pretty, I could already tell. She deserved whatever she had coming to her, too.

***

The next evening...

"So, how is school?"

"I'm finished with school, ma, remember?" I looked into her eyes as she sat across from me in the restaurant.

She'd asked to meet me for an early dinner, and the only reason I was here was because she claimed she would pay. I was sure that she would have some excuse as to why she couldn't by the time the bill came, but she wouldn't get away with it this time. I would straight up pay for my food and leave her ass here to scrub a dub dub in the back.

I really wanted the waitress to hurry up with my food, because she was starting to annoy me. She needed to get to the point and just ask me what she wanted to ask me. The only time my mom wanted to spend time with me was to get information, or brag, so I was just waiting for her to make a move.

"Oh yes, you work for that nail salon you said." She sipped her cocktail.

"It was a spa, and I got fired."

"Really, honey? I'm so sorry. Why did that happen?"

"Because my manager lied and said Lendsey asked her family member for sex, and got aggressive when she told him to leave."

"Lendsey, huh? So what's the deal with you and him?"

"What's the deal? What do you think the deal is? He's my boyfriend and the father of my child."

"I don't know, Matikah. He seems a bit sneaky, like he enjoys

186

stepping out. Do you watch him closely? Never mind, I know you don't. I'm telling you that you should though." She rubbed her finger around the rim of her glass as she spoke.

"Lendsey has done nothing to make me suspicious, Ma. He's a great guy and you should start only speaking on what you know, alright?"

I had the password to Lendsey's phone, and my own fingerprint set up along with his. I used to check his shit morning, noon, and night, but now I didn't feel the need to do that. I knew my nigga, and I would be able to sense if he was fucking around. When he cheated that first time, I felt it in my gut that something was wrong. This time, I don't have anything nagging at me. I can sense his faithfulness, and nobody was gonna knock me out of that happy place. Isabetta almost did, but when I looked into his eyes I was able to get my shit back together.

"I'm sorry, I guess I got the wrong idea when speaking to him. He was a bit flirty with me, but maybe that's just his personality."

"He didn't flirt with you, but he did let me know you gave him full view of your cob web factory down below." Her jaw dropped, and I just stared at her with my head slightly cocked, waiting for a response. "Oh you thought he didn't tell me? Well, he did. Now I suggest we change the subject before I get the urge to jump across this table... Ma."

"So... how is Kimberlyn?" she smiled uncomfortably.

Rhys

It was around 7pm at night, and I was getting out of the shower. There was nothing like taking a nice hot shower, eating a good ass meal, and then climbing into my comfortable ass bed. And even better was the fact that my baby was here with me. I smiled thinking about her as her little voice bounced off the walls from the kitchen area. She and Indiya were best friends she told me, and I made sure she didn't repeat that to her mother. Although I loved the fact that she loved Indiya, I felt like that would hurt Summer's feelings if Bryleigh repeated that.

I slipped my boxers on, some sweats, socks, and then a wife beater before coming out to the kitchen where Indiya and Bryleigh were. They were in a deep conversation, whispering and shit, so I was wondering what the hell they were talking about. I could assume they were just being their silly selves, but I was never one to assume.

"What are y'all whispering about?" I questioned as I sat at the bar next to Bryleigh. Indiya was cooking us a full Russian meal, which included chicken kiev, knishes, and Russian black bread. My stomach was growling at the smell already.

"Can I tell him?" Indiya looked to Bryleigh. That shit really piqued my interest.

"Mommy said not to," Bryleigh whined.

"I know, sweetie, but I think we should because we don't want anything to happen to your mommy, right?" Indiya smiled and Bryleigh nodded.

"What the fuc— what are you guys talking about, Indiya?" I was now frowning up. Summer may not have been my woman, but I wasn't about to let anything happen to her.

"Summer's boyfriend, Hakim, smacked her in front of Bryleigh. She said her mom fell to the floor, and that he was yelling at the both of them."

My heart rate seemed to speed up the more Indiya talked. I already didn't like this nigga, because he was trying to push up on Summer while he knew she was taken. But hearing that he hit her, and in front of my shorty had me 38 hot. I guess that ass whooping I delivered to his ass did nothing, because he was still out here disrespecting me. It was all over with though, because I was gonna do what I should've done that night I caught him holding Summer's hand.

"Rhys." Indiya snapped in my face.

"Oh shit, yeah I'm sorry. I have to make a phone call." I kissed Bryleigh's face, and then went into my bedroom to call my brother.

"What's good?" he answered.

"I need to pick up a pizza tonight."

"So do that then, Rhys. You want some company?" he asked.

"Nah, I need to know the address of the pizza place. I know there are multiple locations, but I need one close to me."

"Oh okay, just call Andrei, that nigga is like a phone book."

"Cool, thanks."

I needed a location on Hakim, and usually I would just tell my father and he would get back to me with what I needed. But now that he was dead, I didn't quite know whom to contact. I guess Andrei was the one who would get my dad the information for me in the past.

Shit was gonna be weird with my father gone, but I knew it would also be better. Did I miss him? A little because the nigga was my damn father, but it was for the best. I had my brothers' back over anybody, so when it came down to it, I had to rock with TQ. In addition to that, Stony wasn't exactly father of the year.

I text Andrei on my burner phone, and by the time I was dressed he'd texted me Hakim's address. Upon reading it, I remembered that I already knew where the nigga lived. He stayed right at the spot that I fucked him up in. Shaking my head at myself, I pocketed the burner phone and turned right around to see Indiya standing in the doorway.

"When will you be back? I want us to eat dinner together."

"I won't be gone long at all. I'm gonna get in there and get out okay?"

"You better make sure you don't get hurt, or I'm gonna have to come out of retirement. And when that happens it'll be all over."

"Come out of retirement? Shorty you ain't no damn thug." I grinned and kissed her smooth forehead. "Calm your ass down." I squeezed her butt. "You gettin' a little more ass on you I see."

"No I'm not." She looked over her shoulder at it.

"Yes you are, and I can't wait to hit it from the back tonight." I pinched it again.

"Ewww!" Bryleigh screeched in the doorway.

"What are you doing spying on me?" I rushed her, scooped her up, and tickled her as she screamed and laughed. Finally stopping, I kissed her cheek and then carried her to the living room. "I will be back in a little bit okay? Fix Indiya's hair for me, it's looking crazy."

"Okay, daddy!"

I kissed Indiya's lips as she rolled her eyes, and then left out to handle this bitch ass nigga.

It didn't take me long to get to his place in Jamaica Plain, and I guess that was because I was speeding like a muthafucka. I wasn't even sure if he was home, but it didn't matter, I would wait until he got there. He was going to die tonight, and that's all there was to it. No nigga was about to be putting their hands on Summer, especially in front of my fucking daughter.

Getting out of the car, I checked my surroundings to see who was outside. I wasn't in my personal vehicle since I had stopped by the warehouse to get one of the many dummy cars we had. But even with that being the case, I still liked to be careful. I wasn't messy with anything. Once I saw it wasn't really anyone outside except a few people walking, I went inside his condo building and took the stairs up, making sure to keep my large hood low, covering most of my face. Once I got to his floor, I pulled my mask down and darted down the hallway to his door. I knocked lightly on it, while praying that he answered before one of his neighbors came up. The sound of his footsteps brought about a smile as I cocked my glock.

"Who is it?" he barked.

I said nothing because I had nothing to say. This wasn't a hotel, so the usual 'housekeeping' wouldn't work this time.

"Fucking stupid yo," he hissed under his breath as he began to unlock the door. "What the fuck?" He yanked the door open. I could see that he was scared, but he wanted to pretend like he wasn't. I was like a lion, I could smell fear in the air, and it was permeating off of him at the moment.

Pushing my mask up I said, "Keep your hands to yourself."

"This nigga," he chuckled and stepped out, half closing his door behind himself. "What you gon' whoop my ass again? I don't even care no—"

PHEW!

I sent one shot through his head, pulled my mask down, and left just like that. Why stick around for conversation? I had dinner waiting for me.

Indiya Nikolaev

A few days later...

I turned into the unoccupied parking space, and shut the car off. I inhaled sharply with my eyes closed, before taking a sip of my water and getting out. Walking slowly across the pavement, all kinds of thoughts raced through my mind, causing my hands to tremble a little bit as I pulled on the door of the restaurant. Once inside, I scanned the room and found the person I was there to meet. A small smile appeared on my face as I toyed with my new Hermes purse Rhys had purchased me for my birthday, along with these very expensive sandal stilettos I was wearing. Pushing one side of my newly dyed dark hair behind my ear, I approached the table and slid the chair out.

"Excuse me, where is my hug?"

"Oh sorry, I'm a bit nervous," I chuckled before moving over a little to embrace them.

"Why, honey?"

"Because I have something to tell you, and I'm gonna need your help I'm sure." I placed my purse into the chair next to me.

"Oh, someone is gonna sit there."

"You invited someone else? I told you we needed to talk in private." I frowned, not understanding her angle. I hoped she hadn't invited Rhys.

"I know, but it will be short, and then we will be alone again." Mrs. Quinton smiled at me.

"Fine," I sighed as the waiter brought me a glass of water.

"Here she is now." She rose to her feet. I turned around to see Summer walking over, dressed like she'd walked off a page of a magazine. She was always a beautiful girl, but today she went overboard. "Hi, honey." Mrs. Quinton hugged her as I gulped some of my water.

"Hello, Indiya." Summer smiled down at me before taking a seat next to me.

"Hi, Summer."

"Umm, Bryleigh told me that you convinced her to tell Rhys what happened. I just wanted to say thank you for doing that, because I wasn't gonna say anything. But when I think about it now, it bothers me to picture him hitting me in front of my daughter. So I appreciate you stepping in. I also want to apologize for the things I said in Trader Joes."

"It's fine, I-I'm sure you were just angry. I don't take too many things personally really," I chuckled lightly. This was so odd for me. Was she really trying to make amends? I had no idea she would come to her senses this quickly. I hope this wasn't some sort of set up.

"You're right, I was mad, but that doesn't make it right. It was hard for me to watch you make someone I love happy, but I had to realize that I loved him enough to allow someone else to provide him something I couldn't."

"You made him happy for a long time." I smiled, trying to make her feel better. What woman wanted to believe she wasn't good enough?

"Yeah, but I couldn't trust him. But I think it will be good for you and I to get along. Bryleigh told me you guys are best friends," she grinned.

"Oh I think it's just because I let her braid my hair when she wants."

"Probably, but maybe she just likes you." Summer half smiled.

"Rhys would love to see this," Mrs. Quinton beamed.

"I'm sure he would, but I have to go. I'm going to lunch and to the movies, so I will see you guys later." Summer rose to her feet and pushed the chair in.

"With whom?" Mrs. Quinton frowned.

"A friend," she giggled, before walking out.

"Mrs. Quinton, how are you feeling about your husband and stuff?" I questioned. I had to know, because I'm sure all of this was a lot.

"To be perfectly honest, most days I feel relieved that I'm not with him and that he's not with us, but sometimes I find myself feeling sad. We did have some good times together, and beautiful children, but I couldn't be with a man who mistreats my kids, I don't care how old they are. Tarenz may be a twenty-seven year old man to everyone else, but all I think about is when the nurse first brought him to me. So when Stony did all of that shit to him, I knew it was time for us to go our separate ways."

"Is there going to be a funeral?"

"Maybe, who knows. He's been cremated already, so I may just throw him into some water." She half smiled and sipped some of her wine. "Enough about him, what did you need to talk about?"

Swallowing the lump in my throat, I grabbed my glass of water and drank some more.

"Well, I, umm, I—"

"Spit it out, Indiya."

I looked into her eyes for a little bit with a worried expression, before finally speaking.

"I'm gonna have a baby." I waited with bated breath for her response.

"Why was that so hard? That's great news, Indiya! Rhys is gonna be so excited!"

"No, he's not gonna be excited. See I told him I was on birth control, and I was. I am. But between working and spending all this time with him, I got a little lazy with it. I swear I didn't do it on purpose, but I know he's gonna think I did. You have to make sure he doesn't kill me."

There was silence between us for a bit, before she burst into laughter. I didn't know what the hell was so funny, but she needed to see that I was dead serious.

"Indiya, he is not gonna kill you. It is an honest mistake."

"What if he thinks I was trying to trap him?"

"If he doesn't know you well enough to know better, then you need to move on, sweetie. Rhys loves you and he would never think something like that about you."

"Are you sure?"

"I'm sure. I know him very well. Despite his rough exterior and personality, he's a sweet boy, he always has been. He's just very passionate, which people mistake for him being crazy. Just tell him and I'm sure he will be okay with it."

"Just don't tell him anything, let me do it."

"Fine, but let me know when you do."

I sure hoped she was right, because Rhys was no joke. I knew he loved me as much as I loved him, but I didn't want him to think I lied. I didn't lie, I was taking it. But being in love, and spending time with him, sometimes it would slip my mind.

I wanted to take Mrs. Quinton's advice, but I wasn't sure about that just yet. My life was always so complicated.

CHAPTER NINE

Britain

I had to go to New York to handle some business, and like last time, my shorty wanted to come with me. She'd completed her internship, and while she was waiting to see if they offered her permanent employment, she didn't have much to do. I hated when Tekeya used to be up under me like that, but with Goldie it was different. And seeing her belly grow more and more was pretty interesting to watch. My kid would be here in just four months, and I was excited to say the least.

I made it up to her condo door, and slipped my key in before entering. When I got in, I heard female voices, but none of them sounded like Goldie. I recognized that one belonged to her sister, but the other wasn't familiar. Making myself known, I walked into the large kitchen to see who the fuck else was in my shorty's crib. I told her ass about just letting every bitch she knew come through here.

"Oh, Britain, this is Hope." Goldie's sister Chenaye introduced me.

Hope was definitely a looker, with blemish free dark skin, short curly hair, and long sexy legs. If I didn't have Goldie, she would definitely be someone I'd smash, but I wasn't on that shit anymore. I prided myself on the fact that even though my track record was terrible, I hadn't cheated on Goldie. I just didn't have the urge to. I didn't know why, but I wasn't interested in finding out.

"What's good? Where is Goldie?"

"She's in the shower. But she's already packed and stuff, so don't worry. She told me to tell you that if you showed up before she got out."

"Oh, okay." I walked out of the kitchen, still feeling some type of way about Chenaye being here. It'd been almost two months since that incident with Ethan, and I didn't see her looking too much.

"You want a drink?" Hope walked out of the kitchen and into the living room where I was, with Chenaye hot on her heels.

"No, I'm good."

"What about some food? It's a long flight you'll be on." She smiled.

"To New York?" I raised a brow. "You need to Google a map or something, shorty," I scoffed as they both giggled like some hyenas.

"Oh yeah, I thought y'all were going to Florida or something like that." She moved from where she was and sat closer to me. "How long have you been with Goldie?" She pushed her chest out towards me. *Damn.*

"Long enough."

"What happened to that other girl you were dating for a minute? What was her name? Tekeya?"

"She moved to Illinois." I scooted over a bit because my dick was getting harder and harder every time I watched her full lips move.

200

"She's a fool. I would've never left something as fine as you back here in Boston. I would be dedicated to you all day."

"Shorty back up a little bit." I noticed Chenaye watching us with devious eyes as she held onto whatever was in her glass. Whatever Hope was doing, Chenaye oddly wanted it to happen.

"Am I bothering you, Britain? I just want to get to know you better. Take my number down, and if anything happens between you and G, let me know."

"How the fuck you gon' be on my girl's couch flirting with me and shit? You up in her crib, drinking her shit, and trying to fuck her nigga," I seethed. That shit had me hot. I didn't like the way she was probably smiling in my shorty's face, and then on her Eartha Kitt shit with me.

"Damn, I see how it is," she chuckled. "I just thought you and I could be cool, but I guess not. Or maybe I should wait it out. When she drops that baby, you may need something extra to help you out during that healing period." She touched my leg.

"Baby, give me like ten minutes." Goldie's voice almost made me jump out of my damn skin.

"Aight." I smacked Hope's hand off of me, and hopped up to go into Goldie's room while she got dressed. That Hope bitch had me feeling some type of way. Closing Goldie's bedroom door behind me I asked, "Why do you have Chenaye here still? She needs to be looking for somewhere else to stay."

"I know, Britain. She's looking and she will be gone soon I promise. I don't want her here either."

"And you need to stop letting her bring random people over here. I bought you this place so you could be safer and still have your own shit, but if you gon' be running some whorehouse, I will be moving you into my spot."

"Okay, baby, relax." She flashed her pretty smile as she pulled on some tights.

"Look at your belly, baby, it's so fucking round."

"Yep, and I feel fatter everyday." She pouted before pulling on a white t-shirt.

"No you look perfect like always." I rose to my feet, and pulled her small body into my chest before leaning down to kiss her gently.

Letting her go, I helped her get her things, and we both walked right past them two hoes in the living room. They said bye, but I didn't speak, and I didn't give Goldie a chance to either.

Once I put Goldie's bags into my car, I placed a call to have cameras installed in her condo while we were gone. I wanted them hoes to *know* we were watching their asses.

I got to the port in no time, and Primo, TQ's pilot, helped us load the plane. He made sure to have all the snacks I told him Goldie and I liked, along with some small meals. The flight would be short as fuck, but Goldie stayed hungry and when she was, she turned into a mean ass crybaby.

Only a little over an hour later, we made it to New York, and were driven to the hotel so we could check in and she could take a nap. While she did that, I changed clothes so I could go handle some business.

The driver I used whenever I was in New York didn't mind that he was no longer working for Stony. In fact, a lot of the people affiliated with QCF didn't mind. I think people actually preferred that it be ran by my siblings and myself, versus one nigga who was drunk with power.

Truthfully I didn't expect such a positive response, I just knew we'd have to go to war and kill a bunch of niggas. Some we did have to take out, but for the most part no one really liked my dad, they were just scared of him. As far as my brothers, sister, and I, niggas weren't necessarily scared, they more so respected us. Don't get me wrong, they knew none of us played any games, but they weren't frightened to sit and have conversation with us like they were with my father.

"Thanks, man," I said to my driver, Daniel, once he pulled up. It was already pretty late, which was perfect because no one was outside. It was a weekday too, and I'd chosen this day purposely.

"No problem, Mr. Quinton."

"Wait here, this will be quick. I'm gonna handle my business, and run back to the car. When I get back in, you just drive off slowly like it's nothing. Do not speed down the street, okay? That will bring attention."

"Got it."

I pulled my black skull mask down before getting out of the car. Taking the safety off my gun, I tightened the silencer onto the front and made my way up the porch steps. Banging on the door, I waited for that muthafucka to answer so I could blow his head open.

"Chto ty khochesh'? (What do you want?)" he questioned lowly in an irritated fashion. I don't think he meant for me to hear, but I was gonna respond anyway.

"Mr. Smirnov, I've come to collect the money," I yelled through the door, and listened to him sigh.

"I call Stony, and he said it's fine," he replied in his thick Russian accent from behind the door.

"Funny, because he sent me to talk to you," I lied like his ass. He blew out hot air again, and began unlocking the door. Pulling it open, he saw my mask and tried to close the door on me but barged in. Backing away with his hands up, he was about to turn to run for it but I yoked him up by his collar. "Stony can't say much from the grave." His eyes almost rolled out of his head upon hearing that my dad was dead. That was most people's reaction these days.

"Please, Britain! I have some things that are going to get me big money! Give me three days! Three days, that is all!"

"Danil, what is going on?" His wife came walking out.

"Times up, nigga."

PHEW!

"Ahhhhh!!" His wife stood there screaming as I dropped him to the floor. His head had exploded and gotten all over her, the walls, and the floor.

I came walking out, closing their front door behind me, and then got into the backseat of the vehicle before removing my mask. Daniel did as he was told, and drove off calmly, taking me to the New York warehouse so he could switch cars, and I could burn my clothes and gun. He then drove me back to the hotel, where I found my shorty in bed watching some scary shit and eating pasta.

"Where did you get pasta?" I began undressing so I could shower.

"I ordered it from downstairs."

"Room service. What about me?"

"I got you one, too. Hurry and eat it because I already know I'm still gonna be hungry after this." She kept her eyes on the TV.

"Come here," I turned her to face me by her chin. "I love you."

She bucked her eyes and looked into mine for a few seconds, surprised.

"I love you, too."

"Are you sure?" I grinned and pushed my sweats and boxers down.

"Yeah you just surprised me when you said it that's all."

I nodded and then turned around to go into the shower. Killing Danil suddenly caused me to smile. I'd been wanting to put his ass six feet under for the longest, and now I finally had.

Kimberlyn

TQ and I had just come from visiting Saya's boo, Pharaoh, in the little room they had him in. It was so weird to see him laid up in there like it was a real hospital. But they had all the staff and amenities needed, so I guess it was a hospital.

He was getting better, even though he lost a lot of blood, and Saya had been staying with him the whole time. I'd never seen her look worried or bothered before, so her feelings for this guy must've been strong. TQ told me they had a little something before he got put away, so I guess it was rekindled when he came out. I'm sure Aries' creepy ass is turning over in his grave.

Now TQ and I were going to the mall because Baby Tarenz was gonna take some pictures. I had him in the cutest little outfit, and I couldn't wait to get these pictures and have them in frames. I was hoping to even get a large one to have on the wall. If so, I would get one for our other babies we had in the future, too. I smiled as I thought about it.

TQ parked the car, and after he got Baby Tarenz out, he opened the door for me. I got the stroller from the trunk, and once my son was in it, we were on our way into the mall.

"How long do you think this shit is gonna take?" He frowned as we walked into the picture place.

"It shouldn't be long, Tarenz, we have an appointment."

I checked in with the lady up front, and then took a seat to wait. I could see from where I was that another baby was getting her picture taken, and she was so adorable. She was laughing and stuff, and I just hoped Baby Tarenz was easy like that. About fifteen minutes later, that baby was done, and was being brought out by its mother.

"She's so pretty." I smiled.

"Thank you. She was crying at first, but once they brought out the toys she was good." The lady smiled.

"He will probably need the same." I pointed to Baby Tarenz.

"He's adorable. Well, have fun." She walked out.

"Quinton!" the lady called, prompting me to stand up quickly.

I pushed my baby to the back, with TQ following behind me. Removing him from the stroller, I sat him in the little chair that they wanted him in so they could take pictures. He was calm at first, but once the lady touched him he started crying and screaming. I picked him up and rocked him for a little bit, before he finally calmed down. I kissed his fat face, straightened his clothes, and then placed him back into the chair. The photographer pulled out some stuffed animals and began talking for them and doing weird stuff, and like clockwork Baby Tarenz began laughing and smiling, which in turn made me smile.

"He's so cute." I looked to TQ.

"He is." He nodded and kissed the side of my face.

The photographer continued snapping pictures as my son

laughed and giggled the whole time. I was anxious as hell to see these prints. When I turned to say something to TQ, I noticed he wasn't by me. I scanned the area with my eyes, and they landed on him standing in the lobby of the mall right outside of the picture place. By him was that bitch, Amikka, and they were having a conversation. My blood immediately began to boil upon seeing him converse with that bitch while his wife and son were here, and when he was supposed to be engaging in what we were doing.

"Mrs. Quinton, Mrs. Quinton." The photographer got my attention.

"Yes, I'm sorry."

"He's all finished. He did great. Just give me about an hour to have them ready for you. You can eat in the mall to pass time, or wait, I don't mind."

"I will go eat, thank you."

I picked Baby Tarenz up, and placed him in his stroller. Walking out of the spot, I kept going right past TQ and that bitch. I was over fighting and going off on bitches because it was all in vain if he was gonna continue to be friendly with them. What the fuck do I look like going ape shit 24/7 just for him to still be cool with them in the end? Fuck that. I felt his eyes on me as I passed him and the bitch, and I knew he was surprised that I didn't stop.

"Kimberlyn!" he called after me.

"Yes?" I turned to him with a raised eyebrow.

"He's done?"

"Yes, he's done. I'm going to get food until the prints are ready."

"Okay hold up and—"

"No, stay here with your friend. You guys look like you have a lot to talk about. I will take my baby to get some food, and you can continue doing whatever you want with this slut ass bitch."

"Hold up, who are you calling a slut ass bitch?" she placed her hand on her wide hip.

"I'm pointing to you, so I'm talking about you, *bitch*."

"Okay y'all need to—"

"I don't need to do shit! Fuck you, Tarenz! And you're lucky I'm not interested in throwing hands over this nigga at the moment, because otherwise I would be dragging yo' ass all over this mall floor." I turned around and headed towards the food court.

"Kimberlyn! Kimberlyn!" I heard TQ yelling after me. I walked past a group of guys and ignored them trying to get at me, as he continued to yell my name. He finally caught up with me, and grabbed my waist from behind. "Why did you do that? I told you to wait."

"Get off me, nigga. And I didn't want to wait on you. You got me fucked up if you think you're about to be friendly with all these bitches that you've fucked. I don't know what the hell you thought this was, TQ, but in case you need for me to tell you, here it is. I am your wife, and this is your son. We need to always come first no matter what. So you know what that means? That means keeping your ass put while your baby takes his first pictures, and not walking out into the mall to converse with some hoe that I told you has disrespected me not once, but twice. If you want the freedom to be able to have friendships with the women that you've stuck your dick in, then we need to divorce. It will be them, or me, but it will not be both."

"Kimberlyn, I can't talk to the girl?"

"For what?! What the fuck do you need to talk to that bitch for, Tarenz?!" I hollered. I didn't give a fuck about what these people in the mall thought.

"Calm yo' ass down!" he hissed.

"I ain't calming shit! Get the fuck out of my face with that bullshit, nigga! If you wanna go have tea and crumpets with that skank then go, but you will not be climbing into bed with me at night while making friends out of your old bed buddies by day!"

I could see in his eyes that he wanted to kill me. His face was calm, but angry. It wasn't twisted up, but I could see how furious he was at my behavior through his blue eyes. I was livid, so I didn't care how mad he or anyone else was.

"You do too fucking much," he stated calmly and walked away. A part of me wanted to call after him, but it was only a very small part. I wasn't wrong, he was, and if he was gonna wait for me to apologize, he'd be waiting forever.

I continued on to get my food, and ate it in the court. By the time I was finished, it'd been a little over an hour since I left the picture studio. I didn't know where TQ was, and I didn't care; I could find a ride home from someone else. Making my way back, I spotted him sitting inside of the studio texting on his phone. I went in and walked right past his ass to the front counter.

"Here you go, Mrs. Quinton. They're so beautiful." The

photographer passed me the big envelope holding the pictures, and pulled one out to show me.

"Thank you, they really are."

I paid her the money, and on my way out, TQ got up. I followed him out to the parking lot, and once I took Baby Tarenz out of the stroller, he put it up. I buckled my son in, and then got in on the passenger side. He slid in on his side, and then cranked the car to drive me home.

For the rest of the day, we said nothing to one another, and I slept in the room with my baby.

Lendsey

"Mr. Quinton, what if I work in your home?" Dominika questioned. I swear every time I looked up this girl was looking for a new employer. I was tired of seeing her face at this point. But because of her dad, and because of an obligation I felt I needed to fulfill, I couldn't turn her away.

"Dom, I live in a condo, and my girl is there all the damn time. I don't think she would approve of someone like you cleaning."

"What? Why? I have man."

"It's 'I have *a* man,'" I corrected her. "But she won't care. How about I give you a job cleaning my father's home? My mother is moving back in soon, once the renovations she ordered are complete. When that happens you can work for her."

"Oh! I would love to work for Mrs. Quinton! Will Mr. Quinton be okay with this?"

"He'd love the idea if he were here. My father passed recently, Dominika. I thought you knew." I gave her a sympathetic smile as if I were broken up about it. I wasn't happy about it, but I wasn't on the verge of bawling either.

"I had no idea. I'm so sorry for your loss, let me make you some black bread." She half smiled.

"That won't be necessary, but thank you. Actually, you know what, I would like some. After all I've done for you, I deserve a nice loaf," I chuckled and she smiled widely.

"I will get right to it. Umm, when would I start?"

"The renovations won't be done for another two weeks. But because we are close, and I care about you, I will write you a check to cover bills, food, and some extra spending money for that time frame. You said rent is $1,000?"

"It's actually $2,600, Mr. Quinton," she giggled.

"What? Why? You moved?"

"Yes, my new job was paying well so we moved to Downtown Boston. It's a beautiful place. We still don't have enough bedrooms for all of us, but the neighborhood is safer."

"All that and still not enough rooms? At least it's safer though, like you said. I'm gonna have to come by sometime and see it. I'm also gonna have to start watching you." I furrowed my brows making her snicker. Pulling out the Quinton Workforce checkbook, I quickly filled out a check for her. "Here. That's $8,000. That should cover rent, and anything else for at least two months until your money starts coming in nicely from my mother."

"Thank you so much! I promise this is the last time I will need to change jobs! Mrs. Quinton and I get along very well." She flashed her pretty smile as she stood up.

"I bet. And tell your man that he needs to help you out. He ain't doing his job right now if you're living the way you are. He needs to relieve some of that burden for you."

"He's looking for job now."

"It's *a* job, Dominika. And he better be. Tell him to come talk to me if he needs help finding work okay?"

"Yes, thank you!"

Once she left I closed my eyes and leaned back in my chair. I was so tired from staying up all night making moves. That bitch, Isabetta, was on my radar, and she was about to feel my wrath like no other. She could do whatever she wanted to me, but my shorty was off limits. I used to actually think her ass had more sense than Dania and Rosie, but she was no better; it just took longer to bring it out of her. They were three disturbed ass bitches, and it was no surprise that none of them could keep a fucking man.

After a couple minutes, I opened my eyes to see my assistant, Alyona, standing there fidgeting… again. I sat up, blew out hot air, and then looked in her direction.

"Baby girl, don't do that! How many times do I have to say that? When you come in here, make yourself known okay?"

"I didn't want to bother you, you looked like you were in deep thought."

"I appreciate that, but I would prefer it if you *did* bother me and tell me what you needed. It's a bit creepy for me to look over and see you standing there."

"Yes, I will keep that in mind, sir." She blushed like always. "There is someone here to see you, can I send them back?"

"Who is it?"

"Janine Hudson."

"No, tell her that you thought I was here, but when you walked in you saw that I had already step—"

"Son in law!" Janine came in boastfully. Alyona just smiled shyly and rushed out, leaving me alone with her predator ass.

"Janine, what can I do you for?"

"You can do me for a lot of things. Namely for a nice orgasm." She plopped down on the leather couch in my office. Her dress was so short, that I was sure her ass was hanging out at the bottom.

"Why are you here?"

"You're not gonna offer me a drink?"

Janine was a very beautiful woman. In fact Matikah looked just like her. They both had big curly hair, slim frames, and light complexions. The only difference was that one was young and had morals, and the other was an old hoe trying to fuck her daughter's man.

"No, I was on my way out so I'm not gonna offer you a drink. Just tell me what you need so I can go. No, I mean tell me why you are here." I changed it when I saw that creepy ass smile appear. This bitch could make a bible scripture sound sexual.

"I decided to stop by because I'm leaving town soon, and I wanted to give you one more chance to get a piece."

"A piece of?" I raised a brow. Please be talking about a going away cake.

"Look, Lendsey, you don't have to play the role with me. I've done my digging already. As soon as my mother told me that Matikah was dating you, I had some old friends find out who you were. What I got back was very interesting."

"Oh yeah?"

"Yes. Turns out you're very important out here in Boston for some reason, and people respect you. I don't even know how Matikah got you. Anyway, what really piqued my interest was the fact that you're a ladies man."

"Not anymore."

"Since when darling?"

"Since your daughter."

"A man doesn't change that quickly for anybody. I don't care how much he loves a woman." She got up and moved closer to me. "I'm not in the business of snitching. It'll just be one time. I know I'm not the only one who is curious about the other." She cocked her head, staring up into my face. "You are so handsome." She reached up to touch my cheek, but I stopped her. "Those blue eyes make you look so innocent, but I know you're not."

Reaching behind me, I pulled my gun from my waist and placed it in the middle of her forehead, causing her to gasp.

"What I'm about to say, I'm only gonna say once. The only woman I'm curious about is my girlfriend, Matikah. I have no interest in fulfilling your cougar meets the cub fantasies in any way, shape, or form. I love Matikah, and she's having my baby. There ain't shit else out there for me, I already looked. Now I want you to walk up outta here, and prepare to go back to wherever you came from. If I see you around again, I will pull this trigger, and trust me no one will care, not even

Matikah. Please don't test me, ma."

She glared at me, and then snatched her purse off of the couch before storming out. I wasn't playing with that bitch. Matikah's mom or not, I would pop her ass in a hurry and go on about my muthafucking business.

My phone ringing snapped me out of my thoughts, and I looked down to see it was my dummy phone. Picking it up, I tapped the green button to answer.

"I got the stuff for tonight," Britain said.

"Cool, did Andrei give you the address for later?"

"Sure did. Only thing is that y'all may not be able to go there until the morning. We can still do the job tonight though."

"Alright cool." I hung up and grinned before getting my shit and dipping.

Goldie

*C*henaye had been bugging me to have what she called a sister's night, and I'd finally agreed. I told her we could do one thing together, but we would not be hanging out the whole night. If I'm being perfectly honest, the only reason I was hanging out with her was because she was my sister. Her personality was whack as hell, and if she were a random bitch we would never be friends. Chenaye was so fake to me, and anybody like that didn't belong anywhere near my circle. That's why all my life I've only fucked with Kimberlyn and Matikah. They were as far from fake as you could get, and that was more my style.

"After you sister," Chenaye beamed, opening the door to this Italian restaurant on Hanover. She chose this place because my mom and her husband used to always take us here after Wednesday night bible class. "Over there." She pointed to a table, and I saw that girl, Hope, sitting down drinking wine.

"Really, Chenaye? Why did I need to come if you have her here?" I rubbed my belly and sighed. I would much rather be eating at Britain's house while he rubbed my feet. I missed him already.

"Hope is my best friend, and I want you guys to get along that's all."

Hope seemed to be cool, but she was one of those girls who

appeared to be sneaky, but you had no proof. I think it was just her facial expressions that threw me off; I wasn't sure. She just gave off the vibe that she was a shiesty hoe. She was the type of bitch to fuck your husband and then try to still be cool with you after. Kind of like how Chenaye did with Ethan. No wonder they were best friends. However, I did find it strange that I'd never heard of Hope until recently. The only friend I remember Chenaye having was this girl named, Cerise, but they just stopped being friends one day, not sure why.

"Wow, you are ready to pop, G!" Hope grinned as I sat down.

"It's Goldie, and yes I know. I can't wait."

"So what is it? A boy or a girl?"

"It's a boy. Hope, how did you meet Chenaye?" I questioned. Hope's eyes darted to Chenaye, before landing back on me. I raised one brow to let her know I was still waiting.

"Well, umm we were—"

"In church," Chenaye cut in. "We both teach Sunday school for the toddlers. She has the 8am service, and I have the 11am, so we crossed paths."

"I see, and you're already best friends. How old are you Hope?"

"I'm twenty-one, same age as Chenay—" she stopped when Chenaye began shaking her head 'no'.

"Chenaye is twenty-six."

"Oh I know." She let out a breathy chuckle before gulping some of her wine.

"Of course you do. Do you have a boyfriend? Are you originally from Boston?"

"No I don't have a boyfriend at the moment. I was born in Portland, but my father got a job in Boston so we moved here about three years ago."

"All the way from Oregon?"

"No from Maine. It's not much different from Boston, well it is, in some areas. But it was easy to make friends here and stuff." Her demeanor was very skittish, so I knew she was hiding something.

I just nodded as her eyes kept going from me to Chenaye nervously. I didn't know what was up with her, but I was sure and the fuck gonna find out. Like I said, Chenaye was a fraud ass bitch, so you never knew what her ass was up to.

The waitress came over to take our orders, and once she left it was quiet for a little while.

"Have any Quinton parties come up?" Hope inquired.

"Why?"

"We'd like to go to the next one that they throw. I hear about them all the time, but I've never been to one. I don't even know how to get invited, but I guess you have to know someone."

"Girl, they are good," Chenaye chuckled.

"How would you know? You've never even been to one."

"That night at the club—"

"That was at the club, an event open to everyone. A Quinton party is never held at a public establishment, Chenaye. Speak on what you know so that you won't embarrass yourself okay?"

"So if Britain tells you about one, you should bring Chenaye and I. I'm sure it would be a lot of fun. Chilling with you, your friends, and the Quintons," Hope giggled in unison with Chenaye.

"Is Rhys still with Indiya?" Chenaye asked.

"Yes, he is. You know he is and I told you to leave that shit alone. Stop trying to mess with him Chenaye. That nigga is crazy and crazy about that girl."

"I saw the way he looked at me at the club that night. You should've seen the way he looked at me, Hope."

"Yeah he looked at her ass like he wanted to strangle her. But in delusional minds like Chenaye's, I'm sure that means love."

"Goldie you don't have to be so mean. Just because Britain is with you doesn't mean that you're better than us. So what you lucked up and got a man, thanks to Kimberlyn," Chenaye spat.

"What does Kimberlyn have to do with me and Britain being together? Yes she was my ticket to the party, but she wasn't there when we talked to one another, spent time, and she definitely wasn't there when we made this baby!"

"You know what I mean. Just like Kimberlyn got you access to Britain, you should get us access!"

"Access to what huh? A Quinton? They're all taken, Naye!"

"Rhys—"

"Is taken! Lendsey is taken, and TQ is taken. We won't discuss Britain because you already know the answer, and that will get you killed."

"Rhys was taken when I met him the first time."

"Okay, you know what, I can't do this."

All I could think about was when Britain told me people would be nice to me in order to get close to them. I knew he was telling the truth, but I didn't think it would really happen like that. Chenaye and Hope were proving him right.

This Hope bitch and my sister were trying to use me to get close to some niggas who wouldn't touch them with a ten-foot pole. And why the fuck would I bring their asses to a party, knowing their intentions? Lendsey and TQ were with my best friends, and even though Indiya wasn't my best friend, I liked her and she was Rhys' woman. For me to intentionally put other women in their faces would be the shadiest shit in the world.

"Stay, Goldie, please. We didn't mean to upset you, we just thought you'd want us to enjoy the same life you have," Hope said, pleading with her eyes for me to sit down.

"You don't need a Quinton to find love."

"No, but you have a new car, condo, and a little bit of hood fame. You can't get that from these regular ass niggas in Boston," Chenaye huffed.

"If we don't change the subject, I'm gonna leave."

"Okay, okay, we can talk about something else, but just promise that we can come to the party. I swear we won't be all in their faces. We'll be chill, right, Chenaye?" Hope looked into her eyes.

"Right."

I wouldn't invite these bitches to a party even if my life depended on it.

onight I was going over to Romeo's house, and I was overjoyed to say the least. We'd been spending a lot of time together, and I wasn't complaining. It reminded me of the days when I first started dating Rhys. Although just a teenager at the time, I was smitten with him and never got tired of being in his presence.

When it came to Hakim, I found myself forcing something that wasn't there, but with Romeo it was natural. Just thinking about him at random moments would make me smile, and I hadn't felt that way in a very long time.

I walked across the street after parking my car, and entered the beautiful condo building that he lived in, in Downtown. I could tell by how the lobby looked that this was a very expensive place. I wasn't surprised though because Romeo was very well off. He was ten years my senior, thirty-four, and I think that's part of what attracted me to him. I liked older men, and that was something that I liked about Rhys, even though he was only three years older than I.

I got off the elevator, and followed the sign to know which direction to walk in. Arriving to his door, I took a deep breath before knocking lightly. As I waited, I smoothed down my casual red dress, and tousled my dreads from one side to the other. The door finally

Summer

You Needed Me 3 • A Love Story

came open, and a woman stood there. She didn't look young, but she wasn't decrepit either.

"Hi, is this the residence of Romeo Smith?"

"Yes it is. You must be Ms. Gillies."

"I am."

"Perfect. Come in honey and let me take your coat. My name is Althea; I am Mr. Smith's housekeeper. He's expecting you, so I will show you to the living room." She hung my coat up and closed the door behind me.

When I say this condo was nice, it was nice as fuck. It reminded me a lot of the one I lived in with Rhys, but somewhat nicer. Thinking about Rhys made me smile a small smile as I followed behind Althea. Sometimes I missed him a lot, but I just had to remember that we would always be in each other's lives. I continued admiring the condo until we got to the living room.

"Wow do you ever have a bad day?" Romeo got up from his huge couch wearing a grin.

He looked so sexy even though he wasn't dressed up at all. He wore black joggers, a plain black t-shirt, and some black socks. His hair and facial hair were freshly lined up, and a chain hung from his neck. His cologne was very prevalent, but it wasn't too much. I loved that he was about his money, legit money, but wasn't a total bore like Hakim.

"I do, but I won't ever let you see them."

"I hope you do, because that means progress. Take a seat, ma. Would you like anything to drink?"

"Whatever wine or champagne you have is fine. I'm not too picky," I shrugged one shoulder as I sat down on his comfy couch.

"Bring the Ace of Spades, Althea. Thank you," he told his housekeeper and she nodded before leaving.

"Ace of Spades? What's the occasion?"

"You." His eyes scanned me from head to toe, making me shift a little bit. I was in love with his demeanor, and had been since the moment I laid eyes on him. He just had that look that told you he had his shit together, and I liked that. Rhys had the same look, he just had a little crazy mixed in, too.

"Tell me something about you, Romeo. I feel like every time we're together, I'm only talking about myself. All I know is that you own a restaurant and you have a very nice condo."

Just as I finished, Althea walked in carrying a big silver tray. It had a bottle of Ace of Spades, two flutes already filled, and a platter with fruit, cheese, and crackers. She set it down on the coffee table right in front of us, before handing off the flutes.

"Dinner will be ready in about thirty minutes, Ms. Gillies. Mr. Smith informed me that you love barbecue ribs, so that's what will be served tonight, along with asparagus and garlic mashed potatoes," she recited before leaving.

"You remembered what I like?"

"Hell yeah I did. I told yo' ass I'm trying to get on your good side. I'm trying to be on all your sides." He licked his perfect lips, causing me to take a nice gulp of my champagne.

"Answer my question, I wanna know more about you, Rome."

"Well I was born in Philly, and I had a pretty poor childhood at first. My father was on drugs, but he still functioned… at first. He was a mailman during the week, and a crackhead on the weekends. Over time he couldn't function so well, and he lost his job. It was like a domino effect after that because he became abusive to my mother, and my brother Romity and I. My mom divorced him immediately, and met a new man, my stepfather, who moved us to Boston when I was ten."

"Wow, where is your father now?"

"He's somewhere in Philly, probably roaming the streets for his next hit. I stopped caring once I got to be in my mid twenties. I tried to save him and shit, but I barely had means for myself. That's when I enrolled in school to study the restaurant business. From there I worked in restaurants and networked a lot. I ended up getting a business loan for a food truck, and that did really, really well, so I opened Melon."

"Wow, that's admirable to know that you worked hard for what you wanted. I like that in a man," I nibbled on my lip. Hearing his story only attracted me more.

"I know you said we talk about you a lot, but how did you end up with Rhys Quinton? That's hood royalty," he chuckled, flashing his gorgeous smile.

"I knew him before all of that in a sense. We met in high school, and I swear only a couple weeks after dating he was my boyfriend. He was always a popular guy, he, his brother TQ, and his older sister Saya, but he wasn't like he is now when I first met him. That didn't happen until like two years after we got together."

"Crazy. You love him?"

"I do. I will always love him, but I can't be with him. I'm not strong enough to be with someone who has cheated on me. I had to come to terms with that."

"Makes sense, not everybody can do it."

"Yeah, I didn't know that at first. I love the kid, but I can't forget what he did no matter how hard I try. My mind does what it wants, and I can't control it I guess."

"Well I can't say that I'm not happy you're single, because I am. Is Bryleigh your only child?"

"She is. I want more though." I looked to see his reaction.

"Good, because I want kids. I almost had a child, but the mother miscarried."

"Who was she?"

"Girl named Jasmine that I dated for a couple years. She was a bit uppity, which I didn't like, but I felt that was who I was supposed to be with since I was getting money. I don't mind a woman who likes nice things, and keeps herself together, but sometimes it's fun to just go hiking and shit without her wearing make up and a Versace dress."

"I don't wear much make up."

"And you don't need it, you have beautiful skin. I see why your ex was a little off. I would be too if you were mine."

"Maybe I will be one day."

"Oh you will be, shorty, don't play me. Once I have my mind and heart set on some shit, I get it by any means necessary. I wanted a food truck and I got it. I wanted a restaurant and I got it. Now I want you and I will have you."

"I like a determined man." I polished off my champagne and straddled his lap. He had me feeling comfortable and I wasn't even drunk.

He slowly licked his lips as his hands and eyes wandered all over my frame. Gripping my torso, he pulled me into his strong chest, allowing our lips to meet.

I could see this going very far. God willing…

CHAPTER TEN

A few days later...

"Hey, shorty, I'm about to go out real quick." I walked into my son's room to see Kimberlyn sitting in the rocking chair with him. She was wearing some pajama shorts and a small strapless top like always at this time of night. Just looking at her had me ready to fuck, but I knew she wouldn't be down for it.

Ever since that shit at the mall, she wasn't fucking with me. I didn't feel like I should apologize and she felt like I should. I was a grown man and I could be friends with whomever the fuck I wanted to be friends with. I wasn't about to limit myself just because she felt threatened by these women. I may have fucked them in the past, but so what. As long as I'm not now, that should be all that matters. But no, Kimberlyn has to have shit her way.

"Did you hear me?" I questioned, walking further into the room.

She just nodded, while keeping her eyes on our son. He was

dozing off more and more as she kept on rocking in the rocking chair. I stood there staring at them both, wondering if I should say anything, but I didn't know what to say. The only thing she wanted to hear was me saying I was gonna cut off all the bitches I'd smashed, and I wasn't about to lie to her. I had no intentions of doing anything with them, so it was no harm in me keeping contact. Feeling slightly stupid for just watching them, I turned around and headed out of my condo to get in the car with Andrei.

After picking up Rhys, and Pharaoh, we headed to this new nightclub that just opened to celebrate Pharaoh's recovery. Everybody knew we would be in the house tonight, so security was loaded up, and all back exits had been cleared for us to enter and exit through. Andrei pulled up around back, and had one of my guys take the car to park it while we were being escorted through the back and up to VIP. As soon as we got up there, the bottles that we'd requested prior were being brought up and set down by some scantily clad hostesses.

"Len and Britain coming?" Pharaoh asked, and I nodded just as they were being escorted up the stairs.

We all dapped one another up and began making ourselves drinks. Like always, we allowed a couple of pretty ladies to come into our VIP and chill. See, it was nothing but company, and if Kimberlyn expected me to cut off women entirely, she was out of her fucking mind.

As I bobbed my head to "Don't Matter" by Iamsu!, I spotted Amikka coming up the stairs, just to get stopped by the security. She flashed her pretty smile and waved to me. I nodded my head up just as security looked at me so he'd know she was cool. He allowed her by, and she came straight over and sat between Rhys and I. I saw how he looked at me, but he should know better; I would never cheat on my wife.

"What you doing here?" I looked at her as she put her chin on my shoulder.

"I knew you would be here, duh," she giggled. Her hand made its way into my lap, and she stopped when she felt the bulge in my pants.

"Chill out," I moved her hand.

"Why, Tarenz? You know I don't mind that you have a wife. I won't say anything. I miss you and I can tell that you miss me, too."

"I don't miss anything. You're cool, so I'm trying to be nice, but you need to chill out Amikka."

"I swear I hate when you do this shit, TQ. One minute you're all in my face and shit, then the next you wanna act like you don't fuck with me. You used to do that shit before you met her, and you're doing it again now."

"I never did that before, and I don't do it now."

"So you've never fucked me and then dissed me in public before?" She looked into my face with tears sitting in her eyes and waiting to fall.

"I don't remember," I lied.

"Of course you don't. And this time, you wanna act like you weren't leading me on, but it's cool."

"Aye I ain't lead shit on. I have a wife and that's all there is to it. Just cause I text yo' ass back and hold a convo with you in public don't mean I'm trying to fuck."

"Then why are you even talking to me? You honestly think we can be friends? You know I have feelings for you, yet you believe that we can be homies and nothing more?"

"I thought we could," I said more so to myself than her.

"Well we can't because I wanna be with you and you know that. I've sat back and watched you do the most. First it was Hayden, and now this bitch."

"Watch your fucking mouth for one, and secondly Hayden was never anything but a friend like you. I was still fucking you when I was fucking Hayden. Dramatic ass." She was irritating me at this point, and I wasn't sure if it was because she was playing the victim, or if it was because I was seeing that Kimberlyn was right.

"A friend. You sleep with and make all of your friends fall in love with you just to play stupid when they see you after you've gotten what you wanted?"

"Amikka, I'm trying to relax, drink, smoke, and listen to some music. If I wanted to argue, I would go home and spark some shit up with my wife, someone that I care about." I looked into her eyes as I watched her silently process what I'd just said.

I knew I'd hurt her by saying I didn't care about her, but I didn't. And I definitely didn't want her going around thinking I cared for her when I had a fucking wife. Hell nah. These bitches weren't about to be out here embarrassing my shorty, having her thinking that her husband was out here giving a fuck about these bitches. TQ didn't give a damn about a hoe, and Amikka needed to see that.

"Bye, Tarenz." She stood to her feet and bumped Rhys' knee as she walked out of the VIP.

"Shorty, don't get shot at being mad because you're a hoe!" Rhys called after her, making all of us laugh. "I don't see why you even converse with these bitches. All they want is some dick, money, and bragging rights." Rhys lit the blunt.

"Don't I know it."

"Yeah, man, don't let these hoes fuck you up like I did," Lendsey added.

"Nigga, never. I love Kimberlyn, I just don't see the problem in having friends. Well I *didn't* see it, but maybe now I do."

"You know they don't wanna be friends, especially if you've dicked them down before. They may act like it in the beginning, but that's only to get close," Britain spoke the truth. When did my little brothers get so knowledgeable?

"I know, fuck." I ran my hands over my face. I hated to be wrong, but I would have to admit it if I wanted to be back on Kimberlyn's good side.

We continued to drink, smoke, and watch the girls in our VIP do the same. It was just what I needed after having such a stressful year so far. I'd gotten stabbed, beaten, married, became a father, and had to kill my own. Shit had changed drastically for me, and even though some of it almost killed me, I wouldn't change a thing.

Around 2am, we all left the club. Andrei dropped Rhys and Pharaoh off at their homes, and then he took me to mine. When I got there, the place was quiet so I knew Kimberlyn was asleep. I wished she were awake so that I could talk to her, but I guess it would have to wait.

I didn't want to wake her because she'd been working hard all week. She'd been designing websites for clients until 1 and 2am, all while making sure Baby Tarenz was good.

I peeled my clothes off and hopped into the shower because I slept better when I was clean. After stepping out and changing into some boxers, I brushed my teeth and then went into the bedroom. I was surprised to see Kimberlyn in our bed, but happy nonetheless. Climbing in behind her, I hugged her body into mine, and closed my eyes to bask in the moment. We hadn't embraced in a while, and I almost forgot how good her body felt against mine. In the middle of my enjoyment, I felt her small hand pry mine off of her body.

"Baby, I'm sorry." I kissed the nape of her neck.

"I don't want you to be sorry, I want you to change your outlook." She kept her back to me.

"I have. I understand where you're coming from. I thought it was extra at first, but now I realize what you meant. I wouldn't want you being friends with a man you slept with either. Shit, I didn't even want you being cool with Gang, and you never fucked him."

"I don't know if I should forgive you. It shouldn't have taken you this long. I'm your wife, and you promised to keep me happy." She was refusing to turn around and face me.

"I know, shorty, and I will. I just... I guess I just needed some time to get it. You know women are smarter than men." She didn't say anything, so I turned her onto her back. After looking into her pretty face for a bit, I kissed her lips longingly. "Kimberlyn, when you met me I was a bachelor, and doing shit that I wanted to do. I had been living that way for as long as I can remember. I'd never been in a situation where there were rules. It was always on some fuck buddy shit. I'm not saying that to excuse my behavior, I'm saying it so that you will understand that with certain shit, I may need more time to understand versus other niggas. Not being able to reply to a text from a girl I hit is new for me. Having to set boundaries when women come around is new for me. Even being jealous of you talking to Gang was new for me. I haven't been jealous since I was in grade school. But because I love you and want nothing more than to be with you, I will do what I need to do to adhere to the rules of being in a monogamous situation. Does that make sense?"

"Yes." She half smiled and nodded.

"Good because I didn't know how to explain it any other way." We chuckled in unison. "So do you forgive me?"

"I forgive you."

"I love you." I grabbed her hand and kissed the palm of it.

"I love you, too."

I pushed her shorts and panties down, before throwing them to the floor. She then helped me pull her top off, and I just ran my pointing finger down her sexy body for a bit. After I took my boxers off, she nudged me back before climbing on top of me. The moment I got inside of her, I swear I saw fireworks and shit. I could never get tired of the feeling of being between her legs, ever.

"You feel so good," I groaned, as I cupped her breasts in my hands.

She rocked her hips back and forth, while gliding up and down on me. Her physique was so perfect to me, and it was mine. Knowing that no other man would ever experience this, only made me harder. I gripped her ass cheeks in my hands, and pushed myself further inside of her, making her cry out softly. I loved hearing her moans in that sweet voice of hers.

"On your knees," I instructed her once she released.

Getting behind her, I eased my way inside, making a moan burst through both of our lips. This woman was my everything, and the fact that I even somewhat jeopardized what we had for some old fuck buddy, was crazy to even think about. No woman was more important than my shorty, and I would never let her think that shit again.

"Mmm, uuuh, aaaah," she whimpered every time I slammed into her with force, and pulled out slowly. I noticed that made her cum the hardest, and that was always my goal.

I tightened my grip on her waist, and thrust into her from behind, letting my full length stay inside of her for a little bit before pulling out. Just sitting there with my dick inside, filling her up, made her cum so hard her body shook. Once she did, I slowly slid out, before doing the same thing again. I knew her pussy like the back of my fucking hand, and I could make her cum in two seconds, or two minutes if I wanted to. The pussy was mine, and not only did she know that, but her pussy knew it, too.

"Tell me you love me," I grunted, feeling myself on the verge of cumming.

"I love you, Tarenz," she sniveled. "You know I love you so much, ahhhh," she cried lowly once I sped up, pounding her spot repeatedly. She was so fucking wet that it made me call out myself.

As I humped her feverishly from the back, I took a handful of her hair to pull. Yanking it up roughly yet gently, I bent her head back and sucked her lips. I had never kissed anyone upside down, but it was the shit. She was calling out into my mouth as I sucked and bit her lips, while beating the pussy up doggy-style.

"Fuck!" I groaned just before filling her up with everything inside of me.

I immediately flipped her onto her back, before lowering myself between her legs. She draped her arms around my neck, as we kissed passionately and hungrily. I have never felt like I needed another human being, but I definitely needed Kimberlyn Quinton.

Matikah

Kimberlyn and I were sitting in Tasty Burger, eating with Baby Tarenz. My old co-worker Annalise said she wanted to talk to me about something, but it had to be in person. Annalise was cool, but she was kind of weird so I asked my cousin to come with me. I could tell she just wanted a friend, but she was too eager which was a turn off.

"So why didn't anyone tell me auntie visited?" Kimberlyn frowned, referring to my mother.

"She came and left so quickly. It's like she touched down, we spent one day together, she disappeared, and then she called me from the airport. Grandma said she wasn't supposed to leave for another week, but for some reason she cut her trip short."

"I'm sure it was because of a man."

"Oh you know it was. That's what she lives for and I hate that about her."

All my mom cared about was getting a man and keeping a man. Anything that didn't involve that, she didn't care about. When we did go out to lunch, all she wanted to talk about was my relationship with Lendsey. Then knowing she came onto him at my grandmother's house was just disgusting. I couldn't even be as mad though because that was Janine; that was my mother. For me to expect her to behave around a handsome man like Lendsey would be foolish on my part.

"Is this your friend?" Kimberlyn nodded towards the entrance of Tasty Burger. I looked up and saw it was Annalise scanning the room looking for me. Waving my arm, I smiled when she saw me and darted over.

"Hi, I'm Annalise," she stuck her hand out to Kimberlyn.

Annalise had red hair, freckles, and fair skin, but she was black. She showed me a picture of her mother, and I was surprised to see that she was brown skinned. Annalise looked white because of her skin, but her facial features were of a black woman. She was a very pretty girl, in a nerdy way.

"Hey, I'm Kimberlyn, Matikah's cousin. And this is my son, Tarenz."

"He's so cute!" Annalise beamed.

"Thank you," Kimberlyn smiled.

"Annalise, what did you have to tell me that you just couldn't text? I could barely sleep last night because my brain was on overload."

"Well, I'm actually surprised you didn't see it all over Facebook. But, Isabetta's shop was burned to the ground. And she was about to get the insurance money, until they found gas cans and all kinds of things in her basement. They somehow figured out that the same gasoline she had in her home, was the same kind used to burn her spa down."

"Oh my gosh? Are you serious?" I bucked my eyes as Annalise nodded with a smile. "So wait, is she in some kind of trouble or what?"

"Is she? Girl yes! She's being charged with arson! They believe she was trying to get insurance money for her shop. I knew she was up to something, taking all of these week long vacations as of late."

"Wow, but at least she won't be in jail for long," I giggled. I couldn't wait to tell Lendsey that karma had taken care of that bitch, so he didn't need to.

"This is Dania's sister?" Kimberlyn furrowed her brows, and I nodded my head 'yes'.

"She may not be in jail for long, but that's only if they don't charge her with her sister's murder." Annalise looked around discreetly before leaning in. "Turns out they think some kind of sibling rivalry was going on, because they found the gun used to kill Dania in her closet. The gun matched the shell casings found on Dania's bedroom floor. They tried to find out who the gun was registered to, but it came up unknown or something. And even worse, her only alibi is that she was home alone at the time of the murder, so no witness can back that up."

When she said that, I pondered for a minute. No, no way Lendsey set her up for that arson shit. But maybe he did because I was sure Isabetta didn't kill her sister, so how did the gun end up there? Lendsey must've planted it there at the same time he planted the gas cans and shit.

"Wow your boss was crazy." Kimberlyn bit her burger.

"I know. So Annalise, what are you gonna do for work? If the place is gone, and Isabetta gets found guilty, you won't have a job. And even if she makes it off, you would still have to wait until it's rebuilt."

"Yeah I know. I had an interview yesterday to work at this other place. They only needed someone to do eyebrows, and since I need the money I took it. I'm hoping to get something else so I can go back to body waxes."

"I hear you. If I opened a place would you come work for me?"

"Girl of course! I would love to work for you!" she grinned widely.

"Cool, I will let you know."

We continued eating and chatting for a while, until I got a text from Lendsey asking where I was. We said our goodbyes and then I left to his condo. I really wanted to talk to him, and see if my hypothesis was true. If so, he was a real fucking criminal, and sadly that turned me on.

Entering the condo, I saw him sitting on his couch shirtless, watching TV. He was sipping on something that was in a white Styrofoam cup, probably a milkshake. He loved milkshakes. He waved me over so that I could sit by him, and when I did, I grabbed his milkshake so that I could take a sip.

"Damn, shorty, I didn't offer that to you."

"I know, but the baby wanted it," I chuckled.

"That's your favorite fucking excuse now." He pecked my lips with his cold ones. "Where were you?" He took the shake back.

"I went to lunch with my cousin and that girl Annalise. She told me Isabetta's shop burned down." I looked up into his handsome face.

"Damn, for real?" he questioned nonchalantly, proving it was him. Then again, Lendsey was just a type B personality guy. It took a lot for him to be surprised or up in arms.

"Don't play dumb, Len. I know you did that shit to her, and I want to say that you're a genius."

"Wasn't all me. Rhys helped me break in, TQ helped me plant the shit in her crib, and Britain helped me burn the place down."

"Only person missing was Saya."

"Nah, she scoped her place out for me and told me when she was gone from her home so the shit could be planted."

"You Quintons really work together." I smiled.

"We do. That's how shit is supposed to be. We ain't supposed to be harming each other like my father was trying to do," he sighed.

"Do you miss him?"

"Sometimes, but I think it was for the best. They say the only way to get out is to die or end up in prison. I think my dad had the option to bow out gracefully, but he was a control freak so he never would have."

"Yes, but he shot himself in the foot. He took things too far and ended up losing his wife, kids, his cotton picking mind, and his life."

"Ain't that the truth."

I touched his face, stroking his beard a little before our lips crushed into one another. It got heavier and hungrier as he leaned me back and got on top of me, setting his shake aside. Pushing my skirt up, he grabbed onto the waistline of my panties before pulling them down. Getting up off of me, he stepped out of his socks, sweatpants, and boxers as I removed my skirt and top completely. Once we were both naked, we got right back to kissing, touching, and groping one another.

"Lendsey," I whispered, already getting way too aroused just from his touch.

I wrapped my legs around his waist, and gasped once I felt his thick head press into my opening. When he got all the way inside, my body relaxed, and allowed him to glide in and out of me seamlessly. I sucked on his shoulder, and rubbed up and down his tatted back as he grasped my ass cheeks in his big hands. My clit tingled, and soon after I exploded on his rod. Feeling him breathe and moan on my neck made me even wetter, and I knew he felt it because he squealed a little bit.

"Matikah, I love you so much, shorty." He pulled away from sucking my neck, and slipped his tongue into my mouth.

"Mmm, uuuh, uuuh, Len, uuh!"

We pressed our lips together as if we wanted to become one, while he continued to thrust into me at the perfect tempo. Feeling him pound my spot repeatedly was euphoric, and I couldn't do anything but cry out and grip his muscular biceps. He pressed my legs into my stomach gently, bit down on his lip, and pummeled my center until we both screamed out in pleasure.

"Why the fuck is your pussy so good?" he frowned, dropping down on me slowly and kissing me deeply.

I just giggled lightly, before hugging his neck and kissing him back just as hard. I swear my nigga was the shit.

Britain

One month later...

Tonight Goldie and I were going to the movies because she wanted to see some little kid film about pets. I didn't really care to see the shit, but since my shorty wanted to I wasn't gonna complain. Life had been good for me since a couple of people had exited stage left, so there was really nothing for me to bitch about. Going to see a children's film with my beautiful girlfriend was the least of my damn worries.

Sliding my key into her front door, I twisted it open and saw Chenaye and that bitch, Hope, chilling on the couch holding glasses of wine. I was dead tired of Chenaye, and I felt like she was using my girl to live rent-free. I wasn't having that shit, and tonight things were gonna change. Yeah this was Goldie's spot, but I wasn't about to be paying the bills up in this bitch just for these hoes to parlay and kick it. Chenaye didn't even do so much as wash dishes or buy food. The most her ass would do is cook some tacos and they were never that good. Goldie may have been too nice to put her sister out on the damn streets, but that's what Britain Quinton was for.

"Evening ladies." I neared them, prompting them both to set their glasses on the coffee table. "Look—"

"Chenaye, remember you said you were going to the store? You better get that cereal before Goldie finishes getting dressed and comes out." Hope stared into Chenaye's eyes. Chenaye looked as if she didn't understand at first, but then something clicked, causing her to rise from the couch like a piece of bread in a toaster.

"Right, did you need anything while I'm gone?"

"No, but thank you."

Chenaye grabbed this little wallet thing from the La-Z-Boy, and then darted out. I sat down in the same chair her wallet was in, and rested my head back while Goldie got dressed. She needed to hurry up, because in a minute I was gonna go in there and watch her ass. She hated for me to do that these days, because she said she looked like Shamu naked. I begged to differ; she was beautiful to me, but that was nothing new.

"Hurry up, shorty!" I barked as Hope kept her eyes fixated on my side profile.

"Okay!" Goldie called back from her bedroom.

Hope finished off her wine and stood up. She began walking over to me, and once she was right in front of me, she quickly straddled my lap.

"Fuck is you doing!" I pushed her off, and didn't care that her ass had bounced onto the laminate floors. "I should push yo' fucking wig back, shorty. Do you know who you're fucking with?" I towered over, removing my gun with the quickness.

"Please, Britain don't. Just help me," she pleaded with her hands up in mock surrender.

"Help you? The fuck is you talking about ma?"

She looked over her shoulder, licking her lips as tears spilled out of her eyes. "Alison, Goldie's mother and her husband Roger are forcing me to come on to you. They convinced Chenaye to get close to Goldie so that she could eventually bring me around to seduce you. And since Chenaye already had plans to get Rhys, she was cool with it. Once I slept with you on video, they would let me fly home to my mother in Maine. My mom thinks I'm on some church retreat because Roger is a pastor, and I thought that's what it was too until I got here. Alison despises her daughter, and she wants me to use you to hurt her. If you could just fly me back to Maine, please," she sobbed.

"Wait, what? What the fuck are you talking about?" I grimaced, just as Goldie slowly emerged from her bedroom, looking astonished at the view before her.

"Your mother is using me to seduce Britain to hurt you." She looked to Goldie. "Please, help me get back up to Maine, that is all I want. Chenaye is in on it, and if she finds out I told I don't know what will happen to me. They don't let me use the phone, and they're always watching me, so I can't get in contact with my family."

"You're being dramatic! Why would my mother do something like that? And what could Roger and my mom really do to you?"

"They said they'd sacrifice me for the Lord, meaning they'd kill me. They said I needed to do this if I wanted to get home with a 'good report'. My mom is very religious and it's pivotal that I get home with your parent's blessing. Please Goldie, I wouldn't lie to you."

"How do I know?" Goldie folded her arms. I knew she was

playing the role because I could see in her eyes how hurt she was by Hope's revelation.

"Let's go to your mother's home and find out," I said, placing my gun back in my waist.

"Britain—"

"Let's go find out, Goldie. If your mom would stoop this low to hurt you, it's no telling what else she may do since this has failed. And if shorty right here is lying, well then I'm sure she knows what will happen to her." I glared down into Hope's eyes. I could see she was being truthful, but you never knew these days.

Hope got up from the floor, and the three of us left out and went down to my car. Goldie directed me to her mother's home in Mission Hills, which was big and beautiful. I didn't know what the hell they did for a living, but I was sure their salaries couldn't afford this shit. Goldie had already told me that her mom was losing the place, and now that I saw it I wasn't surprised.

"Get out," Goldie hissed to Hope as we opened the doors of my car.

We made our way up the porch steps, and I was sure to hold onto Hope's arm. I didn't want her to run, and even if she did, she wouldn't get far because I had aim and speed.

"Who is it?" A man called from behind the door.

"Goldie!"

There was silence for a bit, and then he opened the door. Old man was smiling until he saw me holding Hope by her bicep. He was about to close the door, but I barged in, holding it open so Goldie and Hope could slip by as well. I closed it behind me, put the chain on, and then removed my gun before taking the safety off. Roger's eyes widened at the sight of my 9mm locked and loaded.

"Where is your wife?" I pointed it at his forehead.

"Alison!" he yelled out.

"What Roger? I told you I'm cook—" she paused when she saw Hope, Goldie, and I together in the living room. I wasn't sure if she was more surprised by the fact that Hope was with us, or because I had a gun in her husband's face. "What is going on? Goldie who is this girl?" She tried to play the fool.

"Ma, stop. Hope already told me how you sent her through Chenaye's fake ass to seduce Britain. You hate me that much, Ma?"

"I don't know what you're—"

"Cut the bullshit before I blow this nigga's head off his shoulders!" I roared, causing she, Hope, and Roger to jump.

"I did it because I love you Goldie. I wanted you to see that he was not what you thought he was. That was all," she half smiled as she moved closer to Goldie.

"Stop there, and don't touch her," I stated calmly, and she complied. "Tell her the truth. I know you don't think we believe that, Alison."

"Just tell them!" Hope cried.

"Shut the fuck up!" Roger hissed.

"Aye I'm running this muthafucking show! Keep your mouth

closed, or I promise I will shoot you. Speak before you're spoken to one more time, and I will pull the hammer." I stared down into his eyes, letting my dreads frame my face.

"You shamed me when I came to you for help, Goldie. I am your mother, yet you treated me like a common beggar, just because you're on the arm of some alleged Russian mafia member. I wanted to shame you the same way you shamed me at the restaurant. I hope I succeeded." Hear mother pointed her nose in the air.

"You didn't succeed," Goldie responded calmly. "The only thing you've succeeded in doing is making a fool of yourself, and for years. First you chased behind a broke ass nigga who didn't love you enough to even try to keep a job for you and Chenaye. Then you ran off my father because of your insecurities and bullshit. And now, you are so miserable, that you can't even fathom the thought of someone else having a good life. It's funny because I can't even be mad as I look at you. You're pitiful. I would hate to be you, always angry and envious of the next person. You spent so much time in church, and I hope that you have prayed for yourself and asked God to forgive you for having such a hateful and jealous heart."

"Don't talk to your mother that way, you stuck up bitch!" Roger yelled.

POP!

I dropped him just like I said I would, and then turned the gun on his wife as she stared at me, horrified.

"Please you guys, I am sorry! I get it now."

"Don't say shit to me, I don't know yo' ass. Apologize to your daughter," I frowned.

She turned to Goldie and said, "Baby, I'm sorry. I promise I won't do anything like this again. It was all Roger's idea, honey!"

Goldie just chuckled lightly, and then walked over to me.

POP!

After sending one right through her head, I called clean up and had them pack up the bodies and wipe the place down just in case our prints or anything got anywhere. Once the scene was clean, we drove Hope to TQ's port, and had Primo fly her back up to Maine. She didn't want any of her clothing from Goldie's parents' house for some reason. I didn't really care I just wanted the bitch gone. All we needed to do now was find Chenaye's ass though.

Goldie and I left the port, and went straight home instead of to the movies. She made me some Russian food and dessert, because she said it was a new recipe she'd found. We ate, making small talk here and there, and then got into the shower before climbing into bed naked.

"I'm sorry about your mom, shorty."

"It's okay. It's not like we hung out everyday or anything. I don't even know if I will miss her, because she hadn't been a mother to me since I was a teenager. I wonder if she ever loved me."

"I think your mom only loves her children when their father loves her. Once the dad has moved on, so does her love. It's like she wants nothing to do with the baby if the man isn't there anymore."

"Makes sense."

"But I love you, shorty, no matter what. You know that right?" I moved my dreads out of my face, before uncovering her body.

"I do."

I kissed her longingly, and then trailed the kisses down her body until I was face to face with her center. I pecked her lower lips a few times, gently, enjoying the sweet sounds of her moans. Taking her clit into my mouth, I closed my eyes as I sucked on it with my lips. I held her legs apart as I licked and sucked like it was nobodies business. Her nectar was so good to me, and I wasn't sure if it really was that tasty, or if I just loved her.

"Britain, mmm, baby." She held my dreads back as I buried my face deeper into her middle. "I-I'm gonna cum," she whimpered and sat up on her elbows. She released, but I kept attacking her pussy until I pulled two more orgasms out of her.

I pecked between her legs as she quivered, and trailed them up, taking some time on her belly. I saw her smiling down as I planted small kisses all over her round stomach. Once I was ready to fuck, I made my way inside of her, and began sucking on her lips as I thrust my full length into her. She ran her small hand down my abs as I invaded her body, and the feeling of her soft touch was every damn thing.

"You feel so good, baby."

"You too." She tucked her lips into her mouth for a few seconds, before they were being parted with my tongue.

As I continued to pump myself into her, I admired her beauty and thought about how much I loved her. This time last year I was with crazy ass Tekeya, and not worried about loving anything or anyone that didn't have my same blood running through their veins. But now,

I was on some other shit, acting like that nigga Rhys and shit.

"Ahhh, uuuh!" She scrunched her nose up as she exploded again, getting even wetter than before.

"I love you," I groped the sides of her thighs. "I love you, baby."

Chenaye

About an hour and a half earlier...

I came to my mother's house, looking for her, Roger, and possibly Hope. When I got there no one was home, but the cars were parked outside. I pulled my phone out to dial Hope, hoping she would answer and tell me what the hell was going on. I knew I shouldn't have left her alone, my mother told me she would try some shit if I did.

I looked around as I tried to think of times my parents left without their cars, but nothing came up. My mom and Roger didn't ride buses or anything, so for them to be gone with their cars here was odd.

"The number you have dialed is no longer in service," the automated voice came through on Hope's number.

I pulled the phone away from my ear and looked at my recent calls to make sure I'd dialed the right number. I knew I had because I just pressed her name like always. Now I was starting to worry because this was weird. I was even a little bit scared, wondering if someone had done something to Hope and my parents. *Lord please don't let this be the work of a Quinton,* I thought. As Kevin Hart said, I wasn't ready.

"You stupid bitch! You stupid fucking bitch! I can't believe you told!" I hollered loudly through the house.

It was almost like I'd had an epiphany. That bitch Hope had played me. She made me think she wanted some alone time with Britain, so that she could make her move while Goldie was in the back. That stupid hoe was smarter than I thought. After going to the mall, taking myself to dinner, and dropping by China Sea in Mattapan to see if Rhys was there, I came home to tell my parents the good news about Hope. When I saw they weren't home, I left back to Goldie's only to see no one was there either. Now I'm back here, just realizing my parent's cars were parked the whole time. I really thought Hope was down for the cause. Little did I know, she was planning her fucking escape and betrayal. That stupid bitch.

I was tired of losing, I really was. I should have never agreed to help my mother in trying to break Goldie's heart. I should have just focused on my fucking mission of being with Rhys. Everything was going great for me, and according to plan until I tried to fuse my mother's shit in with mine. I had gotten Ethan killed which was way easier than I thought. I was making Goldie think I wanted to be around her, and I was possibly gonna be at the next Quinton party. But none of that mattered anymore because Hope had blown my cover.

I tried dialing her again before going to sit in my car. She didn't answer, only that same automated voice came on. I bounced my leg repeatedly, trying to think of another way that I could get close to my love. I needed him to see me, and how good we could be together before that new bitch took it too far with him. Why would he even pick her, knowing I was here waiting for him? He knew me before her, yet he skipped over me to be with some bitch that I heard used to be a hoe. And if that's true, he really has me fucked up. I'm not better than some escort? I just wanted to slap him and fuck him at the same time. I chuckled lightly at my thoughts.

Pulling away from the curb, I drove to the apartment I shared with Ethan. Ethan didn't pay half of the rent, I paid it in full, but I wanted Goldie to think that so that I could live with her. Her place was way better and bigger anyway, so I did enjoy staying with her versus my spot. Anyway, I kept up with the rent and utility payments here, unbeknownst to her, because it was all a part of the plan.

Getting out, I hit the alarm on my car and headed up inside. I wanted to take a nice bath, and see if there was a way I could find Rhys tonight. I had the perfect outfit and everything for him to see me in. I wanted to hopefully just get him alone so that I could tell him my true feelings. Once he saw me as more than just a friend, we could be happy together. That was all I wanted, to be loved by the people I loved. My mother and father never loved me, but I knew Rhys would be able to fill that void, that hole inside of me.

I undressed in front of the mirror wearing a smile, because I knew very soon I would be Mrs. Rhys Quinton.

CHAPTER ELEVEN

Rhys

Indiya and I were gonna have dinner tonight at my family's restaurant, Verenich. I wanted to bring her out since Summer had my baby this weekend, and because she'd been acting strange. She barely let me touch her, and the past few times we had sex she wanted to keep on this new big ass pajama top she'd bought. I don't know about other niggas, but I need to see something while I'm stroking the pussy, preferably some titties. And Indiya had the best ones I'd ever seen, so you know I wasn't feeling that covering up shit.

After parking my car, I got out to open the door for her. She was wearing a dress that was tight at the top and got big as it went down. I was hoping she wore one of her tight numbers tonight, but I guess I was unlucky. I kissed her lips, and stared down into her sad eyes for a little bit, before kissing her again.

"Are you okay?" I questioned for the hundredth time this week.

"Yes, Rhys, I'm fine. Stop asking me that," she chuckled lightly, but I could tell it was fake. I was gonna find out why the fuck she was tripping today.

Taking her hand into mine, we entered the restaurant and were met by the hostess, Nika. She gave a warm smile, before escorting us to the back where all of my family members ate when they came here. It was a secluded area that we preferred to sit in if we wanted some sort of privacy. It had a sliding door and everything, cutting you off from the rest of the place. When we got in, I pulled Indiya's chair out, kissed the side of her face, and then went to sit down across from her.

"Mr. Quinton, would you like me to bring some wine for the table?" Nika quizzed.

"Yes thank you, and some water too please." Once Nika left, I turned my attention back to Indiya, whose face was buried in the menu. "You have any idea what you're gonna get?"

"Yes, but it's two things because I can't decide."

"Damn, shorty, you've been grubbing lately. They say you eat when you're happy, so does that mean I make you happy?" I grinned and tucked my bottom lip in.

"Of course you do." She touched my hand, and I leaned down to press my lips against the back of hers.

"So what's been bothering you? You've been acting very weird lately."

"I just haven't been feeling well that's all. I'm getting better though. That doctor your mom got for me is really great. If I didn't know you guys I would be fucked since I don't have health insurance."

"I know, but I'm happy you do know us. What did he say was wrong with you?"

"Just a stomach bug." She grabbed the water out of Nika's hand, not allowing her to set it down.

"Are you guys ready to order?" Nika clasped her hands together.

"Yes, I will have the pelmeni, the schi, and a kompot to drink, thank you," Indiya answered and closed her menu.

"I will have the pelmeni as well, and borsch."

"Do you want the sour cream with the borsch?"

"Yes, thank you." I nodded. "You want some of the wine?" I offered Indiya, about to pour some into her glass, but she shook her head no. "Really? Since when?" I smiled.

"Just not in the mood."

I was about to speak again, but I heard a little bit of ruckus outside of the room we were eating dinner in. It sounded like Nika was arguing with another female, and weirdly I recognized the voice. I couldn't quite put it to a face, but I'd heard it before. I rose out of my seat slowly, just as the doors of our room were being snatched open. Chenaye stormed in with Nika on her heels, who was trying to pull her back out.

"Rhys! Please!" Chenaye begged, with mascara running down her face. Would this bitch ever give up? I'd never even kissed the hoe.

"Fuck are you doing, Chenaye?" I swiftly moved my arm from her reach when she tried to grab for it.

"Rhys, who is this?" Indiya shouted. "Is she the girl from the club?"

"I love you, Rhys! I have no one but you! My parents are gone, and my sister hates me! Please, baby!" she pleaded as Indiya watched with a confused expression. I just shook my head 'no' at Indiya, because I didn't want her getting the wrong idea about Chenaye and I.

"I'm gonna get security!" Nika rushed out of the room.

"You're the reason he treats me like this!" Chenaye cried, looking in Indiya's direction. She retrieved a small gun from her purse, and raised it with trembling hands.

POP!

I immediately dropped her ass with one bullet to the temple. I stared down at her, floored, as blood poured from her head like water. Something told me to kill her ass after she broke Summer and I up, but then I was glad I didn't when I found out she was Goldie's sister. I should have gone with my first mind though, because this girl would never understand that what we had was nothing at all.

"Close the door," I advised Nika when she came back to see Chenaye lying dead on the floor. She did as I asked, while I dialed for clean up.

The clean up crew came shortly after, and got everything straight pretty quickly. Indiya and I decided to just take our damn food home, because who wanted to eat in there after that.

I told my brother Britain to inform Goldie of what happened because I didn't want to. And plus she knew her sister was a fucking nutcase. I'd warned her plenty of times to back up off of me or I would kill her, but she didn't listen so she got smoked. Nobody could say that they didn't see it coming.

As soon as Indiya and I got home, we scarfed the food down

while watching TV. Once we were done, she threw out our trash, and then came back to sit on the couch. I scooted closer to her, and draped my arm around her shoulders; she tensed up. I ignored it and began kissing her lips, but when I tried to rub across her torso, she damn near karate chopped my hand off.

"Rhys, I don't feel like it. I'm gonna go shower and head to sleep." She hopped up from the couch before I could say anything.

I sat there with a hard dick, watching TV and not even paying attention as the shower water ran. After it cut off, I got up from the couch because I was determined to see what the hell was wrong with this girl. I'd let her mope around for long enough, and that shit was about to end.

I made it to the bathroom door, and twisted the knob to enter. It opened slightly, but then she tried to slam it back. I stuck my foot in the door, and slipped in just as she quickly pulled her big pajama shirt over her head.

"Why are you coming in here like that?"

"I always do. What's the problem now?"

"Nothing, goodnight." She walked towards the door, but I grabbed her arm and yanked her back. She moved it around to release herself, but I was way too strong.

"Fuck is wrong with you, huh? And you ain't leaving until you tell me, Indiya."

"Rhys." She shook her head 'no' as tears welled up in her eyes.

"What!" I barked, annoyed by her secretiveness.

She took my hand, put it under her shirt, and placed it against her stomach. It was rounder than usual, and kind of hard. Lifting her shirt, I looked down to see a small bulge in it. I let my hand rub across it a few times as I gaped in disbelief.

"You're pregnant?" I furrowed my brows.

"Yes."

"How long have you been pregnant, shorty? What the hell?"

"Almost four months. I found out a while ago, but I couldn't tell you. I didn't know when I was gonna tell you."

"Why? Whose fucking baby is it?" I stepped back from her. As soon as the other nigga's name came out of her mouth I was gonna strangle her ass to the floor.

It's yours Rhys, I just—"

"Then help me understand why the fuck you kept this a secret? You've been walking around here pregnant and I don't even fucking know? What is wrong with you?" I grimaced, making her tear up even more. "The only reason I could see you keeping it a secret is because the baby ain't mine."

"It is yours! And I didn't say anything because I didn't want you to think I did this on purpose!"

"Did what on purpose? How the fuck could you get pregnant on purpose?"

"Because I messed up taking my pills. And you thought I was on birth control. I was on it, I just slacked a little bit. I'm sorry!" she sobbed.

"Come here, shorty," I sighed and pulled her into my chest. "You can't do shit like this. If we're gonna be in a relationship, you have to be honest. And what did you think I was gonna kill you or something?"

"Yeah," she whined, and we both chuckled.

"See even you realize how fucking crazy that is. I love you. I wouldn't kill you. And I know you well enough to know that you wouldn't do some shit to trap me." I kissed her wet lips.

I lifted her up, and sat her on the sink. She didn't have any panties on, so I just released my dick and rubbed it in between her folds. She bit down on her lip, moaning softly, and then gasped as soon as I got the head in. I continued pushing myself inside of her, and sucked on her bottom lip as she whimpered from me filling her up. Gripping her ass cheeks, I pressed her into me, making sure she took all the dick I had to offer. Her body trembled once she hit the base of my dick, so I let it sit there for a moment. While we sat there, her body tensed up, before trembling again from cumming.

I pulled her shirt from over her head, and salivated at the sight of her perfect breasts. I cupped them gently, and began sucking her nipples while gliding in and out of her tight center nice and slowly. I then brought my lips to hers, and let my tongue snake its way into her mouth as I continued to pump.

"Your pussy is the shit, Indiya."

"Rhyyysss," she cried out, digging her nails into my back through my shirt, as I fucked her with deep ass strokes. I wanted her to feel every inch, and never forget it. "Rhys, I love you."

"I love you too, baby." I sucked on her shoulder.

"Take this off," she moaned and began tugging at my shirt. I did as she asked, and then pulled her body into mine.

"I love feeling your skin," I whispered into her mouth before we began kissing.

Picking her up from the sink, I held her tightly and slammed into her with force as we both yelled loudly. Because we were in the bathroom, we seemed to be louder than we actually were. After a few more deep powerful strokes, I was filling her up and she was spilling on my pole.

"I'm so happy you're having my baby, shorty." I caressed her small stomach as we kissed slowly and sensually.

"Me too."

Life was lit.

Kimberlyn

Some days later...

TQ and I decided to take a trip to Brooklyn, New York so that we could spend some time in Brighton Beach. He told me Brighton Beach was basically like Russia in America, and that his father used to bring them here for family vacations. It was already a pretty interesting place because people knew him here as if it were a small town. I expected that in Boston, but I guess my nigga was a little famous out here, too.

This place was definitely like Russia in America, because every person we walked by was speaking Russian, and barely spoke any English. There were a few people like me who had no Russian background, but they didn't have a Russian guide like I did, so they were having a hard time. TQ said a lot of the residents in Brighton Beach pretended not to know English because they were very distrusting of a lot of people.

Currently we were on the boardwalk, about to eat at one of TQ's favorite places named Tatiana. He said they had the best Russian Cuisine, and he used to love when he and his family could sit at a table on the boardwalk and just watch people go by. I swear I never got tired of learning about his other side. I guess it was just amazing to me how different yet alike we were. Not to mention how sexy it was to hear him speak Russian, especially when he got mad or when he spoke it during sex.

As I was pushing Baby Tarenz in the stroller, I noticed a familiar face. She was walking in the opposite direction of us, holding hands with some man. Her hair was cut differently, and she was carrying a baby on her left hip.

"Is that Hayden?" I pointed subtly in her direction.

"Shit, that is," TQ chuckled.

Once we got closer to her, we stopped to see if she would say anything. She glanced at us, looked away, and then snapped her neck back to us. At first she looked worried, but then a half smile came through, prompting us to reply with the same gesture.

"Tarenz, Kimberlyn," she nodded and then looked down into Baby Tarenz's stroller. "He's adorable. He looks just like Tarenz," she smiled.

"Thank you. Who is this?" I looked towards the big, white guy she was walking with.

"Oh, how rude of me. This is my boyfriend, Ioann, and our baby, Ioann Jr." She introduced him, and both TQ and I shook his hand. He and TQ were about the same height, except TQ may have been an inch taller.

"Nice to meet you. So this is TQ?" Ioann looked down at Hayden and she nodded. "She's told me a lot about you when she first came to Brooklyn."

"Oh did she?"

"Yeah she did, but it's all cool now. As long as you're not here to steal her back from me," he laughed.

"Nah man, not at all. This is my wife right here," TQ furrowed his brows. "But you better be treating her right."

"Of course I am." He pursed his lips.

"Well it was nice seeing you guys. Maybe we can all have dinner before you go back up to Boston," Hayden suggested.

"Maybe," I responded, before the four of us continued walking down the boardwalk in opposite directions. "So I guess she has a thing for Russian guys." I looked up at TQ as we walked.

"I see that," he smiled. "How did you know he was Russian?"

"I could hear his accent, and I could look at him and tell."

"You can look at people and tell that they're Russian?"

"Yes, can't you?"

"But I have Russian in me, so that's not odd for me to be able to tell."

"I have some Russian in me too, every night. Fuck you mean?" I replied and he laughed so hard that people looked in our direction. I had never seen him laugh like that, and I enjoyed it. He was so adorable.

"You caught me off guard with that response," he snickered, and gestured for me to go inside of the restaurant.

"Dobro pozhalovat, Tarenz! (Welcome, Tarenz!)" some man shouted as soon as we stepped foot inside. "Sidet'! (Sit!)" he pointed to a table.

"Fyodor, eto moya krasivaya zhena, Kimberlyn. (Fyodor, this is my beautiful wife, Kimberlyn)," Tarenz smiled.

"Ohhhh." The guy nodded.

"What are you saying?" I looked up at him.

"I just introduced you to him."

The guy pulled me in for a hug, and then he and TQ conversed in Russian for a few, before he took us to a free table on the boardwalk. They talked some more, but since I had no idea what the fuck they were saying, I just paid attention to my menu. I gave little smiles here and there when I was able to tell that they were talking about Baby Tarenz and I. Finally the guy walked away, and let us be.

"I'm gonna have to learn Russian."

"I can teach you. Baby Tarenz will know Russian won't you, son?" he looked to our baby, who was sucking on a pacifier with his blue eyes wide as hell. He was so fucking cute, and he had the fattest little cheeks I'd ever seen.

"All the more reason I will need to understand. I can't have you guys plotting on me."

"We love you, we wouldn't do that."

"I love you guys, too." I smiled.

TQ ordered for us, and got two salmon salads, along with the fish assortment to start. For our main entree, we had the Chicken Scallopini, which was so good, especially with the mashed potatoes. And for dessert, he just got some black currant ice cream, and I got the apple strudel, topped with ice cream and fruit. By the time we finished,

I was so stuffed. Thank God we had to walk for a little bit, because I definitely needed to burn some calories.

After walking on the boardwalk and the beach for a while, we decided to go back to our hotel room. We were staying at the Greenwich, which was a beautiful hotel in New York, New York. This hotel was very different from other ones that I'd stayed in, because it looked more like someone's really nice and clean apartment, than a hotel. I enjoyed that aspect of it, and I also liked that it had a vintage look to it. I felt like I was Marilyn Monroe or something.

After I fed Baby Tarenz and bathed him, he was out like a light. TQ and I then ran a bath for ourselves, and got into the hot water together. Staring at one another from opposite ends of the tub, we shared coy smiles.

"You have fun today?" he questioned as he massaged my foot.

"Yes, I did. I still can't believe we ran into Hayden. Did you know she moved from Boston?"

"Yeah I did. Her mom called me, asking me if I had moved with her," he scoffed and shook his head at the thought. "I guess she was telling her mom some shit that wasn't true."

"Well I'm happy that she left Boston, but even happier that she has her own man to chase after. I thought I was gonna have to murder her."

"No need, you know I'm yours."

"Yes but these bitches don't know, so sometimes I have to show them and not just tell them."

"I'm working on you not having to do either. Before I even tell a female my name I let her know I'm married," he grinned.

"You better. I'm obsessed with you."

"I'm obsessed with you, too, shorty, so that makes it okay."

"It's okay to be crazy about each other."

"It is. So how is it being Mrs. Quinton?"

"It's pretty great. The sex is good, the money is great, and it's been a blast. I always tell myself I can't fall more in love, but then when I spend another day with you, I do."

"Come over here." He tugged my foot lightly.

I made it over to him, and straddled his lap. We just gazed into one another's eyes for some short seconds, before I pecked him gently.

"You know I'm never letting your pretty ass go anywhere."

"I'm never letting you go anywhere either. Will you love me when I get old and ugly."

"You could never be ugly."

"Looks don't last, TQ."

"Your looks only contribute a small percentage to your beauty, Kimberlyn. Your inside and your mind frame was what made me fall in love. All your looks did was bait me."

"Are you just saying this so you can get some?" I grinned and so did he.

"Yes and no. It's the truth. Hayden was pretty, just like you're pretty, but your personality was what shone the most; that's where most of your beauty lies. That's why you had a nigga shooting babies in you and shit." He caressed my back.

"Hayden is not as pretty as me."

"Nah she's not. Not at all. But you get my point."

"I do. That's what makes TQ and Kimberlyn so great. We love each other for what we are on the inside, and see our looks only as a bonus."

"I agree."

He lifted me up and brought me down onto his dick very gently and slowly, making me gasp and coo softly.

"Ya lyublyu tebya, Kimberlyn. (I love you, Kimberlyn.)," he whispered to me.

That was the only thing in Russian that I understood. Hearing him say he loved me, and in Russian, only intensified my sense of touch.

"I love you more, Tarenz Quinton."

Lendsey

That same night...

The family's restaurant was quiet, lit up with candles, and had roses everywhere. I had white ones in a bouquet, and red petals all over the floor. I had gold silverware imported from France, along with wine, and matching gold goblets and plates. Matikah was obsessed with shit like that. I had been planning this night for about a month, and I've never spent so much damn money in all of my twenty-five years. *The money was worth it though*, I told myself as I scanned the big empty dining room for the tenth time in the last ten minutes. I then took a seat, and waited for that text.

Andrei: Pulling up.

Just as I did, my phone buzzed, and after I read the message I went and took my position.

I waited, taking a few deep breaths here and there, until finally I spotted Matikah coming through the entrance. She was wearing a short, white dress that hugged her body, and even showed the small bump in the lower part of her stomach. Her hair was done, but she didn't appear to have on any make up, then again what did I know about that shit? Her walk was slow, as she admired the room that was tinted red due to the color of the unscented candles. She glanced at me in between her scoping, and I just smiled whenever we made eye contact.

"Lendsey, what is all this?" she whispered as she got closer to me.

I didn't say anything immediately, because I wanted to take in the sight before me. She was so beautiful, and there wasn't one thing I didn't love about her. She'd changed me at the drop of a hat, and I wouldn't have had it any other way if I had a choice.

"Sit down." I pulled her chair out at the small, round dining table. She took a seat, and accepted the white bouquet of flowers I handed down to her.

"You remembered that I like white roses."

"I don't forget anything about you, shorty." I pulled the other chair around so that I could sit in front of her. I took her hands into mine once she set the bouquet down. Taking a deep inhale I said, "Matikah, I really don't know where to start but— why are you crying?" I frowned.

"I don't know." We laughed in unison.

"Like I was saying, or trying to say. Umm, I love you Matikah, more than anything in this world. I've never cared about someone so much, other than my family. When we met, I knew there was something special about you, which is why even though I knew I wasn't ready to change I still pursued you. I couldn't let you get by me, and I'm happy I didn't. Even during the times where I felt so defeated, and wanted to give up, I never could. I became determined to make you happy, and I can only hope I've done that.

All my life I thought all I needed was a woman who could please me in bed, and hold a few conversations here and there, but when I met you I realized I needed more. I needed a woman who wasn't gonna deal with bullshit, and someone who was gonna force me to grow up and be a man. I used to wish that I could take back the night I cheated on you, but I think it helped me. You needed to leave me, and make me work for me to see how much you meant to me. I know that sounds bad but it's honest. Never again will I do anything to threaten our bond baby, ever. That time apart was one of the worst periods in my life, and I don't ever want to feel that way again.

I love you so much, that being my girlfriend isn't enough for me anymore. I need more, more of you. So what I want to know is, would you be so kind as to agree to become my wife? You deserve the best, and I promise I will give it to you, or die trying, Matikah." I knelt down onto the floor as she bawled.

She couldn't speak so she just nodded while staring at the ring that almost broke a nigga's pockets. I removed it from the velvet box, and slid it onto her finger. She then grabbed my face in her small hands, before kissing my lips very softly but longingly.

"I love you, Lendsey."

"I love you too, ma. Are you hungry?"

"Yes, when am I not hungry?" She pointed to her midsection. "Did you forget baby daddy?"

"I could never forget."

We shared another kiss, before I waved Nika, who was in the corner snapping photos, over to the table. I took my seat as she approached and popped open that expensive ass wine. After she filled our glasses and said congratulations, she took our orders and left us to converse.

"I can't drink wine, Lendsey," she frowned.

"My mother said you could have one glass and that it was okay. She said it's actually good to have a glass once a month."

"Okay." She nodded and took a small sip. Shit as much as that damn wine cost, somebody was gonna drink it. "Does my grandmother know?"

"She does. Everyone knew about tonight except you. Goldie's ass was trying to extort me to keep it a secret," I said, making us laugh.

"She is so crazy. But she wouldn't be Goldie if she wasn't."

"Good luck to my little brother."

"Excuse me? Your brother is lucky to be with my best friend. Don't get it twisted, nigga."

"Nah I know, all of us are lucky… even Rhys. I know Summer is your friend, but a nigga was happy as hell when he moved on. She was gonna kill my brother."

"Yeah I didn't like him dating Indiya at first, but I think it's better. Summer has someone new as well, Romeo I believe."

"Rhys is supposed to meet him. I told Indiya to make sure he leaves his gun at home, because we know he's a little off."

"That's what makes him Rhys." She took another sip. "So what do you want this to be?" she touched her stomach.

"You know I want a boy, but I don't care. I'm not like my father, so a girl is just as good. I know you probably want a girl though."

"No, I want a boy, too. I'm scared if I have a girl she will run into someone like her daddy," she smirked as I sucked my teeth. "No, I'm kidding. She'd be blessed to meet a guy like her father. There is nothing better than a man who is willing to admit his wrongs, correct them, and grow from them. You're a catch Mr. Quinton, and you're easy on the eyes, too."

"You're alright, too," I replied, laughing along with her. "Nah you know the deal, that's why you got that rock on your finger."

"I can't wait to be your wife."

"I can't wait for you to be my wife either."

We looked at one another in silence, bearing smiles. I think we were both imagining the married life with one another, and enjoyed the idea.

Nika brought out our plates shortly after, and we continued to talk and eat. After dessert, we retired home for some hot and sweaty sex. That shit was fucking amazing. Matikah was amazing.

Goldie

I was lying in the hospital bed, staring across the room at my son. He was sleeping so peacefully, and oddly I enjoyed watching. I never thought I would be someone's mother. I just didn't think it was in the cards for me. Even while pregnant, I was scared that I wouldn't have the maternal instincts needed to love my son. But it all changed when I saw his little face. I didn't even know him but I loved him so much already. He'd only been on this earth for nine hours, yet I couldn't imagine life without him already. What the hell was I gonna do with two Britain Quintons?

"I had to drive around all of fucking Boston for these pastrami chili cheese fries, shorty." Britain walked into my hospital room. It was around 9pm, and all of my friends had just left about an hour ago.

"I appreciate you doing that, baby," I smiled.

"It's the least I can do after what you did for me I guess." Hr shrugged, and then moved his dreads from his face.

It was such a simple thing, but I loved when he did it. That, and licking his full lips always made me hot. There was nothing like watching his dreads swing as he worked in and out of me.

"That's the spirit." I opened the big plate of food, and knew I wouldn't be able to eat all of it.

Britain set my drink on the little table I had lying across me, and after he did, he rubbed my hair back and kissed me. He held his lips on mine for a little bit, prompting me to caress his beard. Pulling away, he looked into my eyes and then kissed me once more before sitting in the chair next to me.

"You sure he's okay? That nigga has been sleep for two hours," he frowned.

"Britain, newborns sleep a lot. He's fine."

"Nah, he's been in that same position for a minute. These niggas got me fucked up."

He hopped up out of his chair and set his food in it. He then left the room as I shook my head and continued eating my fries. A few moments later, he came in with two nurses, explaining that our son hadn't woken up in two hours, and that he hadn't tossed or turn. He was such a big fool, but I was too hungry to chime in so I continued eating as if nothing was happening.

"Mr. Quinton he is fine, see." The nurse picked him, tickled his nose, and then he started blinking very slowly. "Newborns sleep a lot, Mr. Quinton." She looked to me, and I just shrugged.

"Oh alright, y'all need to pay closer attention though still. What if he wasn't just sleep? I would've blown this muthafucka up!"

"Thank you, Ashley," I finally spoke up since Britain still wanted to be ignorant. She nodded hesitantly, and then left out. "Why are you so crazy?" I grinned.

"I ain't crazy, I was just making sure my kid was alive. I thought babies cried all night and shit, and that nigga is over there big chilling like he don' had a steak and a Coors Light."

"Shut the hell up." I shook my head as we both laughed.

"How are you feeling?"

"I'm okay. I'm still sore obviously, but it's not as bad as it was earlier when I'd just had him. I wanted to die at that point."

"That shit was crazy to see his ass coming out of you like that. A nigga almost fainted, but then I couldn't look away."

"Thank you, Britain." I rolled my eyes.

He took a couple bites of his sandwich, and then put it to the side. Scooting closer to me, he laid his head on my lap, gently chewing what was in his mouth. I used one hand to move my food over to my left, and then the other to caress his handsome face. No words were spoken as we just admired one another, processing our thoughts. I couldn't believe I used to be obsessed with this man, and now here we were, in love and parents. I never thought he'd be more than some temporary dick, but it turned out to be *so* much more. I guess it's true when they say you find love when you're not looking.

"How does it feel to be a daddy?"

"It feels great, but then it's kind of scary knowing I have to protect this little person. I have a family now, and that's a bit different for a nigga like me. I've never really had to protect anyone but myself. I mean I've always had my family's back, but they're niggas, even Saya," he snickered lightly. "But you, and him, it's different. I can't be like my father."

"He protected you guys."

281

"Yeah he did, but he didn't show us love. It was like he couldn't do both. Maybe because his father wasn't like that, he didn't know how to be that way. But I don't want to be like him. My kid means more to me than being able to carry on my crime family legacy." He stared at my stomach, but he wasn't even looking at that, he was just in deep thought. I continued to caress his dreads, because he liked when I did that.

"You're gonna be a great father, I can already tell."

"I'm gonna do my best that's for sure."

"Well a Quinton's best is much better than the rest's best right?" I smiled and so did he. "Look how ready you were when you thought he wasn't breathing."

"I'm paranoid, I told you."

"I know."

Picking his head up, he looked over his shoulder at our son, before turning to face me again. He took my hands into his to kiss them, and then brought his lips to mine. Hugging his neck, I ran my fingers through his dreads as we made love with our mouths. He used his strong hands to rub my back gently, while kissing me harder and harder.

"How long is the wait?" he pulled away.

"Just six weeks."

"Just? Fuck you mean *just*? That's a long ass time shorty."

"And you better not touch anything that whole time, or I will cut your dick off with a butcher's knife while you sleep."

"Uh, calm yo' ass down. Ain't nobody about to be fucking these bitches out here. I been turned in my player card for you."

"I'm just making sure you don't go and try to pick the shit back up."

"I won't. I don't need it. Everything I want and need is right here," he said in a low tone, just before our lips met again.

CHAPTER TWELVE

Summer

"Are you nervous?" I looked to Romeo.

"Not at all."

Tonight Rhys and Indiya were coming over for dinner, because Rhys said he wanted to feel Romeo out. I made sure to drop Bryleigh off with my mother, just in case Rhys went there. I knew we weren't together, but he still had a temper, and still cared for me because I was his child's mother. I just prayed that tonight went smoothly, because although Romeo wasn't a thoroughbred thug like Rhys, he was no mouse.

"Good," I smiled and kissed his lips.

I finished setting the table, so he and I began bringing the dishes out. I had fried chicken, rice, broccoli, rolls, macaroni and cheese, and syrniki for dessert; Rhys' favorite. I chose to make something he loved because I wanted to be sure he was in a good mood. Whenever there was a plate of syrniki in front of him, he would always calm down or be cool.

I heard a knock at my door, so I took a deep breath before going to answer it. When I did, I saw Rhys standing there looking handsome as always, and a very pregnant Indiya in front of him. Seeing her carrying his baby did tug at my heart a little bit, not in a good way, but I definitely wasn't as bothered as I would have been when they first got together. Romeo had changed things for me, and I think because I was finally with someone that I liked, Rhys moving on didn't annoy as much. Hakim at the time, I think made shit worse for me.

"Come in. The food is ready, so everyone can just go sit down. I will bring some champagne."

"Let me get it for you, baby, you can sit down," Romeo interjected. "Romeo." He stuck his hand out to Rhys. They were exactly the same height; both tall and fine.

"Rhys, nice to meet you."

"Likewise."

Rhys, Indiya, and I went to sit down while Romeo fetched two bottles of champagne, which were sitting on ice. He brought the flutes as well, and then popped the corks of the champagne before sitting them in the middle of the dinner table.

We prepared to say grace, so Indiya held Rhys' left hand, I had his right, and Romeo had my right. When Romeo tried to grab Indiya's left hand, Rhys shook his head 'no'. Romeo just chuckled and threw his free hand up. We finished praying, and then everyone began to pass the dishes around to pile up their plates. We all filled our flutes with champagne, but I had Romeo get up and bring Indiya some juice.

"What do you do, Romeo?" Rhys quizzed.

"I'm a restaurateur. I own Melon on Salem. What is it that you do?"

"I do a lot of different things. We'd be here all day if I decided to list them. Plus it's nothing too special," Rhys replied.

"Fair enough."

"But a restaurateur, that's dope. I checked you out. I hope you don't mind. You don't have any criminal history, which is cool. I was mainly looking for any pedophile shit, but nothing was there. You've always been straight laced?"

"Pretty much, but just because I don't do illegal things doesn't mean I'm easily frightened."

"Good to hear. I don't want some punk hanging out with Summer and my child anyway. They need to be around someone that would be willing to protect them."

"That's me. What did you think of her ex?"

"Okay, do we really need to talk about that, Romeo?" I looked to him.

"We don't need to bring up exes guys, we just need to talk about the future," Indiya backed me up, making me smile.

"I will just say that I didn't care for him. He seemed weak, and he was very strange. I was happy when that relationship ended," Rhys responded anyway.

"I could sense shorty wasn't happy," Romeo nodded. "But I have every intention on doing what I can to make sure she's always good, financially and emotionally." Hearing Romeo say that made me blush, and I even saw Indiya smiling.

"Good answer, she deserves nothing but the best," Rhys half smiled as he stuffed some food into his mouth.

The subject soon changed to other topics, things that were more interesting, and I was honestly surprised to see Romeo and Rhys getting along so well. They were a lot alike I was realizing, and maybe that's what attracted me to Romeo. They both had that thug edge, but knew how to carry themselves when they needed to be professional. Rhys had his moments, but all in all I didn't have to worry about him getting ignorant in an upscale restaurant. I mean as long as no one tried to get at me.

After having dessert and watching some TV, Indiya and Rhys finally left. But not before Rhys invited Romeo to the next Quinton function, a barbecue. I was actually excited to bring him so that he could see that other part of my life.

"Well what do you think of him?" I asked Romeo once the front door was closed.

"He's cool, but I can tell he's a bit crazy," he chuckled before pulling me closely.

"He is, but he's sweet."

"I said he was cool!" Hr leaned down to kiss my lips, and my clit began throbbing immediately. "I can tell he cares about you and that's good."

I just nodded because my mind was elsewhere now. It'd been a long time since I had some, and tonight I was gonna come off my hiatus. Romeo could sense how I felt, because he picked me up, allowing my legs to wrap around his waist. Carrying me to the back, his hands roamed all over my body, groping and touching different places here and there. I loved the way his hands felt, and I could only imagine how bomb it would feel on my bare skin.

Placing me to my feet, he reached behind me to unzip my dress. It fell to my ankles, just as he neared me and began kissing all over my collarbone, removing my bra. As I assumed, his hands felt like heaven on my smooth skin. Once my bra was off, he took one of my nipples into his mouth, sucking it hungrily as he tore through my panties like the hulk. Any other time I would have been upset, but it just turned me on even more.

"Lie down," he told me.

I laid down on my back, and watched as he removed all of his clothing. His chest was perfectly chiseled under his buttery light complexion. I waited, on the edge of my seat as he removed his boxers. His rod sprang up, staring me in the face and looking so beautiful. He let his eyes dance all over my body as he got down on his knees, yanking me to the edge of the bed by my ass.

"Shit," I moaned once his soft lips and tongue came in contact with my clit. "Rome," I whimpered, massaging his fresh fade.

He was eating my pussy like it was his last meal. I slowly wound my hips into his face, pushing my pussy into his mouth. He kept up his pace, attacking my center by flicking his tongue feverishly over my clit. It throbbed, and my pelvis tightened, sending a feeling through my body that was so good I couldn't help but to scream out. I tried gripping for shit that wasn't even there, because that's just how great of a job he was doing. I got wetter and wetter as he feasted, pulling my damn soul out of my body.

"Please Rome!" I hollered, feeling him lap up my juices from the fifth orgasm. Shit!

Smiling, he stood up and tried to lay me back down. I resisted, taking his long thick dick into my hand. I slowly slobbered on the tip, making love to it with my mouth before easing down. I let it hit the back of my throat, and stopped there for a little bit. That move used to drive Rhys crazy, and clearly Romeo loved it too, because he was groaning. Pulling back, I continued to move my mouth up and down, letting my saliva take the lead. I felt his dick harden just before he grabbed my dreads, pulling me off.

"You fucking beast," he grunted, sinking his teeth into his bottom lip sexily. I just chuckled, and got on all fours. Putting my ass in the air, I looked back at him with a smile. "You are so damn sexy, shorty," he spoke in a low sexy tone, with his eyes squinted as if he'd just smoked a bag of kush.

After placing a condom on, he got behind me, gripped my right hip, and entered me slowly, causing us both to cry out. He started slow, winding his hips in and out of me, clutching my ass in his hands a few times. I loved the way his big hand gripped my little ass. It was like they were made to go hand in hand.

"Mmm," he mumbled as he slammed into me, and pulled out as slowly as possible, causing my body to shiver.

"Rome, shit."

Only certain niggas could fuck slow, and still be good at sex. I didn't know that until I had sex with Hakim. It was only good when he fucked me like a streetwalker. When he tried to make love to me, I would dry up right quick. Rhys and Romeo had no problems getting me to cum with slow motion moves.

"I'm gonna cum, Rome."

"Cum, baby, cum for me," he instructed, groping my ass.

I looked back at him, and was so turned on by his good looks, and the way his tattoos complemented his muscular frame. I loved that he could give me that thug passion, and then go make his money legally the next day. Just thinking about it made me explode.

"Shit, you just came so hard, ma."

After letting me recoup from that mind-blowing orgasm, he began pounding into me until I spilled my juices again, and he filled the condom up. Once we both caught our breath, he pulled out, removed the condom, and then picked me up so we could go to the shower.

I was finally happy for both Rhys and I... apart.

A few weeks later…

"**W**ell what do you think?" I asked Kimberlyn as we walked around the huge condo in Downtown.

"This is beautiful. Whose is it?" she adjusted Baby Tarenz on her hip.

"It's ours. I know we don't need three bedrooms, but I decided to go with this one just in case," I smiled, and took the baby from her. "Your name is on it too, baby. So it's *ours*. That's if you like it. If you wanna pick something else I don't mind."

"No it's beautiful I said. I do want to have someone come in though so I can change some things. I want it to have my style in here, mixed with yours."

"That's fine. The office in here is yours as well. I know you like to have your shit everywhere when you design people's websites and shit, so I thought it'd be perfect."

"Thank you," she giggled. "Do you like it baby?" she walked up to our son and tickled his fat belly, making him kick and giggle.

"I was thinking we could have the movers start ASAP so we can be in here by this weekend."

"I'd like that. And it's a good thing you got that extra room."

"Why is that?" I pulled her closer with my free arm.

"Becaauuuuse," she cheesed. "We're gonna have a new baby." I could tell she was slightly apprehensive about telling me.

I touched the side of her face, and let my fingers snake through her long hair, before pushing her face closer to mine. I kissed her, holding it there for a bit, before parting her lips and letting my tongue dance with hers.

"I guess this means you're happy about it."

"Of course. Anything that has something to do with us makes me happy. You know that. That's why I gave you this." I lifted her hand and kissed her wedding ring.

She hugged my torso as I draped my arm over her shoulder. Baby Tarenz looked down at her, making her grin widely as hell. I loved her smile; that was one of the main things that attracted me to her. And still to this day when she showed it, I would get lost in it.

"You're gonna be a big brother." She tickled his stomach again, making him screech.

I gripped a handful of her hair, tilting her head back, and just looked down into her eyes again before kissing her hungrily, but gently.

Damn was life different... better, but different.

EPILOGUE

Kimberlyn Quinton

One year later...

I checked myself out in the full-length mirror in my hotel room, just admiring my body. I was in very good shape, and my babies gave me more of a womanly feel. My bathing suit was a burnt orange color, which went nicely with my blemish free golden skin. Letting a smile cover my face, I took my long dark locks down and tousled them a bit since I was about to have fun on the beach after lunch downstairs.

Britain and Goldie had just gotten married, and all of us couples were in Punta Cana celebrating. They thought it would be cool for everyone to accompany them on their honeymoon, even my grandmother who was Goldie's biggest fan now. It didn't just happen, she grew to love her over time. I guess before she didn't know Goldie like Matikah and I did, which blocked her from feeling the same way we felt. But Goldie did change and grow a lot too. Anyhow, I was happy that we could all love one another.

After sliding my feet into my sandals, I placed Baby Tarenz and my other son, Terrion in the double stroller. I wasn't about to be carrying either one of them this whole time. When they were new it was easier, but nowadays I could barely walk up the stairs with them.

"Don't put them in there." TQ came out of the bathroom.

"Are you gonna carry them?" I placed my hand on my hip.

"No, but Tarenz can run around and I can carry Terrion," he offered, already removing both of them from their stroller.

"Fine," I sighed just as I heard a knock on the door of our suite. We were staying in this beautiful hotel named Sanctuary Cap Cana, and I swear it had me wanting to move here forever.

"You guys ready?" Matikah asked, adjusting her daughter Lindsay on her hip. Lindsay was the cutest thing in the world, looking just like a blue-eyed Matikah.

Matikah had her own spa now, and she was making a lot of money. Anyone who needed to get waxed, pampered, or anything like that went to *Tikah's Pamper Parlor*. It felt good to see her owning her own spot, because as long as I've known her, which obviously has been all my life, she's talked about owning her own beauty spa. Oh and Isabetta, that bitch was in jail for setting fire to her own shop, and would soon be getting sentenced for her sister's murder.

As for Matikah and Lendsey, they were married of course. They wasted no time tying the knot after he proposed, and oddly he was the one who was most anxious. Matikah tried inviting her mom, but she sounded scared to come she told me. It didn't hurt Matikah any though.

"Yeah, let's go TQ." I called after him.

I looked down to see Baby Tarenz walking, but since he was so little he was too slow. I picked him up and kissed his face, before placing him on my hip. I knew I would end up having to carry one of them. But when we got out into the hallway, TQ and I switched since Terrion was much lighter.

We made it to the downstairs area of the hotel, meeting everyone so we could have lunch. Summer and Romeo were even here, and it was crazy to see us all get along. She was currently pregnant, just like Saya was by Pharaoh, but they both wore it very well. Summer and Romeo were so dope to me, because they stayed traveling together, exploring new places. TQ and I tried traveling a lot as well, but with two little babies it was harder.

"We need more bread for the table," Summer sighed, rubbing her belly.

"I didn't want to say anything but..." Saya agreed, bucking her eyes.

Saya and Pharaoh were like the new age Bonnie and Clyde. Mrs. Quinton said they reminded her of herself and TQ's father when they loved each other. She said Pharaoh was a much better man though, and so far I agreed. As for Mrs. Quinton, she had no interest in dating. The only thing she wanted to do was work a little and be a grandma she said. I smiled at her holding Bryleigh and talking, as I thought about it.

"Ma watch her, she's trying to drink your fuckin' cocktail," Rhys barked, making the table chortle loudly.

Rhys and Indiya had gotten married right after she had their son,

Rhys Jr. He had the damn pastor come to her hospital room because he wanted it done right then. Rhys Jr. was the cutest little thing, looking just like his crazy father. Indiya was still working with Saya and Mrs. Quinton with their little business, but it was more of a partnership between her and Saya now, since Mrs. Quinton stepped down a bit. And now that Indiya was legal due to giving birth and getting married, she was in the process of opening a lash bar. She was really good at it, which I didn't find out until she did Matikah's for her wedding, so it was good to see that she could do something she liked and that was legal.

"Sit, I'm hungry!" Goldie whined to me, holding her son as Britain kissed on her neck.

I told her she was pregnant again, but she swore she wasn't. But with the way she and Britain stayed attached at the pelvis, I was sure I was right. This was the most surprising marriage to us all. Two people, who swore they only wanted sex from one another, ended up married with a kid. I guess that was how shit worked these days.

Goldie had gotten the job with the fashion magazine, making a pretty nice income. She was able to buy herself a Range Rover, so I would say she was doing pretty well for herself. My best friend had come a long way from being the little church girl chasing after whack ass Ethan. It made me happy just to think about.

I was still a little perplexed about Ethan and Chenaye sleeping together, especially because I thought she was a Saint all of these years. But both their shady asses met a terrible well deserved fate though.

"Give him here." My grandma reached for Terrion. I happily

passed his little chunky butt over to her so I could eat in peace.

We started passing around food, making conversation, jokes, and just enjoying one another's company. Everyone seemed to be right where they belonged in life.

As for me, I had a pretty well known web design company, *Beri Designs*. I mean I wasn't being mowed down in the streets when people saw me, but I made a lot of money. I stayed booked, and barely had time to do things like this, but I always made sure I found the time. I loved web design, but my family would always come first. I now understood when Matikah said it was nothing like getting paid for doing something you loved. There were times where I wanted to rip my hair out over a few HTML codes, but for the most part I loved my career. I loved my life in general. I had a gorgeous, attentive, wonderful husband, beautiful babies, loving friends, and a great job.

I never expected for my path to take the turn that it did, but I'm happy with the way things went. I won't lie, I did wish that Mr. Quinton could have accepted his children's partners so he could be here with us, but God makes no mistakes.

I kissed the corner of TQ's mouth, and then placed his cloth napkin in his lap. He lifted Baby Tarenz up so that I could do so.

"You know you will spill something," I laughed.

"What would I do without you wife?" he spoke sarcastically.

"I don't know; you need me."

He looked to me with his piercing blue eyes and said, "I do, more than anything in this world."

FIN

Join our mailing list to get a notification when Leo Sullivan Presents has another release!

Text **LEOSULLIVAN** to **22828** to join!

To submit a manuscript for our review, email us at leosullivanpresents@gmail.com

CPSIA information can be obtained
at www.ICGtesting.com
Printed in the USA
LVOW10s1331300817
546968LV00022BA/583/P